"Oh, Phyllis Burdick, I have missed you," Simon said with deep sincerity. "You'll never know how I've dreamed of this moment and the joy of holding and caressing you, the absolute beauty of kissing you. How utterly foolish of me not to return to New York before this."

"Mr. Simon Phenwick, I've missed you far more than you can ever possibly know," she said just above a whisper, emotion causing raspy huskiness in her throat, a dryness that could only be quenched by several more kisses. She pushed her face toward his, her mouth reacting with a famished hunger. "Kiss me, Simon, before I burst with anticipation," she said, her lips lightly brushing against him as she formed the words. . . .

THE SAGA OF THE PHENWICK WOMAN

#33
Katheryn Kimbrough's
Saga of the Phenwick
Women

PHYLLIS, THE CAUTIOUS

FAWCETT POPULAR LIBRARY • NEW YORK

*SAGA OF THE PHENWICK WOMEN #33: PHYLLIS,
THE CAUTIOUS*

Published by Fawcett Popular Library, a unit of CBS
Publications, the Consumer Publishing Division of CBS Inc.

Copyright © 1980 by John M. Kimbro

All Rights Reserved

ISBN: 0-445-04613-9

Printed in the United States of America

First Fawcett Popular Library printing: October 1980

10 9 8 7 6 5 4 3 2 1

DEDICATED TO
GARY JOHNSON

Prologue

The ranks of those who have been chosen to be called Phenwick women is ever growing. Many have come to think of the tradition as some sort of superstitious legend; and there is considerable question why Augusta I ever began the practice of designating such persons in the first place ... or why it continues. Since I have inherited the position of selecting such ladies, I can only relate that there is a certain quality of character and disposition that sets a so-called *Phenwick woman* apart from other ladies of the family. It may be a dubious honor and distinction at best; still, it is one that has caused rivalry and competition.

For those who have followed the saga of the Phenwick women, it comes as no news that Augusta I decided to reincarnate back into the dynasty which she founded back in the eighteenth century, and that she is presently known as Katherine, the wife of Philip Phenwick. Furthermore, to those followers of the tales of these ladies, it is obvious that the illustrious Augusta II would like to think that she is the reincarnation of her triumphant ancestor. This is pointed out at this time because the conflict between these two Phenwick women is destined to emerge.

Like Patricia and Millijoy, there always has been one of the Phenwick women who has become a dominating factor, and she, too, is destined to take on a role of greater prominence at this time. She returns from San Francisco to take her place among the family as a motivating and commanding force.

And I shall be there with the scent of roses.

Chapter One

1910

The Eternal Light blazed in electric lights, above which was the brightly shining name of AUGUSTA PHENWICK II. Over the years she had established herself as one of the foremost actresses of the theater. One success had followed another and her fame had been acclaimed among the greatest of her profession. It was opening night of what was to become her most triumphant role.

In the early years of establishing herself in her career, Augusta II received little support from her family, other than for her immediate kin and, of course, the notable Millijoy Phenwick, who had seen a talent in the rough and had given her utmost encouragement. While there had been other celebrities among the Phenwick family—Joanne, herself a famed actress,

Susannah, a pianist of renown, like Tommy, and Evelyn, his wife, who was a concert singer—Augusta II would be the most remembered. Now that she had received spectacular recognition, it had almost become a tradition that the Phenwicks would be well represented in attendance for her opening nights.

Her handsome, widowed younger brother Joshua, had become her most ardent supporter, and, in a way, vicariously shared her success. Older brother Edwin, while deeply interested in her career, did not always have the time to take away from Medallion of Portland to celebrate her triumphs. Augusta II understood. Despite the sadness that had befallen him over the years, Joshua was at the Majesty Theater, arrayed in evening finery and appearing as if he were one of the principals of the evening.

Donald and Peggy Phenwick were in his company, along with their cousins Simon and Laura and her husband. Although there was a certain rivalry, Katherine and Philip were also in attendance, as were Philip's brothers Morgan and Jerome. The Phenwicks were well represented and occupied the two best boxes in the house.

The Eternal Light, the fourth effort of playwright Madison Davis, was set in antabellum Georgia. Augusta II played the role of a Southern lady of aristocracy, who was destined to lose all she had over the Civil War, yet remained proud and determined to make the most of the personal tragedy which had dramatically altered her life. The company was comprised of a large cast of actors, with the parts of Negroes being played by Caucasians in blackface makeup and curly black wigs.

During the course of the play, after Atlanta is burned to the ground and the heroine has suffered one disaster after another, she realizes the devotion that many of her slaves had actually had for her. In particular, a young woman named Molly was the one person who would stand by her in the end. The part of Molly was
10

not particularly large, but it stood out as one of the better supporting roles in the play. The actress who took the part was chosen from an open-call audition and it was her first professional appearance on the stage. The actress was nineteen-year-old Phyllis Burdick, who had moved to New York two years previously from Joplin, Missouri. Dark-haired, pretty, with soft features and a pert stance, Phyllis was not only thrilled to be performing on the New York stage but completely in awe over the fact that she was in the same play as the acclaimed Augusta Phenwick II.

Nervously, Phyllis waited in the wings for her first entrance. Trembling with excitement and a touch of stage fright, she was certain that she would be unable to remember a single line. Yet, as she watched Augusta II move about the stage with authority and deliver each line with confidence and precise diction, Phyllis pulled herself together. At the last minute before her entrance, her nose began to itch, then her chin, but she feared to scratch lest she might rub off the blackface makeup.

While Phyllis's performance was not spectacular, she was noticed and singled out as one of the better performers in the play. Even the most accomplished actor could not have upstaged Augusta II in any way. It was her moment, and she took advantage of it. Curtain call after call by the company was interspersed with single calls by Augusta II and she received four bouquets, one of which was collectively from her family.

When the final curtain rang down, the cast gathered around Augusta II to pay compliments for her stellar performance. She knew that she had done a magnificent job. It pleased her to think her fellow actors were so responsive to her efforts. As a gesture of her gratitude for the company's support, a party was planned later that night at her plush Riverside Drive manse, where all those involved in *The Eternal Light* as well

11

as family and friends would be present. Augusta II's parties were gala events in themselves.

The Phenwicks put on a show backstage and in Augusta II's dressing room, but because the actress was inundated with admirers, they would wait until the party to express their praise for her performance.

Phyllis Burdick had overcome her jitters after being on stage for a short while. She soon found that she had become a part of the action, and both her movement and lines flowed with the assurance of one who had had far more professional experience than she had actually had.

"I beg your pardon," tall, handsome Joshua Phenwick said as he accidentally turned into the young actress, who was still in blackface makeup.

"It was my fault. I wasn't watching where I was going," Phyllis returned. "I'm still a little excited."

"Oh, I recognize you. You were Polly."

"Molly," Phyllis corrected. "I suspect you won't recognize me again when I'm out of this makeup. Lawsy, no. Excuse me. Right now I'm anxious to get cleaned up."

Joshua laughed politely and condescended to excuse the young lady with what he thought to be a most provocative figure. He watched her dash to a dressing room which she shared with several other actresses. Although his attention had been closely held to his sister, Joshua had been impressed with Phyllis's acting ability and meant to ask Augusta II about her.

"Darling Joshua!" exclaimed Augusta II when she saw her brother wedge his way into her dressing room. An aisle was immediately opened between the two, and they embraced.

"A dazzling performance, dear sister," Joshua complimented. "You were, as usual, superb. I even had difficulty keeping from not shedding a tear or two there toward the end."

"I haven't seen you cry since," Augusta II caught

12

herself as she recalled attending her late sister-in-law's funeral, "—since you were a boy in short knickers."

"I didn't tonight, but I almost did," he corrected. "You've so many friends, I'll leave and see you at the party."

"You mustn't rush off," Augusta II said. "I've scads of people for you to meet who won't be at the party."

Joshua sighed and accepted his fate.

Tall, esthetic-looking Madison Davis, the playwright, wore a flowing cape over his tuxedo. His angular face was attractive, but not what one would call particularly handsome. Still, he had a quality of looks about him that had an intriguing sensuousness. He stopped briefly in Augusta II's dressing room to praise her performance. Augusta II immediately introduced him around and proclaimed that he had finally proved himself to be *the* genius of the theater in the category of playwrights.

Upon leaving Augusta II's dressing room, Madison went to the stage entrance where two young ladies were waiting to share his cab to go to the party. As the threesome were leaving, Phyllis Burdick emerged from her dressing room. Immediately recognizing the long flowing cape and his pretentious artistic attitude, a sigh caught in her throat along with a feeling of rejection. From the first time she had met Madison—and that was a group introduction with the other members of the company—she had found him so fascinating that she desperately wanted to meet him on a personal basis.

Eager, plain-faced Isaac Bell stepped up alongside of where Phyllis stood in silent admiration of the playwright. He was one of the bit players in the production, who, like Phyllis, was appearing in his first New York show.

"You're going to the party, aren't you?" Isaac asked.

"I wouldn't miss it," Phyllis replied, her face brightening to expunge the look of disappointment she had registered at seeing Madison Davis leave with two other actresses.

"Would you care to ride with me?" Isaac's expression was that of a teenager, although he was well into his twenties.

"Why, I'd be honored, Mr. Bell," Phyllis replied, reverting to the southern accent she used in the play.

"I'm ready whenever you are, Miss Burdick."

As the young couple went through the alley alongside the theater and emerged into the crowd of people who were waiting to get a closeup glimpse of Augusta Phenwick II, Phyllis put her hand in the bend of Isaac's arm and allowed him to pull her forward.

"Maybe I should have left a trace or two of black makeup on my face," Phyllis said, "so that the throng would recognize me as one of the players in the show."

Isaac laughed. "They're only waiting to see one person: Her Highness." They reached the street. "You wait here and I'll hail a cab. It's a bit nippy out there in the wind."

Phyllis positioned herself close to the building and pulled the collar of her coat high about her neck with one hand while the other held the large hat with the dove on it to keep from blowing away.

"Excuse me, did you drop this?" a voice enquired from beside her.

"Oh, you startled me. I didn't hear you come up," Phyllis said. "I don't believe I dropped anything. What is it?"

"This." The handsome stranger was holding a red rose which he extended toward her. *"Even if it isn't yours, I suspect that it was meant for you. Take it."*

"It can't be for me. Nobody ever gave me roses."

"I did, just now."

Phyllis took the perfectly formed rosebud in her gloved hand and examined it as if it represented an omen of some kind. "It is absolutely lovely. I've never seen a flower so beautiful." When she looked up to thank the man, he was gone. "How peculiar?" She stretched her neck to see if she could observe him passing through the crowd. There was no sign of him.

"Here, Miss Burdick, I have one," Isaac exclaimed as he ran toward her. "They're hard to come by. Miss Burdick?"

"What? Oh, yes, Mr. Bell, I'm with you."

During the ride from 14th Street to Riverside Drive, Phyllis had a difficult time taking her eyes or her mind off the rose bud and the singular circumstance under which she had received it.

Some of the Phenwicks had arrived at Augusta II's house before many of the other guests had got there. Mr. and Mrs. R. Pruman Donnally, the former Laura Phenwick, were the first to arrive along with her brother Simon.

"We might as well see that things are got underway until Augusta gets here," Laura said as she entered and appeared to make herself at home.

"Come now, Laura," extremely good-looking Simon Phenwick returned. "This isn't your party."

"Augusta asked me to see to things." Laura's attractive face was lit with the usual excitement she displayed when entertaining.

"She's determined to take over, Simon," Pruman said as he smiled condescendingly to his wife. "And you know how Laura is when she's determined."

"My sister, the gregarious party-giver," Simon laughed. Upon seeing his brother Morgan enter with Joshua Phenwick, he went to greet them. "Well, we might as well all get into the act." He stepped to the door and extended his hand. "Morgan—and Joshua. I'm surprised to see you among the first here, Josh. I thought you would probably wait and accompany your sister—the star of this and practically every other evening."

"I'm only Augusta's brother, not her date for the evening," Joshua returned lightly.

Seeing that Joshua's attention had turned toward the front door and the entrance of Phyllis Burdick and Isaac Bell, Simon discreetly led Morgan away. "You look like you could use a drink, Cousin."

"I believe you may be correct," Morgan replied and willingly accompanied Simon to where the liquid refreshment was being served.

Phyllis immediately recognized Joshua, but he was merely attracted to a new face and did not recognize her as the young actress whom he had bumped into backstage. He smiled and she returned the smile. Isaac took her wrap and disappeared.

"You'll forgive me for staring," Joshua said as he went to where she was standing.

Phyllis raised her eyes from gazing again at the rosebud. "Were you staring?" she asked softly, her eyes glistening with interest.

"I confess that I was. One so rarely views such extraordinary beauty that I am astounded," Joshua stated.

"That sounds like a well-rehearsed line."

"Not really. However, I readily admit that I like to think of myself as a connoisseur of loveliness," Joshua said. "And how appropriate—a red rosebud: beauty to complement beauty."

"You flatter me, sir."

"Allow me. This sir is Joshua Phenwick," he introduced himself.

"How do you do, Mr. Phenwick. I'm Miss Phyllis Burdick." Suddenly her eyes became quite wide before a startled expression changed into a large smile. "You're not one of *the* Phenwicks, are you?"

Joshua found her reaction amusing. "I'm about as much *the* Phenwick as I can possibly be. I'm Augusta's younger brother, Joshua."

"Oh, my goodness! I had no idea." Phyllis tried not to appear to be flustered. "I'm a great admirer of Miss Phenwick."

16

"I take it that you're a friend of my sister. I would have remembered your extraordinary beauty had you been a member of the cast of *The Eternal Light*."

"Lawsy me, Mr. Phenwick, yo' sees how I was so well disguised," Phyllis said in the accent she had used on stage.

Joshua snapped his fingers. "You weren't Polly, were you?"

"Molly," Phyllis corrected brightly. "Many actors feel they might as well be wearing blackface when they appear in the same play with your sister, Mr. Phenwick."

Isaac Bell appeared looking a bit nervous as he saw that Phyllis was speaking with Joshua.

"We must chat again later, Miss Burdick," Joshua commented as he surveyed Isaac's somewhat annoyed expression.

"Yes, thank you, Mr. Phenwick."

Isaac shook his head as he watched the handsome Phenwick man move to join his cousins. "I could tell he was one of the Phenwicks, but I didn't know which one."

"That's Miss Augusta's brother."

"I've seen him at the theater. Shall we go mingle?"

"There's nothing slow about you, Josh," his cousin Simon commented as they met in the large room near the entrance hallway.

"It's time I put away the dreary attitude of mourning," Joshua replied. "My Alice is at peace. The torment of grief is so exhausting. I'm among the living, and it's high time I got back into the mainstream of those who are."

"Admirable!" exclaimed Simon, clapping the other on the shoulder. "Who is the young lady?"

"One of the actresses in the play. She was the slave girl. Molly—I think I got that name right."

"No wonder I didn't recognize her," Simon returned, a curious smile touching his full lips. "Come, Cousin, there are other attractive young ladies present."

"I thought you were a confirmed bachelor, Simon."

"A bachelor, yes, a celibate, no." Simon laughed. "By the by, what gives you the impression that I'm so confirmed? I simply have not made up my mind to take a direct step toward the altar. That's all. Cousin Hayden was the confirmed bachelor—and look what's become of him. I doubt it can be said of anyone that he or she is a confirmed this or that until he or she is dead."

"That's a remarkably broad view to take, Simon."

When Augusta II finally arrived, she entered with remarkable authority and grandeur. She was always on stage. Her hands gestured broadly and her voice was projected as if the most important role she had to play was that of being Augusta Phenwick II. She was immediately surrounded by admirers.

Peggy Phenwick's pretty, round-cheeked face had the appearance of classic beauty, a slender version of a Rubens model. With movement the epitome of sophistication as if each motion was purposely contrived, she was a voluptuous image of charming self-awareness and determination. Elegantly gowned in antique rose satin with billowing leg-of-mutton sleeves, and with enough exposed cleavage to excite the imagination. A glistening array of diamonds and rubies sparkled at her throat, wrists and fingers. The upswept hair, golden-henna for the occasion, was radiant in the gaslight glow. Attention turned to her and remained as if her beauty possessed a tremendous magnetism that compelled both curious interest and admiration.

Donald Phenwick, in black formal attire, presented a perfect escort for his lovely wife. Pride reflected in his expression, even when he saw other men scrutinizing Peggy with salacious interest and entertaining a multitude of obvious notions. He remembered only too well the Peggy that once had been, the glutton, swollen with corpulence and self-incrimination; yet the woman of tremendous will and sheer perseverance who had the desire to set a goal of achievement, and the tenacity to

18

see the tremendous transformation through to completion to emerge the ravishing vision she had become. Let the others ogle his wife all they liked, he knew where her affections lay and to whom she belonged. His eyes twinkled as he observed. In the company of strangers he was a man of very few words.

Having left Simon, Joshua joined his cousin Donald, and the two adjourned to the library to smoke.

Phyllis watched all with wide-eyed interest. Mostly her attention went to the Phenwick women, notably to Peggy, Katherine and Augusta II. Upon close examination, she could discern a definite family resemblance —it was a look around the eyes and mouths. Peggy's beauty was blatant; Katherine's was demure, subtle and conservative with a touch of shyness; Augusta II's beauty was extravagant and flamboyant. There was little doubt in anyone's mind that the latter was a star of the first magnitude and that she intended to remain in all of her stellar magnificence.

As Phyllis observed, she noticed a tension mounting in Augusta II's face as she came in contact with each, Peggy and Katherine, more with Katherine than with the other. Yet Augusta II had almost a look of envy as she appraised Peggy and periodically the actress's eyes would narrow and a line of negative contemplation formed on her lips. Why? For all outward appearances, the female cousins were devoted to each other. Was it all pretense?

"You're being amused by our cousins," a deep baritone voice said as the tall, handsome man came up behind Phyllis.

Pivoting about, Phyllis observed two men, one slightly shorter than the other, smiling patronizingly behind her. "I was curious about the Phenwick ladies. If they are your cousins, I can only assume that you are Phenwicks, too."

"Allow me," the tallest of the two replied. "May we

introduce ourselves? I'm Morgan Phenwick and this is my brother Jerome."

"I'm pleased to make your acquaintance." She curtsied. "I'm Miss Phyllis Burdick."

"Joshua said you performed in blackface," Jerome commented as he beamed an inviting smile. "I remember you well. You were marvelous—wasn't she, Morgan?"

"My memory isn't as elastic as yours, Jerome. Still I'm certain Miss Burdick was capable of the role," Morgan said. "I use the word *capable* advisedly, since I am well aware of cousin Augusta's way of surrounding herself with capable actors, yet those who are adequate without being so outstanding that they up-stage her."

"I didn't realize that," Phyllis returned, feeling herself more a mere fixture than she had before. She frowned.

"Being *capable* is a compliment," Morgan quickly assured her. "That is, unless you have aspirations to be something more than merely capable—as an actress, that is."

"When one is young, Mr. Phenwick, one has many aspirations," Phyllis commented. "Ambition must be refined in time."

"Or defined," Morgan added.

"I must agree," Phyllis returned.

"Or redefined," Jerome augmented.

All three laughed.

"There are those who believe it's wrong for a young lady to have great aspirations and ambitions," Phyllis mentioned as she looked from brother to brother. "I was raised with a certain propriety, but I believe a young lady has every right to express herself in any way she chooses according to her aptitude. That is, if I have talent to act, sing and dance and I can do any one or all of them well, I see no reason whatsoever not to aspire to the height of my ability."

20

"Doesn't Miss Burdick remind you a little of Millijoy?" Jerome asked his brother.

"She sounds a bit like a Phenwick woman, if you ask me," Morgan replied with an amused laugh.

"Are you making fun of me?" Phyllis asked.

"No such thing," Morgan assured her. He pointed. "You see that charming young lady? That's our sister-in-law Katherine. She's married to our brother Philip. She's a Phenwick woman. With all due respect, Katherine is definitely a person of quiet determination—and I might add, ambitious in her own way. Certainly we weren't making fun of you, Miss Burdick, my brother and I have the highest respect for those who are known as Phenwick women."

Seeing that Phyllis appeared to be slightly annoyed, Jerome stepped forward with a broad smile. "I take it by what you have said, and by your attitude, that you do aspire to heights of popularity upon the theatrical stage, Miss Burdick."

Phyllis took a defiant stance. "I do. I don't always intend to appear in blackface makeup, nor will I continually play supporting roles to your illustrious cousin." As she turned she gazed directly into Simon's smiling face. She gasped with surprise.

"An admirable performance, my dear," Simon said as he raised his hands as if he intended to applaud. "Eloquent delivery, flawless timing and, I might add, very real conviction."

"I wasn't acting, Mr. Phenwick," Phyllis fired, not recalling which Mr. Phenwick he was. "I was deadly serious. Now, if you'll excuse me, I have several dances promised." She indicated her dance card. "Furthermore—"

Before Phyllis could finish what she was about to say, Simon took the card from her flailing hand. "You do have several blank spaces. If you don't mind, I'll take this one and this one." He indicated the spaces

21

before he scribbled his name into them. Glancing up, he questioned, "You don't mind, do you?"

Momentarily, she appeared confused before she smiled and replied that she would be honored.

Abruptly Morgan snatched the card from Simon's hand and affixed his signature in two different places. Immediately Jerome did the same.

"Well, my dear," Simon commented as he returned the card to Phyllis, "you are popular tonight—at least among the Phenwick men." He clicked his heels and bowed.

Phyllis smiled, but she was masking a frown. Quickly making an about-face, she headed toward the opposite part of the room.

"It's unkind to make fun of Miss Burdick, Simon," scolded Jerome. "She is obviously a most sensitive young lady."

"Extremely sensitive," echoed Morgan.

"I was not necessarily making fun of her," Simon replied. "I find her quite provocative and stimulating."

"As do I," Morgan responded.

"And I," Jerome chimed.

On the other side of the room, quiet, unassuming Katherine, a singular beauty herself, remained in quiet conference with her husband, since she liked to consider herself more an observer than a participant at social functions. She had been watching another brief encounter between Peggy and Augusta II.

"What do you make of the repeated encounters between Peggy and Augusta II, my darling?" Katherine asked her husband.

"Why do you ask?" Philip studied his wife's curious expression.

"I sense tension," Katherine replied. "Augusta II doesn't like being up-staged—certainly not by another Phenwick woman. And it does seem that Peggy is purposely trying to do just that." She laughed. "It's all such an amusing game, isn't it?"

"It is, dearest?" Philip questioned. "Do you perceive conflict between the two?"

"Not between Peggy and Augusta," Katherine said, a frown coming to her pretty features.

"Another of your enigmatic little remarks, dear?"

"So much of life is often spoken in riddles, isn't it? Oh, yes, I perceive conflict; but the real conflict will not be as open."

"Shall we join Laura and Pru?" Philip asked, aware that his wife was indulging in a psychic premonition.

Katherine's glance had been darting about the room when something caught her interest. "How's that? Oh, no, not for the moment, Philip. Why don't you join them? I'll only be a moment."

Philip knew his wife only too well to know not to object to any of her actions that might appear to be in the least unusual. He merely excused himself.

Katherine quietly moved across the room until she positioned herself near to where Phyllis Burdick was standing. With a curious gaze, she stared at the young actress. Finally, when Phyllis became aware of Katherine's curiosity, she smiled awkwardly and consciously held the rosebud to her nose.

"What a lovely flower," Katherine commented as a means of starting conversation. "You were one of the actresses in the play tonight, were you not?"

"I'm surprised that you recognized me," Phyllis said, flattered that someone at last had done so.

"Only a certain amount of beauty can be disguised," Katherine remarked. "The red rose is very becoming to you. My name is Katherine Phenwick, Mrs. Philip Phenwick. I'm related to Augusta II." Her smiled was warm and reassuring.

"I'm Miss Phyllis Burdick."

"I recall seeing your name in the program," Katherine said. "My husband and I are staying at the Gotham Hotel while we're visiting New York from our home in

Boston. Perhaps if you have free time in the next few days, you would honor me with a visit."

Phyllis could not disguise her astonishment. "That is kind of you to ask, Mrs. Phenwick, but I can't imagine—"

"You can't imagine why I should make such a suggestion, isn't that the case?"

"Yes."

"I suspect that you and I are destined to become friends," Katherine replied. "Are you in the habit of carrying red roses?" She pointed to the flower in Phyllis's hand.

"I don't recall that I've ever previously carried a red rose," Phyllis returned. "A man on the street thought I had dropped it. He was a very strange man."

"Strange?"

"Unusual—not so much in appearance, but more so in attitude," Phyllis related. "A queer feeling came over me when he spoke. It was as if all other sound had stopped and I heard only his voice. Now that I think of it, it was eerie. Furthermore, when I looked up from this rose, he had vanished. I scrutinized all directions. It was as if he had suddenly disappeared." She felt awkward and could only laugh to cover her uneasiness.

"I can see where you would be confused," Katherine said understandingly, "which is all the more reason why I think we should have a little visit—at your convenience."

Chapter Two

Theatrical stages have aromas peculiar to themselves. A combination of makeup, perspiration, cleansing ingredients and liquor mingle together to create a scent which is quite unlike any other. The stage of the Majesty Theater was no exception. A strange, hollow sound echoed footsteps. A singular coldness prevailed in the atmosphere.

The eleven supporting cast members of *The Eternal Light* had quietly entered through the stage door and had assembled in no particular order around the playing area, mingling and quietly talking amongst themselves.

Isaac Bell had singled out Phyllis and was consistently attempting to engage her in trite conversation. But the actress's thoughts seemed to be elsewhere.

Suddenly a door was heard slamming in the distance, followed by the rush of annoyed footsteps. His cape flowing as if to puntuate his indignation, Madison Davis came fluttering across the stage with gigantic strides.

"That woman is absolutely impossible!" the writer shrieked. "She has a reputation to maintain! What about mine?" He seemed to be addressing everyone, yet no one in particular. Holding his hand to shade his eyes, he looked out into the house. "Who's out there?"

There was no reply.

"Damn!" Immediately Madison circled around as if he had not been aware of the other cast members. He shrugged and flapped his arms into the air.

Moments later another doorslam was heard. Madison turned his attention toward it. Upon recognizing Hampton Colwell, he strode toward him. "Were you able to do any better with her, Hamp?"

"The reviews, as you know, Madison, were very good," round, cherubic Hampton Colwell said. "Except there was that complaint about the length. I can't see where a bit of judicious cutting and editing would do anything but improve the play."

"Only one reviewer spoke of the length," Madison retaliated. "And that ass has nothing but outrageous opinions, anyway."

Fatherly, Hampton Colwell put his arm about Madison's shoulders. "Let's just try it as Miss Phenwick has suggested. We'll bring in the producer and let him see it. If we don't all agree that the revisions are an improvement, then I'm certain Miss Phenwick can be persuaded to leave the play as it is."

"She can be utterly impossible at times, and you know that, Hamp!" Madison declared. "*The Eternal Light* is my masterpiece, and she wants to hack it to shreds! Utterly impossible!"

A singular sensation came over Phyllis as she could not help but overhear the conversation between the two men. She moved closer to Isaac.

"What's wrong?" Isaac whispered.

"I don't know, but I have a weird sensation," Phyllis replied. "I just feel terribly uneasy."

26

Isaac fumbled to take her hand and she allowed him to hold it.

A door opened and quietly closed in the distance. Both Madison and Hampton seemed to brace themselves.

"Are we ready to begin?" Augusta II asked as she appeared in a dark gown which she wore for rehearsals.

"We haven't agreed to change anything," Madison blurted.

Hampton quickly pulled him aside. "Listen, Madison, if she walks out on the play, you might as well kiss its success good-bye. The audience will come to see her and not the play without her in it. Remember that."

"But it's my play. I wrote it."

"No one is disputing that fact," Hampton replied. "But Miss Phenwick is the star. She got the greatest notices. Just try it her way. Go out in the house, sit comfortably and damn well try to be objective. I'll handle Miss Phenwick. But, for God's sake, don't have another flareup with her."

Like a sullen little boy, Madison Davis left the director's fatherly embrace. He avoided eyes as he walked across the stage, down the steps and into the darkness of the auditorium.

"We're ready now, Miss Phenwick," Hampton said in a condescending way.

Augusta II crossed to where the director was standing. "Madison hasn't agreed, has he?" she said in a stage whisper.

"He has agreed to watch the run-through," Hampton replied. "You realize, of course, what you've asked is tantamount to asking him to cut off one of his children's arms."

"Madison is neither married, nor has he fathered children," Augusta II stated.

"That is not the point," Hampton returned. "This play is his baby, and he feels a parental protection for it."

27

"Once the curtain went up yesterday evening," Augusta II said, "he released the play into my hands to wet-nurse it into a success—which I did. Now he only has visitation rights, and that is that."

"Yes, I know, Miss Phenwick," Hampton replied. "But you must realize that it is terribly difficult to give up possession of one's offspring."

"You know my ultimatum."

"Yes, Miss Phenwick."

"Then let's get on with this rehearsal," Augusta II demanded and grandly walked into the playing area, sweetly smiling and nodding to various members of the cast. She stopped, her smile diminished slightly, and her eyes met those of Phyllis Burdick.

The look was enough to cause Phyllis to fade back into the scenery. What had she done? Why such a harsh expression which could be best described as contemptuous?

"Is there something—?" Phyllis tried to question.

Augusta II raised her hand and dramatically turned away from the girl. Grandly, she took a chair and glanced at Hampton to begin.

"Since you have all read what the critics had to say about our play," Hampton began, "I'm certain you will recall mention that it was a bit too long. After conferring with Mr. Davis and Miss Phenwick, I have decided to make a few essential cuts."

A moan came from the auditorium. Hampton chose to ignore it, as did Augusta II.

As it turned out, the deletions were largely in the scenes in which Phyllis appeared. Three lengthy speeches were cut down each to two lines, several bits of action which she had were taken away, and in the final scene it was arranged so that Augusta II practically had a monologue, with Phyllis only attempting to interrupt her.

At first the young actress appeared to be in a state of shock, unable to believe that her role had been so severely whittled down. Then anger began to rise and almost overwhelmed her with rage. Still, she treasured the fact that she was working and appearing on the stage. She mechanically did what she was told to do.

After the session, when Augusta II had dramatically gone to her dressing room to change from her rehearsal costume, Phyllis gave vent to her emotions and began to cry. Isaac did what he could to comfort her, but no words of his could possibly soothe the hurt and sense of being persecuted which filled her.

"Is that you, Peggy?" Augusta II responded, after hearing a knock at her dressing room door a short while later. She had changed and was in the process of doing her face. The knock came again. "Come in, come in!" the actress called in her best stage projection. "I'm sorry, Peggy, I was in the midst of—" Her words trailed off as she glanced up at the reflection in the mirror and saw that it was not her expected cousin. "Oh, it's you, Miss Burdick. I was expecting my cousin. I must say I'm pleased by the way you were able to adapt to the changes we made this afternoon. I feel those scenes play much more smoothly now. We must have dropped a good tedious ten minutes from the playing time." Again she glanced at Phyllis's sullen expression. "What is it? Is something troubling you?"

"Why did you do it, Miss Phenwick?" Phyllis asked, barely able to control the tears that wanted to flow.

"Why did I do *what?*" Augusta II addressed the reflection. When she saw that the girl could not express herself, she turned around on the chair and stared until she caught Phyllis's attention. "Why did I do *what?*"

"Have Mr. Colwell cut my lines the way he did," Phyllis managed to say.

"Those lines weren't important," Augusta II replied as she turned back and continued with her preparations, only occasionally glancing up at Phyllis's reflection. "These things happen in the theater. The play must be tightened and that requires snipping a line or two here and there."

"You have several monotonous monologues which could have been trimmed or eliminated completely," Phyllis dared to say.

"I beg your pardon!" Augusta II exclaimed as she again turned back to Phyllis. "I can't believe you had the audacity to say that to me."

"But I did say it, Miss Phenwick, because it is true that you purposely had my lines cut down," Phyllis continued. "Is it because my name was mentioned in the reviews, and at least two reviewers praised my performance?"

Augusta II rolled her eyes. "Good Lord, child, whatever ails you? You speak as if you thought I had a personal vendetta against you. I'm pleased that your named was mentioned in the reviews. You know the play was long. The audience had begun to squirm nearly three scenes before the end. Something had to be cut. Molly is really an incidental role of no great importance. It was only logical to lessen the part even more. So many of Molly's lines are darky jabber, that's all."

"Some that you cut provoked laughter last night."

"I'm well aware of that. But this is a serious drama," Augusta II insisted. "Provoking laughter only takes from the intensity of the drama."

"I beg to differ with you. Comedy only serves to make the emotional drama all the more poignant," Phyllis said.

"Really? Are you so knowledgeable about such things?" Augusta II asked. "I know far better than you what works and what doesn't on the stage."

"Are you upset with me for some reason?" Phyllis questioned.

"I wasn't before you barged into my dressing room a short while ago," Augusta II replied. "But I can overlook such mundane matters. Trivia has always been easy for me to ignore. Now you had better run along, go home, take a little rest and thoroughly go over the changes. We wouldn't want you to make any mistakes tonight."

Phyllis was fuming, but she knew she dare not continue with the intercourse for fear that she would say something that she would later regret. Without a word, she abruptly turned and left the dressing room.

Augusta II remained staring at the reflection of the closed door. A calculating smile moved over her mouth and her eyes flashed back at her with a look of accomplishment. She returned to her preparations.

"Oh, I'm sorry, my dear," Peggy Phenwick exclaimed a short while later as Phyllis stormed through the stage door and nearly collided with the woman.

"I apologize," Phyllis said, followed by a sob that indicated she was on the brink of crying. "I wasn't watching."

"Why are you so distraught? I confess I can't recall your name although I know we did meet last night at the party," Peggy mentioned.

Tearfully, while Peggy indulgently listened, Phyllis explained the situation and what had taken place in the dressing room.

"I see," Peggy returned without removing the puzzled expression from her pretty features.

"I'm certain the whole thing was provoked by the fact that I got mentioned in the reviews, and extremely favorably so at that," Phyllis related.

"If Augusta II was annoyed over that," Peggy commented, "she should realize that the damage has already been done. The reviews have been read. That is basically what is important. I don't see how Augusta could be jealous, much less envious of the mention you received. Still I must warn you that my cousin is quite an emotional—and often childlike—person, who can be eccentric beyond reason at times. If she has indeed decreed such changes, I suggest you go along with

31

them and not attempt to fight back. You would be the loser in the end, not Augusta."

"I simply don't understand her at all," Phyllis sobbed.

Peggy took a handkerchief from her bag and handed it to the young woman. "Here, you must have this. Consider it a gift."

Phyllis accepted the handkerchief and used it to help control the flow of emotional moisture that wanted to pour lavishly from her.

"I had come to look up to Miss Phenwick and love her like a mother," Phyllis said after the tears had stopped. "I do greatly admire her talent. I can't believe that she would do such a petty thing as to become envious of my being mentioned in the reviews."

"I suspect there is more than that behind this," Peggy speculated. "Did you have any sort of run-in with Augusta at the party last night?"

"None whatsoever," Phyllis replied. "I merely said hello to her and complimented her on her performance. I was hardly in her presence at all."

"Well, something obviously happened sometime, somewhere—that is, if this has to do with a personal thing," Peggy allowed. "I'll speak with her—oh, not just right now—and try to get to the bottom of what has happened. In the meantime, I would like you to have lunch with me on Friday. Katherine told me that she felt it would be wise for me to get to know you better. Katherine can be so enigmatic at times. Can you make it on Friday?"

"I believe so."

"Good." Peggy quickly took a card from her purse and scribbled something on it, then handed it to Phyllis. "Call me at this number on Friday morning and we will verify the appointment. Now, stop fretting and just remember that if there is a problem, it is Augusta's far more than it is yours. I'll expect to hear from you on Friday morning—not before ten. Well, then, I must rush. Good-bye, Miss Burdick."

Phyllis stood immobile as she stared in the direction Peggy had gone. She used the handkerchief and began to slowly trudge her way up the alley.

As she reached the street, although her eyes were teary, Phyllis focused on a red object lying on the ground. Curiously she reached to pick it up.

"A red rose?" she questioned aloud and looked about to see if a familiar face could be seen. Then she held it to her nose and the fragrance was almost overpowering.

Chapter Three

"Miss Burdick! May I have a word with you?" came the resonant, articulate voice from the alley. Phyllis turned to see attractive leading man Leslie Brooks heading toward her.

An extremely good looking man in his twenties, Leslie Brooks was actually the secondary leading male in *The Eternal Light*. Eyes of emerald green and blondish-brown hair accentuated his artistically-formed features. He seemed to be perfection personified in a man. Phyllis had often observed and admired him from a distance, as did at least two other young ladies in the company. One remarkable thing about him was that his attention seemed never to stray from his point of interest, and at the present time that appeared to be with Phyllis. His magnificent stage presence caused critics to speculate that he was destined to have an amazing career on the stage. *The Eternal Light* was only his second appearance in professional theater.

"Mr. Brooks?" Phyllis questioned as the actor reached where she was standing. In the past he had merely nodded in her direction with a brief, paradoxical smile.

"I'm off to have a cup of coffee and a bite to eat to fill a gap which feels mercilessly empty in the pit of my stomach," Leslie said. "Would you care to join me?"

"I was about to go back to my room," Phyllis replied. "I've been through an ordeal today."

"I'm well aware of that, Miss Burdick," Leslie said as those vivid green eyes stared impetuously down into hers. "All the more reason for you to take a short respite and put your disappointment aside for a few minutes. There's a cafe just up the block. What a lovely rosebud! It suitably becomes you."

"I—I found it here on the street."

"It was destined to be yours." He laughed with a flamboyant merriment that was typical of many in his profession. He reached for the rosebud. "May I?" Guiding both flower and Phyllis's hand toward his face, he sniffed deeply of the fragrance. "Ah, surely a work of art from the gods!"

"Your words are almost poetic, Mr. Brooks."

"But only *almost*," he corrected. "I won't take no for an answer. I'm certain it will be to your advantage for you to do so; at least it is apt to prove informative, and may well clear the air of some of the questions that are perplexing you."

"In that case, I really have no other choice, have I?"

Together the remarkably handsome young couple walked down the street, a gust of curiosity and speculation arising from all who witnessed them. At the cafe they were shown to a corner table, which was both isolated and quiet. Few customers were in the place and the waiter was eager to serve them.

"Now then, what is this all about?" Phyllis asked after they had ordered. "I sensed urgency in your voice when you met me."

"First, let me say I know you were vastly disappointed

this afternoon with all the cuts that were made in your part," Leslie said sincerely, an almost sympathetic expression crossing his face.

"I was flabbergasted," Phyllis replied. "And I must admit I feel as if I am being punished for some unknown reason."

"Punished?" Leslie laughed with a touch of irony. "No, not punished in the ordinary sense of the word. You are not at fault. Rather I see you as the innocent bystander, and if anything, the victim of circumstance."

"Explain yourself."

"Myself? Yes, I suppose that would be the place to begin," Leslie commented as he took a moment to sort his thoughts. "You see, I can understand you because I have had tremendous theatrical ambitions for as long as I can remember. Only one actor can truly understand what motivates another, and that can only be in part because each of us is different. I suppose in a way we are still children at heart, seeking recognition and praise. Children are natural performers in a constant quest for attention and, if I may, affection. Like children, actors constantly strive for recognition and acceptance. Only by understanding such motivations can one possibly comprehend what compels an actor to do the things he or she does. I trust you realize what I am saying."

"I think I do, but I've never considered it in those terms before," Phyllis commented as she did her best to keep from being magnetically drawn into the charismatic aura surrounding Leslie Brooks. "What has provoked this dissertation?"

"You. Me. The circumstances surrounding the abbreviations made in *The Eternal Light* today," Leslie replied. "Most of all, the person known as Miss Augusta Phenwick II."

Phyllis felt a flush of anger and resentment creep into her face. Her hands trembled slightly. "I confess I do not in the least bit understand Miss Phenwick."

"Miss Phenwick is a star, her name appears above the title of the play," Leslie explained. "She has a tremendous drawing power as far as audiences are concerned. And in essence, *The Eternal Light* is her play. Long after Madison Davis, Hampton Colwell, you, me and probably every other member of the cast are completely forgotten, the name of Augusta Phenwick II will be remembered synonymously with this production. Oh, one day, either you or I may become equally as well known as Miss Phenwick for our acting, but we will not be remembered as being part of *The Eternal Light*. This is her play. We can only hope that we will be seen by the right people, given other roles and somehow, by luck or chance, be catapulted into a position such as Miss Phenwick is in."

"How will the right people see me in blackface, much less recognize that I have talent if the lines are taken away from me?"

"I can't properly answer that, because I don't know," Leslie returned, the intensity of his gaze into her eyes increasing. "Let me explain something else. When a person like Miss Phenwick reaches the place of prominence she has, she must be protective of it and see that she remains where she is at all costs. That is why it would have been far better if you had not received favorable notices for your performance. Once you did, you immediately became a threat to the grand lady."

"How could I be such a threat in an insignificant role?"

"Simply because you received any recognition at all," Leslie said, "it showed that you were talented enough to be praised."

"You received mention for your acting," Phyllis protested.

"True. But I must explain there are two definite factors in my favor as far as Miss Phenwick is concerned, and they both stem from the fact that I am a man," he replied.

"Because you're a man?"

"First, because male actors are not really in competition with female actresses in the sense that they each would vie for the same role," Leslie tried to smile reassuringly. "Second, I was cast in the role of Cavanaugh Ashly because of personal attention I have given to Miss Phenwick."

"Personal attention?" Phyllis suddenly gasped and became wide-eyed with amazement. "Do you mean to say—that is—Oh, dear! *How* personal?"

"*Extremely* personal," Leslie said as a matter-of-fact, and without the slightest bit of embarrassment. "I will go so far as to say that I spend a considerable amount of time at Miss Phenwick's Riverside Drive address. Had I not, I, too, could have been wearing blackface in *The Eternal Light.*"

"You say that so candidly, without any indication of shame."

"Why shouldn't I be candid, and conversely, why should I feel shame? One has to act off-stage as well as on. And an actor worth his salt will do whatever is necessary to obtain the position he wishes."

"Have you no moral reservations or scruples about doing such a thing?"

"None whatsoever." Leslie patted her hand. She immediately jerked it away from his touch. "Have I offended or shocked you? If so, I am deeply sorry."

"Why should you?" Phyllis could still feel the impact of his touch on her hand.

"Sorry? Or offensive and shocking?"

"I'm confused, Mr. Brooks. I think it would be well for me to make a hasty exit from this place," she said.

Again Leslie caught her hand and, by the pressure he applied, it was apparent that he did not intend to let her pull it away. "I have noticed you without giving you my full attention. One must be guarded in such things. You are an extremely sensual and attractive young lady. I noticed you the first day of rehearsals for

The Eternal Light. And what I saw both fascinated and whetted my imagination. I confess I've entertain fantasizing thoughts about you—even during times of intimacy with others."

"What are you saying, Mr. Brooks?"

"That I have become extremely attracted to you," he replied. Again his eyes were staring deeply into hers with a look that was so compelling that she felt a weakening sensation throughout her entire being. "Surely, you must have sensed that."

"Not in the least." She tried to pull her hand from his hold. She must divert the train of conversation. "Why have you told me what you have about Miss Phenwick?"

Leslie smiled. Suddenly the strength lessened in his fingers and he released her hand. "Because I was hoping to make you understand what motivates her and especially her actions toward you."

"Are you implying that she actually does consider me some sort of threat?" Phyllis asked incredulously.

"Only as an actress," Leslie returned. "But, were she to walk in here at this moment and see us together, I've no doubt she might consider you a threat in other ways."

"I have no personal interest in you, Mr. Brooks."

"Haven't you?" His eyes were glistening.

She looked away. "No. From what you have told me, I can only conclude that you are an immoral person, and I have made it a point not to associate with such individuals."

Leslie laughed as he leaned back in the chair. "Then, my dear, I suspect you will have a remarkably limited career in the theater."

"Why do you say that?"

"Are you so naive as to believe that one gets to a position enjoyed by Miss Phenwick by being conservative and moralistic? Nonsense! Poppycock! That's idyllic fantasizing. And I might add, sheer naiveté."

"Why are you telling me this, Mr. Brooks?"

"Obviously I have ulterior motives. I'll be perfectly blunt about that," he returned. "But beyond those, I'm aware that you were deeply hurt today when your role was noticeably reduced in size. My heart went out to you. I'm not an unfeeling person—far from that. Most of all I deplore seeing a sensitive, albeit innocent person, being the victim of a system which you don't understand."

"Then I must immediately consider resigning my interest in acting," Phyllis stated. "For you see, Mr. Brooks, I consider myself to be a highly moralistic person. I confess I have never spoken of such matters to a young man before."

"Yet you're even now trembling with excitement and anticipation." An amused smile. "One does not act with his mind alone, or his eloquent speech with precise diction, but with his entire body, head to foot and back again. Whether you wish to admit it or not, when you are on stage before an audience filled with ogling individuals, you are putting yourself fully on display and titillating the imaginations of all who are watching you. And don't you for one moment think that Miss Phenwick isn't aware of that. Alas, we come to the real reason why she has taken the attitude toward you that she has."

"Which is?"

"You are young, beautiful, seductively attractive," Leslie replied. "She is nearing forty—one side or the other—and she is aware that youth has flown from her and her days of playing youthful heroines are numbered. Although you are dressed in rags and tatters as Molly, there are certain physical attributes which cannot be disguised. It was those very attributes, whether you wish to admit it or not, that attracted the attention of the reviewers. Had you not had physical appeal that triggered their prurient imaginations, their attentions would have gone elsewhere and probably would have remained exclusively with Miss Phenwick."

"I hear you words, Mr. Brooks, but I can't believe what you're telling me. Furthermore, I suspect your ulterior motives."

"I told you from the outset that I did have ulterior motives," he said with a large grin. "To lie about that would be useless."

"In which case I must ask to be excused."

"And if I refuse to let you go?"

"Why should you?"

"Miss Burdick, I predict there will come a time when you will come begging to me because you know I hold the key that could well open the door of success for you."

"That is most presumptuous of you, Mr. Brooks. And I do not care to continue with this discourse." She rose. "Now I insist that you excuse me."

Leslie stood. "May I accompany you somewhere?"

"That will not be necessary. And, in fact, I prefer going by myself. Good day."

"I will see you tonight at the threater," Leslie said with a charming smile.

Phyllis started to move, the stopped and looked back at him. "But you will not look directly at me or exchange pleasantries for fear that Miss Phenwick might see you? Isn't that the case?"

"Ah! I detect a touch of envy in your voice."

"You are incorrigible!" With that she stormed from the restaurant. She could hear the ring of Leslie Brooks' laughter as she departed. Daring not to look back, she hurriedly headed in the direction of the boarding house in which she lived.

Anger, rage, annoyance welled within Phyllis. Still there was also a curious kind of excitement and speculation about Leslie Brooks which she could not escape. Why?

During the two years she had lived in Manhattan, Phyllis had desperately fought to maintain her virtue.

Early on she realized that she could have gotten parts in different shows by submitting to the responses of men of low character. Few directors were the kindly fatherly image that Hampton Colwell was.

Phyllis looked down at the perfectly shaped rosebud which was tightly held in her hand. How very strange it was that she had had two such flowers within two days. Was it significant of something? If so, what? As she contemplated the situation, she thought back to the night before and the curious way that Katherine Phenwick had admired the rosebud.

Out of the corner of her eye Phyllis saw a man who was obviously watching her, standing near a building. Keeping her eyes down and increasing her speed, she moved beyond him before she realized that she had seen a familiar face. But whose face? She wanted to turn around for a second look. Then she recalled that it had been the man who had given her the rosebud the night before. Her head went on an angle with her shoulder and her eyes moved as far to the side as they could. There was no one standing where she had seen the man. He must have moved away. Then, came a disturbing thought: had he been there at all?

Looking back again to make certain, Phyllis continued to move until she felt the impact of collision with another person.

"Oops! My dear! How dreadfully absentminded of me!"

"It was my fault, sir, I assure you," Phyllis replied as she glanced up to recognize a familiar face. "Oh, goodness, Mr. Davis!"

Madison Davis, the playwright, took a giant step backwards so that he could get a comprehensive look at the young lady. A smile came to his lips which only moments before had been uttering profanity as he dwelled on his bitterness toward Augusta Phenwick II and what she had caused to be done to his play. "You know my name, but I confess, although I recognize your face, I don't know yours."

"I'm Miss Phyllis Burdick."

"Ah, yes, Molly!" exclaimed Madison as he adjusted his cape back over his shoulders. "How interesting it is that we should meet when I was thinking of you only moments ago."

"You were thinking of me?"

"This is such a congested place, isn't there somewhere we can go to chat a few moments?" Madison asked, taking what he considered to be a poetic stance.

"There's the square across the street."

"It's become a bit breezy and I fear we both might take a chill," Madison said. "I love autumn in New York, but the weather is so unpredictable, isn't it?"

"What is it you wish to say to me?" Phyllis asked.

"I feel terribly alone and outcast at the moment," Madison said, affecting a dramatic expression of woe. "I simply would like to have someone with whom I can talk. Do you mind?"

Phyllis sighed. In a sense she realized that she, too, didn't want to be alone. "I would suggest that we have coffee or tea somewhere, but I must admit I've had my quota for several hours."

"Were you a man, I would suggest a tavern," Madison returned. "But there's the Chelsea Hotel. We can sit in the lobby in a nice secluded corner. Hotel lobbies can be so accommodating."

That agreed upon, the pair entered the building and, avoiding the curious eyes of bellhops, they went into the lounge where three elderly ladies were holding conversation. Because of Madison's spectacularly eccentric dress and manner, the aforementioned ladies looked at him with raised eyebrows and haughty expressions.

"Don't pay any attention to those old bats," Madison exclaimed loudly enough that he was certain they could hear him. "We're not here to mind their business,

43

they should show us common courtesy in the same manner."

Phyllis tried not to laugh, but she found the situation amusing.

After they had ensconced themselves in comfortable library chairs, Madison asked if she minded if he smoked. He offered a cigarette to Phyllis, but she politely declined. She was certain their appearance in the lounge was sufficient enough to disconcert the three ladies; besides, she didn't smoke anyway.

"Is there something in particular you would like to discuss?" Phyllis questioned when Madison sat in silence for several minutes.

"How's that? Oh, forgive me. My mind is deeply distracted today. The curse of being a creative artist!" Madison again took an esthetic pose. "I'm certain you can understand how I must feel."

"Why such certainty?"

"Because you were intensely affected by what happened," Madison replied. "I awakened this morning with a sense of elation that my play had been so fondly received. I felt as if I had the world securely in the palm of my hand. Then came the message that I was wanted at the theater. My sense of premonition immediately reacted and I knew that all was not well. Miss Phenwick made me feel as if I had prostituted myself and my art simply to see that my play continued to run. Although I've had three other plays on the boards, I am basically an impoverished writer. A playwright doesn't make a fortune. I've tried my hand at novels, without success. The truth is, some people were born to be playwrights, and others novelists, and still others poets. Rarely is there the person who can do all three well."

"Still you are devoted to your creative talent, aren't you, Mr. Davis?"

"Extremely." He sighed. "She—I refer to Miss Phenwick—has had her way all along. I've written and

44

rewritten to please her. Right or wrong, she will have her way. Now today—oh, I don't want to speak of it—yet how can I ignore it?"

"I have been led to believe that I am to blame for the changes that had to be made today," Phyllis said softly.

"Miss Phenwick would very much like to have a one-person play written for her—a gross monologue," Madison explained. "She has a tremendous ego and she's terribly self-indulgent. I loathe her with a crimson passion!"

"Why did you ever become a writer in the first place?"

"I couldn't help myself, it was as if I was born with writing talent and it was an absolute necessity that I fulfill my destiny," Madison exclaimed. "Oh, God, had I only been born with the talent to dig ditches and that sort of thing, it would have made life far easier. But I do have this inner drive to express in words, to tell stories, to flesh out characters of my imagination. There's no escaping. At times I think it is a curse, at other times a blessing. What I need is an ally."

"Haven't you friends?"

"Does the Pope play baseball on Sunday?"

"Surely you must have some friends," Phyllis persisted.

"I have a few acquaintances," Madison admitted. "But have you any notion how lonely a profession writing can be—and how disheartening it can become when others tear my creations apart to fit their own needs?"

"I can only guess," Phyllis replied.

"There is little time for friendship in one's ambitious struggle toward fame," Madison explained. "It is a solitary road one must take. Yet how terribly lonely it becomes at times."

"Can't we become friends?" Phyllis found herself asking.

Madison eyed her suspiciously. "*Intimate* friends?"

"No, just close friends," Phyllis corrected.

"Isn't that what intimate friends are?"

"Oh. I thought you meant—" Phyllis blushed a bright red.

"Gad, no, Miss Burdick! I didn't meant to imply physical intimacy," Madison said. "I fear I would be most inadequate to you in that sort of a role. I am a romanticist with words, but not in actions. The quality of a dreamer is poetic and far too idyllic to be practical. But couldn't we be friends and confidants? After all, we have one very strong point in common besides our interest in the theater."

"What is that?"

"Our dislike for Miss Phenwick."

"I don't believe I truly dislike her," Phyllis explained. "I am disappointed in what she has done. Still, if it's possible for me to be objective in the matter, I can see her position and realize why she has done it."

"I should think that you would despise her for what she has done. You've practically been reduced to a walk-on," Madison exclaimed. "Oh, dear, where is my Christian charity? I'm at such odds with myself today."

Phyllis studied the man for a few moments. Then, ever so gently she placed her hand on his. "Mr. Davis, I believe I should very much like to be your friend."

Looking up, tears seemed to well in his eyes. Madison put his other hand atop hers. "Do you really mean that?"

"I do."

"I shall write a play for you, that's what I'll do," he declared, "one in which you will be the leading lady. Suddenly I feel as if I have something to live for. How revengeful that will be!"

"Revengeful? What are you talking about?" Phyllis questioned.

A multitude of thoughts were splashing around in Madison's mind, vindictive yet creative ideas. "I swear to you, as I am sitting here, Miss Burdick, that I will do everything in my power to cause you to become a far bigger and greater personality on the stage than Augusta Phenwick has ever been! Together we'll soar like triumphant eagles! And when we fly over Miss Phenwick, we'll drop something nasty on her head!"

Phyllis was overwhelmed. However, reason told her that she must not become too enthusiastic over what might only be a pipedream on Madison Davis's part. Still she couldn't divorce herself from speculative thoughts.

Chapter Four

The performance that evening was rife with tension. Augusta II was her usual grand self, but even she felt the uneasiness that prevailed amongst the cast. Her timing was off and she had difficulty with three different speeches in which she turned the lines around. The audience was unaware, of course, of the situation, but those who knew were aware of the problem she was having.

"The second night is always the hardest," Augusta II said at the end of the second act, confiding to Hampton Colwell when he questioned about her performance. "I thought I was fully aware of all of the changes, but I was conscious of having to make them. A few more rehearsals and it will be smooth and perfect." With that she flounced to her dressing room where her maid Cynthia was waiting to help her change costumes and prepare for the last act.

Hampton Colwell watched her leave, shaking his head

as he did. He had pampered and appeased her as much as he possibly could. That was part of a director's job. Still with Augusta II it had become more of an ordeal than he had anticipated. And he was only too aware of disappointed feelings among other cast members who had had parts of their roles cut, especially Phyllis Burdick.

Upon Augusta II's departure, Hampton went to the dressing room which Phyllis shared with two other actresses. She had been crying and had to replace the black makeup that had been smeared.

"May I have a word with you, Miss Burdick?" Colwell asked as he stepped inside the dressing room.

"Just a moment, please, Mr. Colwell," Phyllis replied as she hurried to put finishing touches on her makeup.

"I'm sorry about all of this," Hampton said a few minutes later immediately outside of the dressing room. "I meant to speak to you after the rehearsal this afternoon, but, as you know, I was preoccupied with Miss Phenwick."

"I'm aware of that, Mr. Colwell."

"As I say, I'm sorry. There is little more to be said right now and I don't want to further upset you," He explained. "We'll talk more at another time. I have noticed, however, that your performance is a little down tonight, ragged at the edges. That is perfectly understandable to me, because I'm aware of what you must be experiencing; however, the audience doesn't know that and they didn't pay good money to come and watch actors with personal problems."

"Forgive me, Mr. Colwell, I'm just not myself tonight," Phyllis explained. "I will try harder in the last act—but . . ." She hesitated and felt a stifled sob. "Most of the cuts were made in the third act. I'll try to remember them."

"I'm certain you will." Colwell gave her a reassuring hug. "Do your best and we will all be pulling for you. If it's any consolation, everyone in the company is with you and pulling for you. Give it all you've got."

Phyllis remembered all of the alterations that were made in the third act. When she came on for a curtain call at the end of the performance, she received a larger ovation than she had the night before.

"What the hell did she do to deserve that?" Augusta II questioned almost under her breath to the stage manager, who merely shrugged in response. Shortly thereafter, the star was out before the audience. Was it her imagination or was her own ovation only slightly more than what Phyllis had received?

"A gentleman would like to see you, Miss Burdick," the stage manager said after knocking on the dressing room door after the actors had left the stage.

"A gentleman?" Phyllis asked curiously. "Did he leave a card?"

"No, Miss Burdick. He said he would be waiting at the stage door for you."

"Is it by any chance Mr. Davis the playwright?"

"No, Miss Burdick, I know Mr. Davis," the stage manager replied. "Excuse me."

Phyllis was in a quandary about not knowing who was asking for her, as she wiped the grease and black makeup from her pretty face.

"You certainly got an ovation tonight, Phyllis," one of the actresses who shared the dressing room commented. "What did you do, show your bloomers?" She giggled.

"I did nothing but react to Miss Phenwick's lines," Phyllis returned. "I hardly had a thing to say, so I simply reacted."

Cynthia, the plain-faced maid who attended Augusta II, entered the dressing room and informed Phyllis that Miss Phenwick wished to see her before she left the theater.

"You may have reacted too much," the other actress remarked.

"Perhaps I did," Phyllis replied, a feeling of uneasiness

coming over her. She hurriedly changed into her streetwear, then hesitated before going to Augusta II's dressing room.

"Come in, Miss Burdick," Augusta II commanded. She was still in her dressing robe with a scarf tied about her hair.

"You sent for me."

"Only for a brief word," Augusta II said. "Do you know what the term 'up-staging' means?"

"It means standing further back on the stage than the person with whom you are playing," Phyllis recited.

"It also means doing anything that will detract from the actress who is delivering her lines," Augusta II stated, an edge of sarcasm to her voice.

"I merely reacted to the lines you were saying, Miss Phenwick," Phyllis insisted. "I was doing exactly what Mr. Colwell instructed me to do. I did identically the same thing before my lines were taken away."

"I see." Augusta II narrowed her eyes. "Well, then, I guess I must speak of this matter to Mr. Colwell. That will be all."

Phyllis started to leave.

"There is one other thing," Augusta II interrupted Phyllis's exit. "Did you have friends or relatives in the audience tonight?"

"Neither, Miss Phenwick. I have no relatives in New York City, and very few friends, none of whom could have afforded to come to the theater tonight."

"Hmm. That will be all. You may go." Augusta II watched through the mirror as Phyllis left. "I may have made a mistake, Cynthia."

"How's that, Miss Phenwick?" the maid asked.

"It's not important," Augusta II replied. "There is something about that girl—I can't explain what it is, it's just a feeling I have. I'll ruminate on that tomorrow." She used a large powder puff to dust over her cheeks and nose. "I can't help but distrust her," she uttered under her breath, but Cynthia heard it anyway.

51

When Phyllis arrived at the stage door, she was surprised to find Joshua Phenwick waiting to meet her. Again, because she had met so many gentlemen the night before named Phenwick, she was not certain which of the men he was. She did, however, recognize him as a Phenwick. "Why, Mr. Phenwick, this is a surprise."

"I trust you don't have other plans for the rest of the evening," Joshua said. "I mean, for the respectable part of the rest of the evening."

"Since I can't eat before the performance," Phyllis explained, "I usually have a bite to eat and go to my room where I read for a while."

"Have you established such a routine after only one night of playing?"

Phyllis laughed. "Well, let's say that is my intention."

"May I offer to join you for that bite to eat?" Joshua asked.

"If you like."

Isaac Bell arrived at the stage door. He started to speak to Phyllis, but seeing that she was occupied, he merely nodded good night and hastily departed.

"Would Lüchow's suit you?" Joshua asked.

"Lüchow's? Oh, my goodness! I've heard of it, of course, but I never dreamed—I mean—Why, yes, I believe that would be suitable."

They both laughed.

"I find it curious, Mr. Phenwick," Phyllis said as they rode toward the famed restaurant.

"Find *what* curious, Miss Burdick?"

"That you waited for me outside the theater. Am I mistaken—that is—I met so many Mr. Phenwicks last night that I'm a little confused—but aren't you Miss Augusta Phenwick's brother?"

"I am."

"Then why didn't you simply meet me inside?" Phyllis asked. "It is a little nippy in the night air."

"I didn't enter the theater for the very reason that I am Augusta's brother," he replied. "Had she seen me, she would have insisted that I accompany her and whomever she was with—and I didn't want to do that. I love Augusta dearly, but escape from her occasionally is most desirable."

"I see." Phyllis delicately covered a smirk with her gloved hand.

"I live in Portland, Maine," Joshua volunteered, "where I work with my father in the family business. We Phenwicks are a peculiar lot. Whenever we get together in any one place, we have several days or even weeks of celebration, making a regular holiday of it. Augusta opening in a new play was an excuse for several of us to make an occasion of it. Although the family is scattered about the country now, we—at least some of us—manage to keep in close contact."

"How much longer do you plan to be in New York?"

"I'm not certain. It depends on various things."

"That seems to be to be a rather vague answer."

"At this point it is the only answer I can give."

When they arrived at Lüchow's, the maître d' showed them to one of the best tables, which Joshua had reserved in advance. Shortly thereafter they ordered. Phyllis sat in amazement as she observed the people, the decor and the excitement that was generated by the arrival of several well known celebrities.

"You're like a child at the circus," Joshua observed.

"I've never seen so many famous people all in one place," Phyllis replied. "I'm overwhelmed."

"I noticed that your performance was considerably different tonight than it was last night," Joshua commented after the first course had arrived.

"It was."

"Was it my imagination, or did you have less to say?"

"Quite a bit less, thanks to your sister, Mr. Phenwick," Phyllis stated, then went on to tell him precisely what had happened.

"I can believe that of Augusta," Joshua remarked with a smile. "I warned you that she is eccentric, or if I didn't, I should have. But that eccentricity is what makes her the great actress that she is."

"Why should she be envious of me? My role was not large to begin with. And during rehearsals, I thought she was quite outgoing to me and responsive. Now, it's as if she suddenly turned on me. I feel as if I must be cautious about everything I do."

"Would you like me to speak to Augusta in your behalf?"

"Would it do any good?"

"Probably not." Again Joshua laughed. "Although I've been close to her over the years, I never have fully understood her or what has motivated her. Still, like Joanne Phenwick, a distant relative from another era, Augusta is the grand Phenwick of the theater. But enough of my sister. I am interested in knowing more about you."

"Knowing about me? I can't imagine why."

"Can't you?" Joshua asked with subtle innuendo. Perhaps it was too subtle. "I'm curious about your ambitions, your desires, where you intend to go in life."

"You sound if you were wanting to write a book about me."

"I'm not a writer," he replied. "I simply find you interesting and I would like to know more about you."

"Well, I desire to become a great actress—as great and as famous as your sister is."

"That *is* ambitious."

"I come from a large family from a small town in the mid-west. No one has ever heard of it, so it is unimportant. I am third eldest of nine children. For years I was simply known as number three. We were raised on the Bible and moralistic teachings. My father was a ranting and raving Baptist, who dominated us with a strong hand and a leather strap if we misbehaved."

"Spare the rod, spoil the child," Joshua recited.

"Maybe I wasn't spoiled, but I did have a mind of my own," Phyllis related, "which led me to several confrontations in the barn with the leather strap. Quite early I learned to swallow my annoyance with Daddy and I would go into the cornfield and emote, yelling my rage and indignation to the jackrabbits and cornstalks, none of which were a particularly appreciative audience."

"I should think not. Even if jackrabbits could applaud, with furry paws their clapping could not be very encouraging," Joshua joked.

"Are you making fun of me, Mr. Phenwick?"

"Perish the thought!"

"Anyway, there was a traveling show that came to our town," Phyllis continued. "They weren't especially good, and they performed on the street, then passed the hat. I used to sneak away from doing my chores to watch them. They were finally run out of town and I experienced my last session in the barn to the tune of the leather strap. I was sixteen, then, and my teenage pride was hurt far greater than my backside. I had earned a little money doing odd jobs. I ran away from home."

"Ran away? I've heard of boys doing that sort of thing, but I didn't think girls did," Joshua interrupted.

"You would be surprised about that, Mr. Phenwick," Phyllis related. "I ran into several girls who had, and I learned that there are certain ways that girls are able to get by. I would have no part of that. I was determined to be an actress."

"That must take some determination."

"I went to Chicago, where, after a few weeks of washing dishes and scrubbing floors, I heard that a traveling show required a girl to replace one of the actresses who had run off with a drummer. I applied, and, although my acting left much to be desired, I was given the role. After I learned my part, which was rather small, one of the older character actresses gave me acting lessons, for which I paid by sewing for her.

55

"I was nearly six months with that company," Phyllis continued, "before it closed. By then I had saved enough money to purchase a railroad ticket to New York. Oh, I was starry-eyed and full of illusions, only to be faced with the grim reality of how things really are. I had been warned by members of the company that there would be hard knocks ahead, so I braced myself for what I eventually had to endure. It wasn't easy, and I won't bore you with the sordid details. But I will state that I emerged unsullied and holding steadfast to my virtue. There was many a day I went hungry, but I survived by doing whatever I could to get by without lowering my standards."

"You amaze me, Miss Burdick. And you finally got cast in Augusta's play?"

"That's it."

"I'm impressed. And I can understand what motivated you."

"Because of your sister?"

"Not only because of Augusta," Joshua stated. "You see, my late wife Alice had had theatrical ambitions. I met her indirectly through Augusta. In all modesty I won her away from her true desires—or at least I thought I had. We were married and had two children before she took desperately ill and ultimately died."

"Oh, I'm sorry."

"That is over and done with," Joshua said with a wave of his hand. "I don't mean to sound nonchalant about it. I was deeply grieved over her passing. I've only recently come out of mourning for her. My distant cousin, the noted and respected physician and psychologist in Boston, Dr. Joseph Ornby, now an elderly gentleman, perceived that Alice's illnesses were brought about by psychological factors, what they call psychosomatic sickness. I or the children were not her first love: it was the theater. I often wondered if she had become contemptuous of me for having lured her away from that which was closest to her heart." He placed his hand on hers. "I would like to be your friend, Phyllis—that is, Miss Burdick. I know better this time than to attempt to alter your ambitions."

"You say that in a singular way, Mr. Phenwick," Phyllis observed, "as if you had taken an extreme personal interest in me. But how could that be when we've only recently met?"

"I know my heart."

"Dear Mr. Phenwick, I must make one thing perfectly clear to you, and that is I am not in the least bit interested in marriage at the present time, and for you to insinuate that I might be is terribly presumptuous on your part."

"Did I give you that impression?" Joshua asked.

"I'm afraid you did," Phyllis replied. "It sounded to me as if you were holding an audition for a replacement for your late wife."

"Perhaps I am," Joshua said with a sigh.

"But I should think you would seek such a replacement in another sort of woman, not one who aspires to the stage as your first wife did," Phyllis said. "I've been told that there are girls in the theater who are simply there to attract husbands of wealth and means, which is not the case with me. When I marry it will be for love—*if* I permit myself to fall in love."

"How very much like Augusta you are," he remarked. "She has never married because of her ambition. I misjudged you. Augusta never appeared as sweetly innocent as you do. You lack her hard veneer and an almost artificial quality that she seems to have. Still, perhaps if we were to get to know each other quite well, we might find a point of mutual agreement."

"I do not say that that is impossible, Mr. Phenwick," Phyllis replied, realizing that she had offended him with her earlier statement and that she could tell that he was a sensitive individual.

"May I call on you—from time to time?" Joshua asked.

"If you like," Phyllis replied. "But you do know that I am busy at the theater every night."

"I'm aware of that," Joshua said. "We can spend time together while I'm in town. Then, if you're so inclined, I would enjoy corresponding with you after I return to Portland."

"I think that is possible." Phyllis turned her attention to the small orchestra playing conspicuously on the podium. "I find it very exciting being here tonight, Mr. Phenwick. I shall always remember this."

"And I find you very exciting to be with, Miss Burdick."

Phyllis glanced over at him with a wry smile. "I could be flirtatious and lead you on, Mr. Phenwick. But I won't. I've been perfectly honest with you and I trust you will respect me for it."

"I do, of course."

The conversation settled into banal topics at Phyllis's instigation. She felt it only fair to discourage a romantic mood. However, after the final course, Joshua again approached the subject of romance and marriage. The wine had loosened his tongue along with his emotions.

"Mr. Phenwick," Phyllis finally said. "I have stated my position, and I must expect you to respect it."

"I do, Miss Burdick. Am I being out of line? I'm sorry. Forgive me."

"It occurs to me, because of what happened today," Phyllis said, a short time later, "that, were you to take an interest in me, I wonder what your sister would think."

"Augusta?" Joshua blinked.

"The results could be disastrous," she speculated. "I must, at all costs, be cautious—especially around Miss Phenwick because my career depends on my relationship with her—at least for the present."

"I can deal with my sister," Joshua assured her. "Besides, her attitude might change toward you if she thought we had a mutual interest in each other."

58

"For the better," Phyllis questioned, "or for the worse?"

"I beg your pardon," Joshua said, slurring his words. "Oh, I see what you mean. I hadn't thought of that. Still, although Augusta and I are close, we're not that close that my personal life should affect hers."

"But at the moment, I *am* that close to your sister, Mr. Phenwick. The matter of romance is closed for the time being," Phyllis stated. "We may become friends. I should like that, but *only* friends. If you have other notions, either eliminate them, or I will not be able to consider the matter of friendship a possibility. Is that perfectly understood?"

"Yes, I'm certain it is."

Shortly after Joshua paid the check and delivered Phyllis to the boarding house wherein she lived. Because the man had become unsteady and had fallen against her several times during the ride, she insisted that he remain in the cab and direct the driver to his hotel. She was appreciative of his generosity and the excitement of the evening, but she displayed concern for his well-being and insisted he go immediately to his hotel.

Alone, Phyllis climbed the steps to the boarding house. Her thoughts were still with Joshua Phenwick, who had told her that he had been named for the first Augusta's husband, the woman who had established the dynasty of Phenwick women. Because he had become inarticulate when he tried to explain about the legend of the women chosen to receive the title of Phenwick woman, Phyllis had paid little attention to it.

After reaching her room, Phyllis disrobed and prepared for bed. It had been an exhausting and an emotional day, to say the least. So very much had happened. And that day following the celebration of the night before, had left her weary. She prayed that another rehearsal wouldn't be called the next day. Rest was needed.

Before she turned out the lights, Phyllis's attention went to the two red rosebuds she had placed in a waterglass on the dresser. Curious, she went to examine them. What struck her as being odd was the fact that they were both still perfectly formed buds and neither had opened. What a singularly strong fragrance they had. Had that heady aroma not been present, one might have mistaken them for being artificial.

Carrying the glass with her, Phyllis placed the rosebuds beside the bed where she could enjoy the powerful fragrance as she drifted off to sleep.

With one last look at the rosebuds before she turned off the last light, Phyllis's thoughts went to the man who had given her the first one. Had he actually given it to her, or had he simply mistakenly thought she had dropped it and retrieved it for her? What a singular thought. Then she recalled seeing him again that afternoon after she had found the second rosebud. Was it only an odd circumstance that he had been nearby at that precise time? And why had he suddenly seemed to have disappeared as he did the night before? Such questions disturbed her. Why was he such a mystery? And why red rosebuds?

While the scent of roses surrounded her, Phyllis returned her thoughts to Joshua Phenwick, himself a man of mystery in many ways. She felt compassion for him, perhaps pity. Yet she knew only too well that he was courting trouble and more heartache if he were to seek the same sort of person he had in the past; an actress. Was he so swept away by the fantasy of his sister's profession that he idealized actresses? That could be a possibility. She couldn't continue dwelling on the subject. It was best to put it from her mind.

Phyllis yawned and snuggled into a comfortable position for sleep. Thoughts of the day began to fade as a half awake, half dreaming state enshrouded her and the fantasies of her subconscious began to dance through her mind.

"Red roses suit you well, my dear," a man's voice seemed to say. *"You have been chosen and the rosebuds indicate my choice. There will be more—many more before your realize the truth of what is happening to you."*

The voice was so real to her that Phyllis shook her head and forced herself out of that dream-beginning state. Her eyes opened and tried to penetrate the darkness of the room. Switching on the light, she scanned the room for evidence of any other presence there.

No one. The light out, she settled back into a sleeping position.

"Red roses suit you well, Phyllis, my dear, and you are destined to become a Phenwick woman."

No, Phyllis thought when she decided not to turn the light on again, it is only a voice that comes out of dreams. Still she could not help wonder why even a dream-voice would say such things.

Chapter Five

When Phyllis awakened on Friday morning, aware of a faint mood of depression that had come over her, she suddenly remembered that she had promised to have lunch with Peggy Phenwick. Scrambling about, she finally located the card which the lady had given her. She slipped into casual attire and went to find the nearest telephone.

Peggy invited her to meet her in the lobby of the Waldorf Astoria at noon.

At first Phyllis wanted to decline the invitation, certain that nothing in her limited wardrobe would be suitable to wear to such a select place. Still, because of circumstances that had transpired over the last few days, she was anxious to get to know other members of the illustrious family. She wore her best dress, which was adequate but hardly fashionable. Over the green cotton dress, she wore her heavy coat. A large, somewhat cumbersome hat was pinned securely to the hair which she arranged in a large bun atop her head. She would simply have to pretend that she was gowned differently. After all a person's attitude was as important as her attire.

Peggy Phenwick, a vision of beauty and fashion, was waiting in the lobby when Phyllis arrived. Impetuously the older woman greeted the actress with a kiss which confused Phyllis. Still it was a warm welcome of friendship and she accepted it as a beautiful gesture. Arm-in-arm they went to the dining room.

"Do I confound you?" Peggy asked after they had ordered.

"Confound me? What a curious question."

"I confess I would be confounded if I were in your position," Peggy replied. "We will dine alone, but we will be joined by another in a half hour."

"Another?" You make it sound mysterious," Phyllis responded.

"A bit enigmatic, but not totally mysterious," Peggy replied with a light ripple of laughter. "I wished to speak to you in private."

The thought that struck Phyllis was that they would be joined by Joshua Phenwick, but she did not voice it. "I must admit that I am both pleased and perplexed that you should wish to have luncheon with me, Mrs. Phenwick. I'm practically a stranger to you."

"Which is one of the precise reasons I wished to have this meeting," Peggy replied. "Miss Burdick—mayn't I call you Phyllis while you address me as Peggy?"

"If you like."

"Very well, Phyllis, let me begin by telling you that I have had quite a discussion with my cousin Augusta II. Don't let that alarm you. We're not particularly close, the reason being that Augusta II rarely lets anyone get close to her—at least as far as family is concerned. When she and I first met, Augusta II was especially cold and passive toward me; she has not changed much

63

since then. However, we do converse, and I have made every effort to get to know her better."

"You are distant cousins, aren't you?"

"My father is half brother to her grandfather." Peggy laughed at the expression Phyllis reacted with. "Let me explain that the Phenwicks are unusual in that several cousins or distant cousins have married over the years. My grandfather, Peter, was twice married, the second time when he was on in years. His first wife bore him four children, all of whom were grown and some with children of their own before Grandfather married a second time. Four other children were produced during the second marriage, my father being the third of four sons. Augusta II is the daughter of Leo, the second child of grandfather's youngest son by the first marriage. Oh, dear, this does sound so confusing. I'm certain you've no idea what I'm talking about."

"Only that you are distantly related to Miss Phenwick," Phyllis replied since she had almost been able to follow the genealogy.

"Let me get back to what I began to say before I got sidetracked with Phenwick history," Peggy said as she delicately forked a dainty salad. "I must start off by saying that you are most fortunate to still be a part of the cast of *The Eternal Light*."

"Why is that?"

"Because Augusta II is, what shall I say, envious of you, to put it in a nutshell," Peggy explained. "For some reason you pose a threat to her in more ways than one."

"I don't see how that can be."

"Nor I, still that is the situation," Peggy said. "Augusta II is respected for her talent, but there are few in the family who have much admiration for her personal life."

"If that is the case, why do so many of the family make a pilgrimage to be present at her opening nights?" Phyllis questioned.

"I suspect it has to do with family pride—and curiosity."

"Curiosity?"

"About Augusta II's present state of mind," Peggy informed her. "It seems Augusta II believes she is the reincarnation of my great-great-grandmother, Augusta I. That notion has somehow affected her—well, her mind. I don't wish to imply that her sanity is involved, but it well may be. The first Augusta was a strong, powerful, determined woman who meant to have her way at whatever the price. The second Augusta has done everything conceivable to identify herself with our ancient relative. Undoubtedly, that is how she happened to become an actress in the first place— because she had tried to be someone else."

"I can see how such a situation could affect one's sanity," Phyllis observed.

"As you must know an imagination is an essential part of being an actress," Peggy continued. "But an imagination not balanced with reality can be detrimental to an individual. I'm quoting from Dr. Joseph Ornby—another distant cousin. And that can lead to false imaginings, if you understand what I mean."

"False imaginings?"

"In your case, Augusta II has begun to imagine that you have purposely set about to depose her. It is foolish of her, but for some reason she sees you as a threat simply because you received favorable notices for your opening night performance—and you were the only actress who did besides herself. Don't you begin to see the picture?"

"There I was in blackface and tatters," Phyllis protested, "in what can only be called a minor role. How could she possibly think—?"

"It's simply the outpouring of a twisted mind," Peggy replied. "I hate to say that about my cousin, but it is true. I fear Augusta II's only reality is a singular kind of illusion, her imagination is carrying her rather swiftly into a world that has no actuality whatsoever save in the confines of her own mind."

"You paint a grotesque picture, Mrs. Phenwick."

"It could well be that I am perceiving a very accurate account of Augusta II," Peggy responded. "I've tried to reason with her concerning you, but she becomes abstract in her ramblings, and, I confess, doesn't always make a great deal of sense. I tell you this because I believe you should know the sort of person with whom you're dealing, therefore, be warned."

"May I ask why you've taken such an interest in me?" Phyllis asked.

"Since the night of the party at Augusta II's home on Riverside Drive," Peggy replied, pushing the remainder of the salad away from her, "I have had conversations with several of the men in my family, notably Joshua, Augusta II's brother. It seems you have attracted the interest of not only Joshua, but Morgan and Jerome as well. Of the single Phenwick men, only Simon has not spoken to me about you."

"I am flattered—I think."

"You should be flattered. The Phenwick family is extremely wealthy and affluent."

"Before you go any further, Peggy, let me tell you what I told Mr. Joshua Phenwick. I am not at the present time interested in any man, much less in the prospect of marriage. My one desire is to become a great actress."

"And that may be your downfall, my dear."

"Why do you say that?"

"Because your aspiration towards greatness in the theatrical world may be what Augusta II perceives and feels threatened by," Peggy said. "It could well be that she is responding to your attitude, which, although you are unaware of it, you are projecting on all sides of you."

"Is that wrong?" Phyllis questioned.

"No, not at all. But I might suggest that it is foolish

of you to close your life to masculine influence and, with all due consideration, to love."

"I haven't closed myself to men and to love," Phyllis argued, "merely to the idea of letting either/or be paramount in my motivations of the moment."

"I suspect you are more calculating than I had at first supposed you were," Peggy commented, taking an appraising pose.

"If one has determination and ambition, one must be calculating, mustn't one?" Phyllis returned.

Peggy studied her for a full half minute before her eyes began to twinkle and a smile grew on her quizzical expression. "You know, I like you, Phyllis Burdick. In some ways you remind me of my sister-in-law Olga; in other ways, you very much remind me of myself. I do hope that we will become the best of friends. In this day and age, where women are beginning to come into their own with the suffrage movement and all, a person of your fortitude is good to know."

Phyllis believed her. And the tension was broken that had previously existed between them. In the next fifteen minutes they shared intimate topics of conversation. Any casual observer would have thought they had been close friends for years.

Finally Peggy examined her brooch watch to discover that it was later than she thought it was. "Oh, dear! Where has the time gone?"

"Do you have another appointment, Peggy?"

"I actually do have one in forty-five minutes. I'm to meet my husband in the Wall Street area at the Stock Exchange."

"Weren't we to have been joined by someone else?" Peggy asked.

"We were."

"Might I guess if it was to be Mr. Joshua Phenwick?"

"You might guess that, yes, but you also might be mistaken," Peggy replied with an almost whimsical smile. "Joshua has impressed you, hasn't he?"

"I find him an interesting person, most attentive and quite eager to please," Phyllis returned, hoping to give a somewhat evasive answer. "I hold only admiration and respect for him. Yet he does have a way of being overbearing, and erroneously convinced that he will eventually have his way in certain matters."

"There is that quality in many of the Phenwick men," Peggy allowed. "Yet I detect a tone of cynicism in your voice when you speak of him that tells me you are not convinced he will have his way in those matters."

"Did you know his first wife?"

"Funny you should put it that way, because I didn't ever meet her," Peggy responded. "Much of my life was spent in San Francisco and it has been only comparatively recent that I have had the opportunity to meet Cousin Joshua. I developed a fondness for him instantly. Why do you ask about his wife?"

"Did you know that she aspired toward a career as an actress?"

"I had heard something to that effect."

"Joshua has admitted to me that his marriage to her thwarted her ambitions, and ultimately becoming discontent with a life alien to her desires, she developed a psychosomatic illness which eventually resulted in her death."

"Poor thing," Peggy sighed. "Oh, I see what you're getting at. Now Joshua is practically turning around and attempting to get himself right back into an identical situation. I could tell that he liked you very much, but I hadn't fully realized what he was doing. I must have a long talk with him, or perhaps Donald should."

"I simply don't want to hurt him, because he has been kind to me."

"Yet you are treading on rather thin-shelled eggs, aren't you?" Peggy noted. "If you don't handle Joshua's interest properly, he could influence his sister's opinion of you—and that could become unpleasant. In which case, I think it only judicious that a heart-to-heart be had with him at the earliest possible time." Again she examined her brooch watch. "Time is hurrying by, isn't it? My husband has the patience of Job, unless he is detained from business matters. And since we are meeting to mutually sign documents, I fear I am going to have to leave."

"Who am I to expect?" Phyllis questioned.

"Why, Cousin Katherine. I thought I had told you."

"Mrs. Philip Phenwick?"

"Katherine," Peggy said. "Now I must beg that you will excuse me. Donald is liable to be upset if I'm terribly late."

Words of departure were expressed, along with hopes on each of their part that they would have the opportunity to repeat the experience again. Moments later, Peggy left, attracting the attention of those she passed.

As Phyllis ruminated about the meeting, she wondered what precisely had been behind it. She liked Peggy and felt that she had made a favorable impression on her. Still she was puzzled.

A waiter approached the table, looking starched with a stoic expression. "Miss Burdick?"

"Yes."

"I was instructed to present this to you," he said, handing her a single red rosebud on a silver salver.

"From whom did it come?"

"I do not know, miss. I was only instructed by the maître d'. That is all I can tell you. May I freshen your coffee?"

"Yes, thank you." Phyllis replied absently, since her attention was incredulously held on the flower.

During the next few minutes as the table was cleared and coffee was poured, Phyllis concentrated her interest on the rosebud and was hardly aware of the action taking place before her. This was the fourth such flower she had received. Moreover the other three were still as fresh and as unopened as they were at the time

she got them. Her impulse was to go to the maître d'
and enquire who had sent it. Why did she get such an
eerie feeling when she gazed at it? What was the
meaning behind it? It was all so enigmatic and
perplexing.

She was still staring at the rosebud when she became aware of Katherine moving toward her. She
quickly put it aside and rose to greet the lady.

"What has become of Peggy? Am I that late in
getting here?" Katherine questioned after she had
greeting Phyllis with a handshake. "The streets are so
crowded this time of the day with everyone rushing
somewhere. We have lovely shopping areas in Boston,
but I do get much better bargains here in Manhattan."
She sat opposite Phyllis. "It must sound peculiar to you
for a Phenwick to be bargain-shopping, but even the
wealthy like to cut edges where they can. I'm sorry I
missed Peggy, but I was almost certain that I would."

"She had to meet her husband to sign some documents."

"Yes, I know." Katherine paused to catch her breath.
"Dear me, I have been hurrying."

"Why were you so certain that you would miss Peggy?"

"I believe I previously mentioned to you that I have
premonitions," Katherine answered. "I'll explain all
about that to you sometime."

"Sometime?"

"Why do you say it like that?" Katherine asked.
"You see, I believe we are destined to become close
friends. I knew that from the moment I laid eyes on
you. Again I have to label that a premonition. But I
mustn't dwell on that aspect of my character for fear
that you will think that I'm peculiar or eccentric, or
something like that. I'm not, really." Her eyes went
from Phyllis's lovely face to the rosebud still on the
salver. "Oh, my, Adam is really at it, isn't he?"

"I beg your pardon. Do you know who sent me this
rose?"

"No, I don't suppose I do."

"But you mentioned the name of Adam."

"I believe it's too early to tell you about Adam. I perceive your information and understanding of such matters is limited," Katherine replied. "What religion were you rasied in?"

"Hard-shell Baptist," Phyllis said. "I was exposed to it, but I don't believe a great amount of it rubbed off on me."

"Interesting," Katherine mused. "Do you believe that life is an ongoing thing, I mean after the transformation which we call death?"

"I've never really given it much thought. I suppose I believe in a heaven and a hell—at least I was taught that such places exist."

"I don't believe in either of them as actual places, more as states of mind," Katherine remarked, "but I am certain, from experience, that life or the spirit is a continuous thing, like a gigantic string of beads. Each bead is an individual life in the flesh, while the string connects it with the spiritual aspect of man."

"Are you speaking of reincarnation?" Phyllis asked. Where had she had a discussion about that recently? She couldn't recall.

"It would not be inaccurate to say that."

"I am merely familiar with the term," Phyllis confessed, "I know nothing of the theory or concept of such a premise."

"If you are meant to know about it in this expression," Katherine commented somewhat whimsically, "you will learn. And the knowledge of it will be an awakening in your far distant memory. But however did we get on such a topic so early in the game?" She motioned for the waiter and ordered tea and a dainty French pastry.

Phyllis had been watching her with a close scrutiny. When she thought the moment was right, she asked, "Why have you taken such a deep interest in this

71

rosebud, as well as the one I was carrying the night of Miss Phenwick's party?"

"You might say I am partial to roses," Katherine replied in a nonchalant manner. "In another life I was particularly fond of violets. Who knows what it will be in still another?"

"Are you being evasive with me, Mrs. Phenwick?"

"If you can call Peggy by her given name, why can't you call me Katherine?"

"My question still stands, Katherine."

"Evasive? That was the word you used, wasn't it?" Katherine rolled her eyes and suddenly wore a pensive expression. "Before I reply to that, I would like you to answer a question for me."

"Which is?"

"What has become of the rosebud you were carrying at the party the other night?"

"It's very much as it was when you saw me with it," Phyllis replied, a strange prickly feeling at the back of her neck. "It's most curious. This is the fourth rose I've received since that night. The other two have remained unopened and perfect as the first. I keep them in my room beside my bed. Why do you ask?"

"Just as I expected." Katherine sipped from the cup of tea which had been presented to her. "It is an omen, you know."

"I didn't know, but I had become suspicious that most peculiar circumstances surrounded the rosebuds," Phyllis said. She reached across the table and put her hand on Katherine's. "*You* know what it means, don't you?"

Katherine lost her quiet composure for a moment, before she regained it and the smile returned to her face. "For some mysterious reason you have been drawn into a situation as an innocent third party. Yet I wonder how remotely innocent you actually are in the somewhat explosive situation that exists."

"I don't follow you."

"Nor do I expect you to at this time," Katherine said enigmatically. "Let me ask you one further question. Since you have had the rosebuds in your possession, have you by any chance heard any strange and inexplicable sounds?"

"Sounds?" Phyllis frowned. "Do you mean such as a voice that seemingly comes out of nowhere?"

"Yes, that would be it. Your question leads me to believe that you have. Isn't that the case?" Katherine tried not to stare too eagerly as she awaited Phyllis's answer.

"On the night after I had found the second rosebud," Phyllis related as the prickly sensation at the back of her neck intensified, "after I had retired with the lights out, I thought I heard a man's voice just as I was about to fall asleep. There was something unearthly about it, and I was convinced that it was only a voice that comes when one is on the verge of falling asleep, the early part of a dream."

"What did the voice say?"

"I recall 'red roses suit you well,' and then something about being chosen for something and that the rosebuds were an indication of it," Phyllis recited, now trembling as the prickly sensation seemed to inundate her entire body.

"Chosen for what?" Katherine persisted.

"I can't tell you that. I'm afraid it would sound most peculiar and you would think ill of me," Phyllis replied. She looked down and reacted with a cold shiver. "I feel as if I'm about to break out with a cold perspiration."

Katherine smiled understandingly. It was her turn to reach over and touch Phyllis's hand. "I can appreciate what you are experiencing, my dear. You see, without a doubt, I know precisely what you were chosen to be. This Adam, of whom I earlier spoke, once was very close to the Phenwick family, and he had been in a life previous to this one in which he was known as

73

Adam Truff. In that other existence he was known as Clayton Latshaw, a close friend and confidant of the first Augusta Phenwick. And that first Augusta was quite a woman in many ways, aggressive, domineering, determined, and the creator of the initial Phenwick fortune. She believed in the inalienable rights of women long before there was such a thing as the suffrage movement. She was a powerful force with which to be reckoned. Because she believed in what is now known as the feminist cause, she decided that she wanted a strong line of Phenwick women to follow in her footsteps, women whom she would chose—even from the other side of the grave while she was in the so-called spirit world."

"You're frightening me," Phyllis declared.

"Am I? I don't mean to, but I can see how speaking of this sort of thing could unnerve a person unfamiliar with such concepts," Katherine replied as gently as she possibly could. "Bear with me. As you gain understanding and awareness, you will discover that it isn't all as mystifying as you think it might be. Shall I speak of something else and drop the subject for the present?"

"No," Phyllis returned, hardly able to form the words because of her inner tremblings, "my curiosity is up, and I've seemed to developed a somewhat morbid interest. Please, go on."

Katherine chuckled softly. "If you are certain you want me to do so, I will. The first Augusta supervised the choosing of the Phenwick women from the spirit side for many years. Her choices were not always the best, but she did well, all things considered. Then it came time for her to return into physical form and she chose to come back as another Phenwick woman."

"As the second Augusta Phenwick?" Phyllis asked.

"No, although Augusta II would like to think that that was true. It isn't. And that is where the great conflict is bound to arise," Katherine said. "But let me

74

go back for a moment. You see, at the time the first Augusta was to be reincarnated, she selected another to take her place to supervise from the spirit side the determination of those who the successive Phenwick women would be. Since Adam Truff was at the point of departing earthly form for a while, and he had been extremely close to the Phenwick family and in particular to several of the Phenwick women, he was elected to that role. In as much as the first Augusta made her spirit presence known as well as her choices by the scent of violets, or on some occasions with the materialization of the actual flowers, Adam decided to use roses—red roses. He has been extremely clever, I might add, at causing them to materialize."

"You have totally confused me, Mrs. Phenwick," Phyllis admitted, "and I confess I feel emotionally shaken by your disclosure."

"Then you think this all a frabrication of my eccentric imagination?"

"I would like to think that. Cold reason tells me that that has to be the case," Phyllis said, now sensing a warm glow coming over her as the trembling subsided. "Yet something deep within me wants to acknowledge that what you say is the truth. I don't know when I've ever been so bewildered and, at the same time, singularly intrigued."

"That is the awakening," Katherine suggested, "the remembrance from time gone by. Eventually you will sort it all out in your consciousness and the perplexities that now trouble you will be gone. Then, I dare say, you will wonder why it is so difficult for others to comprehend what you innately perceive as fact. It wasn't meant that all mankind should know such things; but when an individual is ready, the perception will come. That's simply the way it is."

Phyllis considered Katherine's words in silence while the other delicately forked the pastry. Suddenly Phyllis frowned before a look of annoyance moved across her

75

countenance. "To become a Phenwick woman," she said at last, "I would have to marry a Phenwick man. Isn't that the case?"

"It is, since you weren't born into the Phenwick family as Augusta II was."

"Are you suggesting then—or is this Adam whatever-his-name—that Mr. Joshua Phenwick and I—?" She could not bring herself to complete the sentence.

"Oh, not necessarily Joshua," Katherine quickly replied, which nearly caused her to choke on a bit of pastry. "My goodness, no, there are many other eligible Phenwick men. You've only met four to my knowledge, but rest assured there are others. But I would not completely discount Joshua for the moment. You may find that he learned his lesson with Alice and that he has become far more flexible in his thinking as a result of his experience with her."

Phyllis emptied her lungs in a resolute sigh. "Have I no choice in this matter?"

"You have every choice you could possibly want, Phyllis. This is no arbitrary thing," Katherine said. "In the roster of Boston society there are many debutantes who would leap at the opportunity—prompted by their parents, I might add—to marry into the opulent and influential Phenwick family. Many are enthralled, few are chosen."

Phyllis swallowed hard. Her throat felt dry and cluttered with queer emotional reactions. "This disclosure hasn't in the least altered my goal of wishing to become a great actress."

"I should hope not," Katherine returned sweetly. "You must first and foremost be true to your own ambitions. Since you have been chosen by Adam, and you obviously have, rest assured that the Phenwick man will fall in love with you, and you with him. And, I dare say, he will be instrumental in helping you obtain your goal."

Again Phyllis fell into contemplative silence while

Katherine finished the pastry. Her mind was a collage of multi-directional thoughts, prompted by conflicting emotions.

"I don't wish to speak any further about this, Katherine," the young actress said, "not now. Perhaps later, when I've given the topic consideration and can discover some grain of logic in all that we've discussed. But before we drop the matter, there is one last question I would like to ask. Supposing all this is true, the omen of the rosebuds and all, am I to know who the reincarnation of the first Augusta Phenwick is?"

"If you feel it important."

"I do."

Then I suggest you close your eyes for a few moments and use concerted effort to put all conscious thoughts from your mind," Katherine instructed. "As you sit in that silence, aware of the very here and now and nothing more, you will perceive a thought, perhaps a name, or receive the mental image of a person."

"I've never done that sort of thing before."

"Try it. You might be surprised about your inner perception," Katherine stated. "I assure you that I will verify what you perceive, if you perceive correctly."

Feeling somewhat conspicuous, but curiously driven to try the experiment, Phyllis closed all active thoughts, questions and confusion from her mind. It took extreme effort and she was only able to quiet her conscious mind for a few seconds at a time before another alien thought intruded.

The waiter approached the table while Phyllis was in meditation. Katherine motioned for him not to interrupt. After a shrug, he quietly went away.

Phyllis's eyes popped open with an expression of alarm.

"What is it, Phyllis?"

"I keep getting one thought, one name and one mental image of a person," Phyllis replied incredulously as she gazed into Katherine's kind and understanding eyes.

77

"Do you wish me to verify it for you?"

Phyllis blinked. She took a swallow of water without taking her eyes from Katherine's. *"You?"*

Katherine smiled and gently nodded her head.

"But how could you possibly be the reincarnation of the woman you described as the first Augusta Phenwick?" Phyllis questioned. "You're the antithesis of what you depicted her to be."

"The pendulum swings back and forth from one extreme to the other in the path of the soul. One must seek balance of extremes until the distance between those opposites is reduced to a mere hair's breadth. Katherine Phenwick is indeed quite the opposite of the Augusta Phenwick she had been. That is the very nature of how the principle of reincarnation works. This, too, you will comprehend in time. Consciously, from what I know of the life which that Augusta Phenwick led, I am repelled and want to reject it thoroughly as being completely alien to what I am; still I know it is what I must have been. We'll discuss it no further at this time. And, for that matter, I believe it is time that we brought all discussion to a conclusion for the present." She motioned for the waiter. "Don't you agree, Phyllis?"

Phyllis did not. Her interest had been so aroused and so many questions were entering her mind that she wanted the visit to continue. Judiciously, she knew that that meeting must come to an end.

"And don't forget your rosebud, Phyllis," Katherine said as she began to move away from the table where they had been seated.

Phyllis went back for the flower. Upon picking it up, it occurred to her that that simple flower was part of a mystical experience which she sensed was destined to affect the rest of her life.

When she returned to her room, Phyllis placed the fourth rosebud in the glass with the other three. Then the thought came that she should purchase a far better container for the roses.

Suddenly drowsy, Phyllis felt the need to nap to refresh herself for that evening's performance.

Shortly after she got beneath the covers, Phyllis anticipated that she would again hear that mysterious voice. She did not. Then, putting all conscious thoughts, questions and pictures from her mind, she drifted off into rejuvenating sleep.

Chapter Six

That same evening, Joshua, in the company of his cousin Simon, went to the Riverside Drive address to have an early dinner with his sister. When Augusta II had invited Joshua, he told her that he had previously arranged to dine with Simon. As a result Augusta II invited both men to be her guests.

The large manse was four stories high, constructed of brownstone in a design peculiar to the Victorian era. A gloominess prevailed in the downstairs areas, rooms which were rarely used. Except for social occasions and times when she entertained in a pretentious way, Augusta II preferred to spend most of the time in her private chambers on the second floor where she had an unobstructed view of the Hudson River and the pretty park that ran alongside it.

Joshua and Simon were shown to the first floor sitting room by the officious butler, Carlyle, a man who cherished his position and who was extremely devoted to and protective of his mistress.

"Carlyle was perfectly cast in his role," Simon observed as the butler left the room.

"A more proper and dedicated man could not be found," Joshua acknowledged. "He knows his place and can be trusted beyond the shadow of any doubt. Augusta is fortunate to have him. As to being theatrical, there is no part of my sister's life that is not that. You don't suppose she would incorrectly cast, do you?"

Simon laughed. "I don't know your sister that well, I must admit. I've only been associated with her in the presence of others. This will be the most intimate with her that I will have had the honor to be."

"It's a pity you're returning so soon to Boston," Joshua said. "You might find it enlightening to get to know my sister better."

"I'm certain that I might," Simon returned politely. "However, Pru has to get back and I do have a law practice to maintain. Dad will think I've deserted him as it is, since I've been away so long."

"It's not inconceivable that Augusta may one day perform in Boston," Joshua seemed to be thinking aloud. "I've been hoping to encourage her to take *The Eternal Light* to Boston once it completes its run here in New York. So far Augusta thinks it's only an interesting possibility."

"That would be something to look forward to." Simon appeared preoccupied with other thoughts.

Joshua went to help himself to a glass of brandy and offered one to his cousin. While he poured, he glanced over at Simon several times. In Joshua's opinion Simon was one of the most handsome of all the Phenwick men, masculine and sensible in appearance, polished and dignified with an excellent mind and a congenial nature, both appealing and friendly.

"I find it difficult to comprehend how a man of your stature, presence and personality can have escaped so long from the clutches of matrimony," Joshua commented as he presented a brandy snifter to the other.

"You used the right word to define my position in the matter," Simon returned with a light ripple of laughter. "*Clutches.* I'm not a man who likes to be possessed, I never have been. My father claims I have an extremely independent nature, which, in his opinion, should be rectified." Again he laughed, showing teeth. "Dad is of the old school of morality, a tad prudish and conservative."

"Uncle John has always impressed me as being progressive and flexible in his thinking," Joshua returned. "I greatly admire him."

"I admire my father, don't get me wrong about that," Simon said. "In my opinion the only other Phenwick man who comes close to him in prominence is Uncle Thadius. Since Mother's death, I have become a little concerned for Dad. He seems lonely, yet rejects the idea of going out to meet other women. Both Laura and I have tried to arrange for him to meet new people, but our choices seem to widely differ from his. Despite her illnesses over the years, Dad was staunchly devoted to Mother. I sometimes think that women are far better equipped to deal with the loss of a mate than a man is. Oh, I'm sorry, Joshua, I didn't mean to rub salt."

"That's perfectly all right, Simon, I understand," Joshua replied. "I'm used to being a widower, but I don't intend to remain a single man the rest of my life. When Alice died, a part of me went with her. I finally realized that a man has many other parts, most of which have not been fully explored. The hardest part for me was to learn to live in the present here and now, and *not* in the past that will never be again. Nor can I permit myself to speculate too greatly about the future."

"A here and now existence is the only kind to have," Simon agreed. "Love, laugh and be gay, for tomorrow may never come, as they say."

"I thought it was 'eat, drink and be merry.' "

"It's whatever you want it to be, Josh." Simon emptied the glass at the same moment Carlyle arrived to announce that Augusta II was awaiting their company in the dining room.

"Brother, dear!" Augusta II exclaimed as she rose from the chair at the end of the large dining table. She was gowned in electric blue, shimmering velvet. A long string of pearls hung about her neck and her overall demeanor was both dramatic and condescendingly pleasant. "And Cousin Simon! What a pleasure this is! I'm honored by two extremely handsome men."

Greetings were exchange with kisses and embraces.

"I've asked Carlyle to sit the two of you opposite each other at my end of the table," Augusta II said. "I'll have to project my voice enough the rest of the evening without having to do so over dinner, if you don't mind."

"Intimacy is always desirable to distance," Simon remarked.

"I like your philosophy, Cousin Simon," Augusta II returned. "We must find the opportunity to get better acquainted. Ah, the theater of life! 'All the world is a stage,' etcetera. Shakespeare."

"The etcetera was your ad-lib, no doubt," Simon teased.

"And you have a quick wit," Augusta II said. "Had I thought in advance, I would have invited your sister and her husband to join us."

"Laura and Pru had other plans which had been scheduled quite in advance," Simon explained.

"Well, just the three of us will be just fine for tonight," Augusta II returned. She turned her concerted attention from Simon on her right to Joshua at her left. "I trust you've been keeping yourself sufficiently occupied while visiting New York."

"I always do, you know that, Augusta." Joshua adjusted his napkin in place and leaned aside while Carlyle served.

"I am told by the theater manager that he has seen you at the performance practically every night this week, Joshua. Is that true?" Augusta II questioned a while later.

"I've been at the thater, but I didn't think I had been recognized." Joshua looked a bit uneasy.

"Perhaps you should have worn a false beard and heavier eyebrows," Simon joked.

"Why is it that you did not come backstage to see me after the performances?" Augusta II asked, greater intensity in her voice.

"I feared you would be busy," Joshua explained. "Besides, I had other plans for afterwards."

"I was informed that you attended the theater unaccompanied," Augusta II persisted.

"That is true, Sister, quite true, which does not mean that I hadn't made arrangements for after the show."

"That would lead me to suspect that such arrangements were made with a member of the cast of *The Eternal Light*," she continued.

"Not necessarily, Augusta. I don't know why you are persisting in this." Joshua sounded annoyed. "I'm sorry, Simon, if I live to be a hundred and forty, I will always be Augusta's little brother, ergo, treated in a manner befitting that situation. I happen to be quite grown-up, Augusta, and I don't need your mother-hen concern hovering over my private life."

"You are testy tonight. I was merely curious, that's all." Augusta II again turned her attention to Simon. "And you, Cousin, have you kept yourself nicely occupied while visiting here?"

"Laura, Pru and I have done quite a bit of looking around, enjoying the sights, the entertainment and fabulous food," Simon replied. "I've had a few adventures on my own, but nothing spectacular, nor none which I care to relate."

"You sound secretive, Simon," Augusta II commented. "Not naughtily secretive, I trust."

"Would it make a difference?" Simon questioned, without sounding defensive.

"Not to me," Augusta II returned, "but it might have made you be a bit more pleasant."

"Do you find me unpleasant?"

"Not in the least," Augusta II quickly assured him.

"Then why was the matter brought up?"

"Here now, you two, what's provoked all of this?" Joshua intervened. "I'm shocked at both of you."

"You needn't be shocked, Joshua," Augusta II returned. "I'm merely having a little game with Simon, a verbal romp as it were."

"Your games have an incisive sting to them, Cousin Augusta," Simon said. "Would you have liked me to have said that I have been courting trollops, bedding sleazy showgirls and patronizing dens of sin?"

"Have you been?"

"No. But I got the impression that that is what you would have liked to hear. Sorry if I disappointed you."

"I suspect a full moon tonight," Augusta II commented as she again turned her attention back to her brother. "Everyone goes crazy at the time of a full moon. We notice it most in the theater where tempters are rife with short fuses, and explosions regularly occur anyway. It's all so very dramatic."

"So it would seem," Joshua commented.

Suddenly Augusta II's mood appeared to do an about-face. "But Joshua, I've been made privy to the information that you've been seen practically every night this past week at the stage door of the Majesty theater. Is that the case?"

"I don't know who your informant is, but he may be mistaken," Joshua said with a coldness in his voice.

"But only may have been," Augusta II inserted. "Furthermore, another informant told me that you were seen twice at Lüchow's after the performance—and not alone."

"All right, Augusta, that's enough of this little game," Joshua declared. "I came here to dine, not to be interrogated."

Augusta II was instantly sugar-and-spice sweet, although a sarcastic edge lingered on her words. "I only persist in this matter because a curious thing has been happening every night during the curtain calls."

"What is that, Augusta?" Simon asked.

"Each night a particular young lady in the company who plays a diminutive role receives a rather pretentious ovation for a performance hardly worthy of mention. I've had the audience watched, and it seems the instigator of such impetuous applause is always in the immediate area where Joshua is seated."

"I applaud equally as loud for you, Augusta," Joshua stated.

"Equally? *Equally?*" Augusta II asked indignantly. "My own brother applauds my performance equally as robustly as he does that of a bit player? *Equally,* indeed!"

"I can't possibly applaud any louder than I do," Joshua defended himself. "I'm liable to get blisters."

"Then you could clap with less gusto for that other person," Augusta II suggested, her jaws tight and the words spat out with mounting rage.

"I'll remember that next time, if I happen to attend another performance, Sister dear."

"You do that, Brother dear!" Augusta II snapped. Suddenly a honeyed smile. "I fear my brother would applaud a tramp who dropped his pants to get a cheap laugh—or should I say *her* pants?"

"That is enough, Augusta! I'll not sit here and listen to any more of this! You're being impossible." Joshua was about to push himself away from the table.

"Brother, Brother," Augusta II said as if she were emoting her best line of the evening, "you're quite right. Your private life is your own—and I have absolutely no right to interfere with it—as long as it doesn't affect me. However, fraternizing or socializing or whatever other kind of 'izing' you do with a member of my company does become my business. Not only am

I among the best, if not the most prominent in my profession, but I am also a Phenwick woman, and to have it bandied about that my very own brother is being seen in the company of an incidental bit player comes back to me as a personal insult."

"That's enough, Augusta!" Joshua rose and stood behind the chair with his hands clutching to it. "I'll not sit here and listen to this!"

"Have you gotten to know Miss Burdick well—and I imply this in the Biblical sense?" Augusta II bit.

"That's none of your damned business!"

"Did I come here to witness a sibling row, or to dine?" Simon asked in hopes of breaking the tension that was mounting. "And if it's the former, mayn't I be made aware of whom you're bickering about?"

"Miss Phyllis Burdick." Augusta II enunciated the name as if it were a vile phrase of profanity.

"Stop it, Augusta!"

"Miss Phyllis Burdick?" Simon ruminated as if the other display was merely incidental and unimportant. "Ah, yes, wasn't she present at the opening night party here?"

"She was."

Joshua moved around the table until he stood at the opposite end from where Augusta II was seated. Putting palms flat, he braced his arms on the table and leaned forward. "Listen, both of you, I want to get one thing straight. I am very fond of Miss Burdick. I find her physically, mentally and romantically stimulating. But I assure you both that she is every inch a lady and a fine example of propriety. To insinuate anything cheap or shoddy about her is a direct insult to me, and I take offense at it. Is that clear? Is it, Augusta?"

"It has to be full moon," Augusta II managed to say after a dramatic pause for effect. "Well, Miss Burdick can be replaced."

"You have her replaced, Augusta," Joshua declared, "and I will never speak to you again as long as I live.

Furthermore, I will go on an all-out campaign to malign you to every member of the Phenwick family, and consciously do everything I can to turn them irrevocably against you. Is that clear?"

Again a dramatic pause before Augusta II slowly pushed herself up and, with outstretched arms, proceeded to go to where Joshua was standing. "Poor baby brother, I am so sorry. I never realized you were as serious toward Miss Burdick as you apparently are. My only complaint is that you had the audacity to applaud as loudly—equally as loudly—for her as you did for me, and by so doing inciting others to join you. That's all. Here I was blaming Miss Burdick for receiving such an outrageous ovation when I should have been putting the guilt on my loving baby brother." She wrapped her arms around Joshua and cradled him.

"Augusta, what are you doing to me?" Joshua all but sobbed.

"Holding you as I always have. Now you come back to your chair like a good little boy and finish your dinner," Augusta II coaxed. "I've planned your favorite desert."

Simon found it difficult to believe what he was seeing.

Contrite and almost whimpering, Joshua permitted himself to be led back to the chair. What strange mysterious hold did Augusta II have over her brother? Simon wondered. When he offered to assist, his help was ignored.

During the rest of the time spent at Augusta II's home, nothing out of the ordinary happened and the conversation settled into trite mundane topics that seemed to be purposely used to keep from a recurrence of the dramatics that had happened before. Both Augusta II and Joshua reverted back to their old selves, the way Simon had always known them.

Because Augusta II had to be at the theater, the visit was cut short and Simon suggested that he and Joshua go to a private men's club that had gymnasium and sauna facilities, where he hoped to get a better insight into his cousin's problem.

Augusta II had kissed both her brother and cousin good-bye in the dining room, permitting Carlyle to show them to the front door and out. Once they were gone and she heard the front door close, Augusta II plunged both hands into her hair and pulled fists full of it out to each side. Her face became a fiery red and she glanced about to find something of not tremendous value to smash.

"Did you drop something, Miss Phenwick?" Carlyle asked as he quickly entered the dining room to find a plate shattered to pieces.

"It must have slipped from my hand," Augusta II replied with a wild-eyed look in her eyes and a twisted mouth that seemed to snarl contempt. "I don't know how it could have happened."

"I'll get something to pick it up," Carlyle said, excusing himself to go to the kitchen.

"That tart! That trollop! That she-devil!" Augusta II screamed as she connected with another plate and let it fly.

The crash so alarmed Carlyle that he returned from the kitchen without the broom. "Are you quite all right, Miss Phenwick?"

"Perfectly. And, as a matter of fact, I feel infinitely better. I've been wanting to get rid of that tawdry set of dishes, anyway. Has there been any word from Mr. Brooks?"

"He said he would be here in time to see you to the theater, Miss Phenwick."

"In that case, I'll be waiting for him upstairs. He knows which room," Augusta II said grandly and paraded from the dining room as if nothing in particular had happened.

Carlyle shook his head as she disappeared beyond the doors. He had observed her in such a state of temper tantrums—if that is all that is was—over the last several years. He was of the opinion that one of her problems stemmed from the fact that she had gone through a string of young men, most of whom were ten to fifteen years her junior. Yet, since most of them were actors or those who were aspiring to be actors, they had attracted her fancy and she had offered them assistance in seeking their goals in exchange for personal favors.

As Carlyle was finishing with the broom and dustpan, he looked up to see Leslie Brooks watching him.

"Problems, Carlyle?"

"Oh, Mr. Brooks You startled me."

"I let myself in. I didn't want to disturb you."

"Have you a key, Mr. Brooks?"

"Yes. Miss Phenwick gave me one last week. This is the first opportunity I've had to use it," the young actor said, his bright eyes flashing.

"I see. Very well, Mr. Brooks. Miss Phenwick is in her room awaiting you. She said you would know which room she meant."

Leslie examined his pocket watch. "We're due at the theater in forty-five minutes."

Stoic Carlyle made no comment, but went directly to the kitchen to deposit the broken piece of china. Leslie merely shrugged at the butler's reaction and went to take the stairs two at a time to the second floor.

"You're late," Augusta II fired, when he entered the room after knocking.

"I'm terribly sorry, Miss Phenwick. I was unavoidably detained," Leslie apologized. He beamed a radiant smile and his green eyes radiantly glistened. "As a matter of fact, just as I was on my way here, I ran into one of the people in *The Eternal Light* who had a bit of a problem. If I had not helped her, she wouldn't have made it to the theater on time."

"She?" Augusta II arched one eyebrow. "What precisely was *her* problem?"

"She had broken one of the heels of her shoes," Leslie

explained. "She was hobbling along at such a slow pace that I went to her rescue and lent her enough money to buy a new pair."

"That was extravagant of you, Leslie," Augusta II returned. "Never mind that. Take off your things and come join me on the bed."

"Is there time, Miss Phenwick?"

"We'll make time, won't we?" she cooed and wiggled her way into a welcoming position.

As Augusta II watched the young man disrobe, her curiosity again began to fester. "Which of the actresses was it who broke the heel of her shoe?"

"I forget her name," Leslie replied as he skinned out of his last garment. "I called her by her play name."

"Which is?"

Leslie got beside her. "Is it important?"

"*What* did you call her?" Augusta II hissed between clenched teeth.

"Molly. Why?"

"Phyllis Burdick! That—that—"

"I don't believe I've ever seen your face that red, Miss Phenwick."

"That floozy!" She grabbed him by the hair, using both hands as she shook and jerked him about in response to the fierce anger welling within her. Then, when he looked properly terrified and, she hoped, repentent, she navigated his face to hers, stared deeply into his eyes and began to laugh almost hysterically.

"Augusta has been that way for as long as I can remember," Joshua said, sitting in the altogether in the steam room of the club, "that is toward me. She's a little less the matriarch with Edwin, but she never let him get away with much, either."

A wet towel around his head as his only attire, Simon glanced over at Joshua through the steamy vapor. "I was surprised. I will say that."

"Augusta has had flare-ups before," Joshua explained,

"but I've never seen her in the rage she was in tonight. It was foolish of me to mention Miss Burdick's name. I should have known better. Augusta was so infuriated that Miss Burdick's name got mentioned in the reviews for *The Eternal Light* that she seems to have developed a tremendous resentment for her."

"Miss Burdick? Miss Burdick?" Simon repeated, trying to recall the face that went with the name. "Oh, yes, *that* Miss Burdick. I danced two dances with her at your sister's party. She's very pretty, as I remember. Beauty, youth, talent—it's no wonder that Augusta is envious of her."

"Miss Burdick wishes only to be my friend," Joshua lamented. "I shouldn't have told her about Alice and her aspirations to be an actress. At times I verge on being stupid."

Simon reached over and patted his cousin's thigh. "Don't chastise yourself, Joshua. The problem is Augusta's, not yours."

The steam became progressively thicker until the cousins could only see each other's gray silhouettes. Simon moved away from Joshua and entertained private thoughts. But no matter how he tried to take his mind away from the incident that occurred in Augusta II's dining room, he could not elude the images that replayed in his mind, nor the questions he had that accompanied them.

Chapter Seven

"Although I was born in Phenwick," Laura Donnally said shortly after she had accidentally met Phyllis in the lobby of the Waldorf-Astoria hotel, "I wasn't chosen to be known as a Phenwick women. I don't understand what it's all about, or what difference it makes, but those who possess the title seem to covet it with protective tenacity." She laughed merrily, as if it wasn't important.

"Still there must be some distinction to be known as a Phenwick woman?" Phyllis questioned. She had come to meet Madison Davis and had arrived fifteen minutes prior to the appointed time.

Laura shrugged. "It's of no consequence to me. I'm perfectly content being Mrs. R. Pruman Donnally. Of course, in Boston Society I'm known as one of the famous or infamous Phenwicks, as the case may be. Like my first cousin Lola, Peggy's younger sister, we were somehow overlooked by the powers that be who choose. Simon teases me about it."

"Simon?"

"My brother," Laura returned, her attractive face wreathed in smiles of admiration when she spoke of Simon. "Simon and I are the only children of John and Isabelle Phenwick. Mother had the distinction of being known as a Phenwick woman, but I couldn't see that it made much difference in her life. She's gone now. Poor Daddy is alone."

Seeing a distant look come to Laura's eyes as she spoke of her mother, Phyllis thought it prudent to alter the course of the conversation. "I've never been in Boston. Has it become as conservative in its thinking as they say?"

"I don't know what they say—whoever they may be—but Bostonians do have a conservative and prudish attitude," Laura replied. "We have so many churches, and the religious advocates wield tremendous power. You certainly don't see the things in Boston that you see in New York. Katherine's brother-in-law, Richard, has become a hell-fire and damnation preacher. An arch-conservative and religionist, I find him extremely disagreeable to be around, and I make no bones about telling him so. Donald, his younger brother, and his sister Polly upbraid me for my attitude. I simply don't care. Frankly, I don't believe either Donald or Polly is that sympathetic toward Richard's persuasions, but they are devoted, loving siblings. We are a complex family, aren't we?"

"It would seem so."

"Our closets rattle with skeletons," Laura added with a touch of whimsy. "Still the Phenwicks are strong and powerful . . . and rich. If you're ever in Boston, you must come and visit."

"I will do that."

Laura suddenly peered into Phyllis's face.

"What is it, Mrs. Donnally?" Phyllis asked, becoming embarrassed by the probing scrutiny.

"There is something about you that I find amazingly

94

familiar," Laura said. "Have you ever known that to happen? I mean to say, encountered someone who was basically a stranger and had the feeling that you knew them from somewhere—only you couldn't have possibly known them, because in tracing back each of your backgrounds there is no possible way that you could have met."

"I've encountered strangers whom I've seemed to instantly know."

"Yes, that's exactly how I feel about you for some peculiar reason. I hope that doesn't bother you."

"Not in the least." Phyllis felt the need to change the subject again. She wished Madison Davis would arrive. "What line of work is your husband in?"

"He is in manufacturing as a sort of subsidiary of Medallion Enterprises, which is the Phenwick family business," Laura replied. "I orginally met him through my father, who was handling legal matters for his father. It was a marriage of arrangement or convenience. I'm deeply in love with Pru, and he with me."

"Have you children?"

"No." Laura looked away. "I'm unable to bear children." She brightened. "If he ever marries, Simon will have to supply Daddy with grandchildren."

"You're close to your brother, aren't you?" Phyllis said, unable to mistake the expression of admiration Laura got when she spoke of Simon.

"There's just the two of us," Laura replied. "They say that twins run in families. My mother was so relieved that neither Simon nor I was born with a twin that she didn't want to have other children for fear she would be tempting her luck. Mother had an identical twin—at least they were identical in appearance—so much so that Aunt Elena could take mother's place and no one would be the wiser. At least she tried to do that on more than one occasion. I'm certain that Simon and I would have detected the difference. Listen to me, just running on this way. I must be boring you beyond belief."

"Not at all. I find it interesting."

"Well, you've been saved by the arrival of my husband and Simon," Laura stated as she caught sight of the two men heading toward them.

"Darling," Pru said as he arrived at his wife's side, "you must forgive our tardiness."

"My interview took longer than I had anticipated," Simon interrupted. "I told Pru he needn't wait for me."

"And I wasn't about to leave without Simon," Pru added.

Seeing that Simon's attention had gone to Phyllis, Laura introduced, "May I present Miss Phyllis Burdick. This is my husband, Mr. Donnally, and my brother, Mr. Phenwick."

"We've met," Simon returned, his eyes held with curious interest on Phyllis's face. "As a matter of fact, we enjoyed two dances together at Augusta's party the other evening. It's good to see you again, Miss Burdick."

"Thank you, Mr. Phenwick, I'm honored," Phyllis said, doing her best to control a butterfly that seemed to be fluttering about in her solar plexus.

"I, too, am honored, Miss Burdick." Pru Donnally said as he shook her hand. "I'm sorry that we can't take longer to visit, my dear, but we are running behind schedule."

"So we are, Pru," Laura agreed. She had been watching her brother's expression of interest as he gazed into Phyllis's face. "We'll only be a few minutes, Simon, if you wish to wait for us here."

"That will be fine," Simon replied.

"We'll not be long," Laura said as she took her husband's arm and they hurried toward the elevators.

"You must forgive my sister, Miss Burdick," Simon commented after the Donnallys had moved away from them. "Laura gets flustered at times, especially when delay is involved."

"Why do you say that?"

"She didn't bother to say good-bye."

"That is of no consequence," Phyllis assured him. "We only met today quite by accident. I'm here to meet a friend."

"A friend? A gentleman friend?" Simon questioned.

"The playwright, Madison Davis."

"Oh, yes, I recall meeting him at the party." Simon was pleasant and did not appear to respond in a negative way to the mention of Madison Davis. "Why don't we sit over there? Your friend may be a while yet in arriving."

Phyllis consented and led the way to a nearby upholstered sofa.

"There, now isn't this better?" Simon asked as he turned toward her. "I confess I've been on my feet most of the day, running here and there, taking care of last-minute business in New York before we leave tomorrow. So many things to accomplish, and so little time to do it in."

"Business matters, did you say?" Phyllis was trying not to stare at him.

"I'm working on a case which involves a New York company," Simon said. "Then, too, I've been interviewing with a few law firms here."

"Interviewing with them. Are you out of work?"

"Not hardly." Simon laughed. "I work with my father in Boston. He has a law firm. Recently I've been bucking a lot of resistance from some of the older members of the firm who believe that I'm being given special privilege because I'm the son of John Phenwick. They have a way of making certain conditions uncomfortable for me, not in obvious ways but by little subtle means. I've considered taking up with another firm, if they will have me, prove my merit and then, when Dad is definitely ready to retire, go back to Boston. On the other hand, I may find that I like New York better than my home city and decide to take up permanent residence here. At times I find the religious conservative attitudes in Boston both stifling and limiting."

"Since I've never been in Boston," Phyllis commented, "I can't imagine what it is like."

"It's a far cry from what New York is." Simon looked away, then back at Phyllis. "I suspect the theater keeps you limited to New York, doesn't it?"

"New York is where the theater is," Phyllis replied. "I have appeared in Chicago, but most plays originate in New York. That's why I'm here."

"I understand you're having a bit of a problem with my cousin," Simon said as a means of changing the subject.

"Mr. Phenwick—that is, Mr. Joshua Phenwick, isn't any problem. Actually I enjoy his company and his friendship. He has been able to show me more of New York than I've ever seen before."

Simon found that amusing. "I suppose I should have specified. I was alluding to my cousin Augusta."

"Oh!" Phyllis blinked. "I'm not really having a problem with Miss Phenwick—as long as I comply to her wishes. She is a leading lady, I'm merely a bit player. I admire Miss Phenwick's acting ability, and I've learned much from working with her. As in all things, one must learn one's place and remain in it."

"Does that mean you will always take a back seat to the likes of Augusta?" Simon questioned.

"I don't intend to do so," Phyllis replied. "But at the present I must. I try to put myself in her place and realize what it must be like to maintain oneself on the top. I suspect it's like with anyone who obtains power in a higher echelon, there must be concern that someone will come along who might topple you and usurp your position."

"And do you have such ambitions as far as Augusta is concerned?"

"Not to topple her, goodness knows," Phyllis assured him. "I have no desire to take anyone else's place. I want to make my own way and become my own person. I've never been one to be competitive in a vicious sense.

Fact is, I believe there is room at the top for more than one. Maybe when I reach the position Miss Phenwick has obtained, I'll alter my opinion about competition. I suppose much depends on the place of perspective where one stands."

"You amaze me, Miss Burdick. On occasion I have met several actresses and aspiring actresses, largely through my cousins. Most of them proved to be vacuous little nobodies, ready to sell themselves short for a chance—any chance—to perform. You're different—quite different."

"I can be objective about most things," Phyllis replied. "The other actors are primarily subjective in everything they do until the forest gets obscured by the trees. I guess the secret is getting oneself out of the way, becoming detached, and simply expecting to see the forest."

"I must say you surprise me, Miss Burdick," Simon commented. "When I met you the other night, I had no idea that you had such opinions. Few men have such a philosophy."

"Once I left home," Phyllis stated, "I was forced to develop a positive philosophy, set goals, and go after them."

"Can this be a frail woman speaking?" Simon teased.

"While I am a woman, I've never considered myself in the least bit frail. God help me if I were."

Simon laughed loudly. "If I didn't know otherwise, I would swear I was speaking with a Phenwick woman."

"That seems an odd observation to make," Phyllis commented.

"I am noted for making the odd observation periodically," Simon said. "It is for that very reason that I often lock horns with my father. I like to think of myself as progressive. Dad has a tendency toward conservative attitudes. I think Boston has affected him that way."

As Phyllis looked beyond the intensity of Simon's

gaze, she beheld the arrival of Madison Davis. "The gentleman I was awaiting is approaching us."

Simon turned. "Oh, yes, I recall seeing him." He stood. "In that case, I don't wish to interfere. I've enjoyed the chat, Miss Burdick. Perhaps we will have the opportunity to resume it at another time."

"I trust that is so, Mr. Phenwick."

"Ah, there you are!" Madison exclaimed in a theatrical way as his cape rustled behind him. He took Phyllis's extended hand and kissed the back of it.

"Have you met Mr. Phenwick? Mr. Simon Phenwick?" Phyllis asked.

"I believe we've been introduced, Mr. Davis," Simon said as he shook Madison's hand. "I suspect it was the other night at my cousin's party."

"Ah, yes, one of the cousins," Madison commented. "There are so many I can't keep them all straight." He looked from Simon to Phyllis and back again, an unuttered question forming on his lips.

"I was just preparing to leave," Simon explained. "It was pleasant seeing you again, Mr. Davis." His eyes went to Phyllis. "And, Miss Burdick, I shall be looking forward to another visit."

"He seems to be an affable person," Madison commented as he watched Simon depart. "Despite some of their peculiarities, the Phenwicks do have great charm. Even Miss Augusta has her delightful side, I'm simply at a loss to appreciate it at the present time."

"I was speaking with Mr. Phenwick's sister earlier," Phyllis said as if she felt an explanation was necessary. "Mrs. Donnally and I were here when her husband and brother arrived. That is how Mr. Phenwick and I happened to be in conversation."

"Whatever the reason," Madison returned, "I should think you were lifted by the encounter. Your cheeks are quite rosy, your eyes twinkle with an unusual brightness, and your smile has almost a naughty, seductive look to it."

"Madison! Really!" Phyllis was embarrassed. "No more about Mr. Phenwick. I suspect you read far too much into things."

"Do I? I wonder." Madison looked pensive before he took the folder from beneath his arm and swung it through the air with a flourish. "I have here sketched out an outline for a new play, entitled: *Triumph and Passion*, which I have conceived for you, Miss Burdick. It may be my masterpiece."

"Why don't we go someplace less public to speak about it," Phyllis suggested, noticing that Madison's gestures and vocal projection were attracting the interest of passers-by.

"Whatever you say, dear lady," Madison returned. "There's a quiet lounge not far from here."

A short while later, Phyllis sat opposite Madison at a corner in the aforementioned lounge. She watched carefully as the writer untied the folder and neatly put papers out before him.

"The *Triumph and Passion* sounds like quite a grand title," Phyllis observed as she watched the man thumb through papers.

"I rather like it." Madison was all smiles when he looked into her face. "Furthermore, I had breakfast with Hampton Colwell this morning and told him about the story of the play. He loved it. And, as a matter of fact, he was so enthusiastic about the play, that he suggested that once the first act was in condition to show, he would gladly take it to the producer, Mortimer Gree, and attempt to sell him on the idea."

"That's very exciting."

"I also told Hampton that I had conceived the idea of the play as a starring vehicle for you, Phyllis," Madison said with an appropriate gesture.

"What was his reaction to that?"

"Hampton likes you very much," Madison explained. "He thinks you have potentially strong talent. What you lack is experience."

"I'm well aware of that."

"But—and this is the interesting part—the more disenchanted Hampton becomes with Miss Phenwick—and she has given him no end of problems in the past as she is doing in the present—the more likely are the chances that he will consider taking the new play on as a project with you in the leading role."

"Why should he do that if he thinks I lack experience?"

"Like with myself, it is more for the purpose of knocking Miss Phenwick off her pedestal than it is for personal reasons, as far as you're concerned."

"That isn't exactly complimentary," Phyllis remarked.

"You mustn't misunderstand," Madison hurriedly inserted. "We both think you have talent, Phyllis. Hampton said you were like a diamond in the rough. I believe he would work diligently with you, if he likes the play and he thinks that you can do it. It's as simple as that."

"Anything worth winning is worth gambling for," Phyllis stated.

"You realize, of course," Madison continued, "Mr. Gree would not put his own money into the play. He would go for investors. Unfortunately, investors like to invest both in a good play and an actress who has proven herself as a drawing card on the stage."

"You are gently leading me to a possible letdown, aren't you?"

"One must be realistic."

"Well, I'm realistic enough to accept your new play as a challenge," Phyllis returned. "And once challenged, I fight to the end to achieve victory."

"I wonder if Miss Phenwick was as you are, early in her career," Madison said after a few moments of consideration. "I suspect most people who achieve success have that similar determination to accomplish. In my way, I have, I must admit that. With a writer, however, there is a difference: one's work is down in black and white. Fortunately, I'm not inflexible, therefore, I am willing to alter—to a certain judicious degree—that which I have written." Again he took a few minutes for reflection. "Although you may never have the opportunity to use it, I suggest that you learn Miss Phenwick's lines in *The Eternal Light*."

"Whatever for?"

"The purpose would be twofold," Madison replied. "First, if Hampton knows that you have memorized Miss Phenwick's part, he may well consider working with you. Miss Phenwick refuses to have an understudy. Whatever happens to her, she is bound that the show will go on. So the secondfold reason would be that you were ready to go on, should anything happen that Miss Phenwick couldn't."

"Oh, I don't see how I could do that."

"But you could—if you knew the part perfectly and Hampton had worked with you," Madison assured her. "Miss Phenwick's behavior has become progressively erratic. While she can be depended upon to give a satisfactory performance onstage, her situation offstage has become most peculiar. There is concern about her. Let me leave it at that. You would be doing yourself a tremendous favor by learning her role."

Phyllis thought about the situation. A rush of excitement went through her. In the past she had heard of situations wherein understudies took over roles in plays to prove that they were far better able to handle the parts than the experienced actors who played them. That was one means by which a lesser known actor stepped up from mediocrity to success.

Madison Davis walked Phyllis to the theater. The breeze was nippy, but the stroll was refreshing. Phyllis would have liked to have gone by herself so that she could speculate freely about all the things which the writer had told her. Her mind was filled with stars, but she realized that she had to keep her feet planted firmly on the ground.

When they parted at the stage door, Phyllis agreed to meet Madison two days later to discuss the new play. That would give her sufficient time to mull over the prospects of doing it, as well as to make up her mind about unofficially understudying Augusta II.

As she was going toward the dressing room that she shared with the two others, Phyllis encountered Augusta II, who was on the way to her own dressing room.

"Good evening, Miss Phenwick," Phyllis said politely.

At first Augusta II glared, then she found a strained smile. Why did she consider that girl to be such an adversary? Why a threat? The meeting was brief, and Phyllis hurriedly moved away.

"Is there something wrong, Miss Phenwick?" Leslie Brooks asked as he came up behind where Augusta II was standing.

"I have the strangest reaction to Miss Burdick," Augusta II said. "This may seem odd, but I would like you to get to know Miss Burdick better—in a detached way—and see if you can discern what she's up to."

"What makes you think she's up to anything?" Leslie asked.

"It's just a feeling I have. I don't trust her."

Leslie stared at the actress with his lower jaw hanging. "What do you want me to learn?"

"I don't know—just anything you can," Augusta II stated. "We'll discuss it later."

When Phyllis entered the dressing room, she tried to put the memory of her encounter with Augusta II from her mind. There were too many other things there to be bothered with petty personality problems. She went about the process of preparing for the evening's performance.

Her face blackened and her costume in place, Phyllis was alarmed when the stage doorman came knocking and called out her name. She was even more startled when she opened the door to him and saw that he was carrying a bouquet of a dozen long-stemmed red roses still in bud.

"For you, Miss Burdick."

"There must be some mistake."

"None whatsoever. There's a card."

After dismissing the man, Phyllis took the roses to her dressing table while one of the other actresses filled a container with water to place them in until after the night's performance.

The card was addressed to Phyllis, but the message simply said, *"From a secret admirer."* It wasn't signed.

Immediately Phyllis suspected that the flowers had come from Joshua Phenwick. She felt honored.

As the flowers were arranged in water, Phyllis stared at them with curious interest and thought it most peculiar that they were red roses.

Chapter Eight

The Pythian Club for men of New York, which gave reciprocal privileges to members of the Pythian Club of Boston, was housed in a midtown gothic-like structure and offered a place of retreat for men of affluence. The atmosphere was stodgy, and that description could be applied to many of the members. Being a place strictly for men, the employees were also of that gender. Within its walls many business deals were made, profitable transactions and new alliances.

Simon Phenwick had made an appointment to meet Cyrus Hart of Hart, Hart, Hart & Fagan, a law firm, at the club that evening. After waiting half an hour in the smoking lounge, a place of high-backed, leather-upholstered Queen Anne chairs, oak panelling and heavy maroon draperies, a note was delivered to Simon by messenger from Mr. Hart, in which the attorney expressed his regrets that unexpected business had come up and he would have to postpone their meeting until another time.

Simon was disappointed, since he had hoped to form a business alliance with the law firm through his association with Cyrus Hart. Still, he was a man who believed that there was a proper time for all things, and, if such an alliance was meant to be, it would materialize when it was supposed to. Since he was not to have the pleasure of Cyrus Hart's company, Simon decided to go to the exercise area, later take a swim, enjoy the relaxation of the sauna and steam, and indulge himself with a relaxing massage.

During the next hour he struck up acquaintances with several men who were working out in the gymnasium, but largely he kept to himself. A strange attitude had come over him, and he couldn't quite decipher what it was all about.

After pushing his physical endurance as far as he dared, Simon stripped and went to the sauna room where the dry heat cleared his head and forced perspiration to bubble on his finely structured physique. Fifteen minutes of the dry heat, a brief cooling-off period, and he was ready to go to the steam room.

On the previous times he had been at the club, Simon had been aware of a pungent wintergreen aroma in the large mist-filled room. The absence of that scent gave the atmosphere a sweaty smell that was slightly repulsive to him. Since it was the hour when most of the club members were dining, the steam room was virtually unoccupied. Only one gray silhouette was visible. Simon sat on the tile-covered bench on the opposite side of the room from where the figure was seated.

His brow became liquid, perspiration rolled over his entire body, giving him a sense that all of the toxins and impurities were being driven out. Ultimately he stretched out on the bench and breathed deeply of the steam as he attempted to make his mind a blank and simply enjoy the here and now pleasure of what he was experiencing. Still, curious thoughts popped into his head and almost as quickly he popped them out.

It was subtle at first, that delicate sweet fragrance that wafted on the steam. Not wintergreen. Simon raised his upper torso and braced himself with his elbows. The scent was becoming stronger.

"That's a perfume for women," Simon said aloud. "It smells like flowers."

"Roses," a voice said from the other side of the room.

"Yes, now I recall," Simon returned, and breathed in deeply again. "I miss the wintergreen."

"The wintergreen will return."

"None too soon as far as I'm concerned."

"Do you dislike roses?"

"I always associate flowers with women."

"Are you so uncertain of your masculinity that you cannot appreciate roses?"

"That's a queer question," Simon replied, now arranging himself into a sitting position. The silhouette opposite him was vaguely visible. "I have no doubt whatsoever about my masculinity." He thought a moment and waited for the other to speak. "My name is Phenwick. I'm visiting New York from Boston."

"I know Boston quite well. Oh, excuse me, my name is Truff."

The aroma of roses saturated the steam room.

"I don't know who's dumping all of that perfume into the steam," Simon commented, "but I wish they would let up on it."

"I find it pleasant."

Another period of silence.

"The Phenwicks have never much established themselves in New York," Simon said as a means of continuing the conversation.

"There is an actress."

"Yes, my cousin—second cousin, I believe she is," Simon returned. "Have you ever seen her act?"

"Yes, I have."

108

"Actually, I came with other members of my family to New York to see the opening performance of Augusta's new play."

"Can I assume by that that you are a patron of the arts?"

"Only passively so. I'm an attorney. I'm with my father's law firm in Boston. If you know Boston, perhaps you've heard of John Phenwick."

"I knew your father when he was a boy, along with your uncles, Thadius, Paul and Daniel Louis, the latter of whom came to a tragic end as a youth."

Simon searched his memory. "Truff? Truff? The name has a familiar ring to it. Perhaps my father mentioned it."

"Perhaps."

"Are you a resident of New York? Or are you here on business?"

"You might say I'm on business—the kind of business I'm in now." There came an amused chuckle. *"My last such business was in San Francisco with your cousin Hayden."*

"With Hayden?" Simon questioned. "Shouldn't I know you?"

"Not necessarily."

Pause. Simon laughed awkwardly with a touch of irony. "I recall my mother speaking of a man named Truff. He was sort of a harbinger of—" He suddenly remembered. "Well, it isn't important. We Phenwicks have a few skeletons as well as other mysteries in our closets."

"Explain yourself."

"I think it would be better if I didn't," Simon replied. "I've heard the tales, of course, but I never pass them on for fear that those who hear me will think me peculiar."

"Peculiar? In what way?"

"According to Mother, who is now deceased," Simon

related, "this Truff individual, if that is what he can be called, is not presently in the flesh."

"Not in the flesh?"

"Never mind."

"Do go on. I'm curious about what you have to say."

"It came up at the time my sister Laura was engaged to Pruman Donnally," Simon explained as he rose and went to the other side of the room so that he could speak in lower tones. "My sister was certain that she was destined to become a Phenwick woman—a rather dubious distinction at best. Mother told her, in my presence, that if it was meant to be that she would be known as one of the chosen few, that she would be visited by this Truff—uh—whatever he is."

"An entity in spirit?"

"I suppose that is it, or at least what Mother would have liked us to believe," Simon replied. "Since Laura hadn't had such a 'spiritual' encounter, she perceived that she might as well marry Donnally, whom she loved deeply, I'm certain of that. And I told her that she would be foolish to give up a man's love in hopes that she might one day be selected to be known as a Phenwick woman. I know this all sounds pretty silly and hardly the thing which two grown men should discuss."

"Did your mother tell you how this Truff individual made his presence known?"

"I believe she did, but I don't recall it at the moment. It's unimportant. Sheer fantasy, if you ask me."

"You're a very practical man, aren't you, Simon?"

"I try to be." Simon wiped perspiration from his face. "I once spoke of this to my cousin Philip, thinking that we would have a good laugh over it. But Philip told me that he had also encountered this Truff fellow and that's how he knew that his future wife—now present wife, Katherine—was to be known as a Phenwick woman." He laughed. "I promise to say no more about it."

The door to the steam room opened, allowing a cool draft to enter along with another patron.

"For God's sake, let's talk about something else," Simon whispered. "Any stranger hearing us discuss such things might think we both need mental investigation. Perhaps you will permit me to buy you a drink after we get through in here."

"Thank you all the same, Simon."

"For some reason, I feel a desire to continue our conversation."

The gray shadow of a man's form passed in front of Simon, walked a few feet and paced back.

"Plenty of steam in here today," the newcomer commented as he passed Simon a second time.

"Quite a bit. I like it," Simon commented.

"A little too much wintergreen in it, though," the other remarked. "I'll get used to it."

"Wintergreen?"

"They put wintergreen oil in the steam spout."

"Wintergreen? A tingling sensation came over Simon. "Truff, do you hear that? Truff?"

"I think we're the only two in here," the other man said as he paced back again. The voice was familiar, but Simon couldn't place it.

The scent of wintergreen mingled with the odor of roses and soon overpowered it. Simon began to wonder if the fragrance of roses had actually been there at all. That eerie sensation continued until he felt compelled to leave the steam room and see if he could locate the man called Truff.

As he emerged from the vapors, a curious thought crossed Simon's mind. "How did he know—I didn't tell him my given name was Simon," he muttered to himself. Moving over the tiled floor, he looked in all possible places as he asked each man he encountered if his name was Truff.

When he had exhausted all possible places where anyone might be, Simon returned to the steam room.

"Did you see another man in here when you entered besides myself?"

"It's difficult to see much of anything," was the reply.

"And no one left when you opened the door to enter?" Simon persisted.

"I saw no one. What's the problem?"

"I—I don't know." Simon sat on the tile bench. "I think I've been hallucinating."

"How's that?"

"Never mind." Simon ruminated over what had happened. "You don't smell roses in here, do you?"

"I beg your pardon."

"Forget I asked."

As Simon replayed that last several minutes in his mind, he recalled the cold draft that came into the steam room when the pacing man had entered. Truff had said something to him after the other had arrived. Yet Simon didn't recall any other draft after that. Had that Truff person simply vanished in the steam? Or had he ever really been there at all? "I think I'd better get some fresh air. The steam is getting to me."

After showering, Simon wrapped himself in a sheet and sat in a lounge chair. He wanted to cool off somewhat before he took a swim. As he stretched in a comfortable reclining position, he found it impossible to put the strange chain of events from his mind. He had a desire to converse with his cousin Philip.

Simon was in the swimming pool for fifteen minutes. He was an expert swimmer. Concentrating his mind on what he was doing, he was able to expel memories of the steam room incident from his thoughts for the moment. Another shower and dried off, he again wrapped the sheet about him and reclined in the lounge chair. There was a wait before he could get a massage. His initial desire was to take more steam, but he felt, under the circumstances, that he didn't want to return to the vapor again that day. Had it in some way affected his sanity?

112

"Well, well, Mr. Phenwick, I didn't recognize you at first," Madison Davis said as, sheet-wrapped, he took the lounge chair beside Simon. "You don't mind if I join you, do you?"

Simon recognized his voice as that of the man who had been pacing in the steam room. "Be my guest."

"I'm already a guest of one of the members," Madison returned. "I've been trying the place out, now that I can afford membership in such an exclusive establishment." He positioned himself on the lounge. "I'm not all that affluent yet, but I intend to be one of these days." He sighed dramatically. "The steam is exhausting, and at the same time invigorating. I've been sweating out the plot for my new play."

Simon snapped his fingers in recognition. "Oh, yes, you're that Madison fellow, the writer of Augusta's play."

"The writer of my own play, which Miss Phenwick happens to be in," Madison corrected.

"I'm sorry, Mr. Madison, but I don't recall your first name."

"My first name *is* Madison. Madison Davis."

"I recall now. Accept my aplogies. I'm a bit confused this evening," Simon admitted.

"I've decided to take out a membership in this club," Madison said a short while later after they had engaged in small talk. "The steam room is a perfectly marvelous place for me to pace out plots. After you left a while ago, I was talking out dialogue and even acting out scenes. Unfortunately another man came in and I had to contain my dramatics. The facilities are lovely, and exactly what I need."

"Are you certain there was no one else in the steam room when you entered other than me?" Simon asked.

"I couldn't be positive in all that fog," Madison replied. "but I was almost certain. Why do you ask?"

"It's not important."

"Oh, but it must be, or you wouldn't keep bringing it up."

Simon chose to change the subject of conversation. "Did you have a cozy little meeting with our actress friend?"

"Meeting? Actress friend?" Madison looked perplexed before a joyous expression lit his countenance. "Oh, you mean Miss Burdick! I'm writing a play for her, you know."

"No, I didn't."

"Well, I am. I believe that Miss Burdick is remarkably talented, with an even greater potential than perhaps even she realizes." Madison struck a pose, which was a bit awkward in the sheet wrapped around him. "With all due respects, Mr. Phenwick, I believe Miss Burdick can be a greater actress than Miss Phenwick."

"You needn't aplogize for saying that, Mr. Davis. My cousin and I aren't particularly close. However, it seems to me you're a bit premature in creating a play for Miss Burdick to star in. She hasn't had a vast amount of experience in the theater."

"There are natural-born actors who gain experience from everyday life," Madison stated. "Acting is second nature to them. Which I believe is the case with Miss Burdick . . . and possibly with Miss Phenwick. Mr. Colwell, the director of *The Eternal Light,* thinks Miss Burdick can easily become a leading performer. He likes the idea of my new play. And once her approves of the first act, he will approach Mr. Gree, the producer, about it and about Miss Burdick playing the main role."

"If Mr. Gree is the successful producer that I have been led to believe he is," Simon speculated, "he would have to be a tremendous gambler to take a chance on putting a virtual unknown in a starring part."

"Every producer is a gambler, staking a fortune against outrageous odds," Madison said. "I've only spoken with Mr. Gree a half dozen times or more, but I

114

have found him to be innovative and willing to break out of the mold of tried-and-true methods. Also, Mr. Gree let it slip once that he *is* influenced by his backers, those who heavily invest in his productions. That could be where there could be a problem as far as Miss Burdick is concerned."

"You mean convincing the money people even after the producer has decided to take the gamble?"

"Precisely."

"Do you have a card, Mr. Davis?" Simon asked.

"Not a professionally-printed card, Mr. Phenwick. However, I have a blank upon which I can place my name and address."

"That will suffice. I want it for future reference," Simon remarked. "I'm considering making a move to New York, and it has occurred to me that there must be attorneys who specialize in theatrical ventures, everything from legal counsel to arranging and handling backers and other financial aspects of the business. I find myself curiously aroused by the prospects involved therein. It's only an idea now. But, should I decide to make the move and further investigate the theatrical business, I should very much like to call on you for advice."

"You honor me, Mr. Phenwick."

Simon was called by the masseur. Madison returned to the steam room.

While being rubbed, pounded, soothed and abruptly slapped to bring the blood to the surface of his skin, Simon considered the conversation he had had with Madison Davis. He had never aspired toward acting as such, yet as an attorney he realized he put on quite a performance each time he appeared in court to defend a case. It wasn't exactly the same, but he could recognize a similarity between court-acting and stage-performing.

Simon liked the glitter and excitement of the theater. He especially had a fondness for New York and the reaction he felt toward the whole of the show world. The harder the masseur rubbed him, and the little stings were soothed into pleasant reactions, the deeper his thoughts dwelled on the matter of the theater and his possible move to Manhattan.

Dressed and feeling wonderfully refreshed, Simon made certain that he got Madison Davis's address. His parting words to the writer were not encouraging as far as Phyllis Burdick was concerned, especially the prospect of elevating her into the leading actress category, still he conceded that all things were possible.

"Simon! Wait up a moment!" a man's voice called behind him as he prepared to enter a cab. He turned to see his cousin Philip running toward him. "Philip?"

"Do you have a few moments?" the other asked, winded and making aspirant sounds.

Simon examined his gold pocketwatch. "I have half an hour. Hop in the cab with me and we'll go over to the theater district. What's on your mind?"

"Nothing of vast importance," Philip replied, his handsome smile beaming.

"Laura, Pru and I are catching the early train for Boston tomorrow," Simon said as the cab began to move. "I feel I should say farewell to Augusta."

"I thought Katherine and I would have been home by now," Philip commented. "I do enjoy these trips to New York, but I am always delighted to return home. Katherine is talking in terms of taking an apartment here so that we can come to the city more often. There is something about Manhattan that magnetizes one to it."

"Yes, so I've observed," Simon returned. "What is it you wanted to speak to me about, Philip?"

"It's nothing urgent. I just happened to see you on the street and thought it would give us time to get together for a chat."

"Earlier you sounded as though it was of vital importance."

"I didn't mean to do so," Philip returned. "Yet I suppose, if one analyzes it, that there is some importance."

"Explain yourself."

"I love my Katherine dearly, a man couldn't ask for a finer wife," Philip related. "But she does have her moments of being extremely confusing, especially when she gets off on her psychic premonitions and notions of that sort."

"Psychic premonitions?" Simon laughed. "I know you've mentioned that before, but I confess I've not put much stock in such things."

"As I didn't—*at first.*" Philip leaned back and sighed.

"What is it?"

"Katherine has a weird bee in her bonnet all of a sudden," Philip related. "Frankly, she suggested that Augusta II may be losing her sanity. I scolded her for making such a speculative statement. I have a fondness for Augusta II."

"Have you ever known Katherine's predictions to be accurate?"

"Nearly 99% of the time," Philip replied. "It's uncanny. That's why I was disturbed when she said what she did about Augusta II." He thought a moment. "Did you have an unusual encounter today, one that left you in a quandary and doubtful that you had actually experienced what you experienced?"

Simon's immediate reaction was to deny it; then he remembered the singular incident that had occurred in the steam room. "Why do you ask?"

"Katherine said this morning over breakfast that just that would happen. Naturally, I wanted to believe she was mistaken."

"I may have had an unusual encounter," Simon said. "Did Katherine think it important?"

"Of vital importance," Philip answered. "You don't have to respond to this, but I'm curious if you also encountered a remarkable fragrance in a most unusual place—at least unusual for such a fragrance to be where it was."

The tingling sensation moved over Simon's neck and shoulders and all the way down his spinal column. He felt as if he were about to break out in a cold sweat. He laughed nervously; his usual reserved composure had been affected. "Is that another of Katherine's predictions?"

"Yes."

"I have to admit that she was correct," Simon commented.

"Since that is the case, Katherine is convinced that your days of bachelorhood are numbered."

"She must be jesting."

"Katherine was most serious when she predicted what she did," Philip returned. "I hasten to add that she said such a situation would not take place for a year or more, but that the seeds of romance will have been planted before you leave New York."

Simon laughed and withdrew change from his pocket to pay the cab driver as they neared the Majesty Theater. "I must make a point of speaking privately with your wife back in Boston. As you know, I've steered clear of matrimony with a passion."

The two cousins went into a small tavern near the theater and ordered a glass of wine apiece.

"May I make a guess?" Philip questioned after he had lifted his glass in a toast to Simon.

"A guess about what?"

"The unusual fragrance you experienced today."

"Do you have premonitions, too?"

"No. Katherine was curious to have me ask you." Philip traced his index finger over the rim of the glass. "Was it the scent of roses?"

Simon felt as if he had suddenly grown conspicuously pale. His hand trembled so that he had to place the glass on the counter. His eyes darted over Philip's face as if they were attempting to ask a dozen unspoken questions. When he tried to smile, his attempt was awkward.

"You needn't voice your response, Simon," Philip said. "Your physical expression says it all. Katherine was correct."

Simon said nothing for several seconds as he made a concerted effort to regain his composure. "What do you know about a man named Truff?"

"Adam Truff?" Philip asked. "I was just a boy when he passed away at Greenfield. Before he took desperately ill, I used to visit him quite often. He was a remarkable man with a bagful of stories and more. Mother told me that he had always been very close to the Phenwick family. In a sense he was kind of a hero."

"Oh, yes, I remember him now," Simon stated. "Funny how he just sort of disappeared from my memory for a while. I recall I was somewhat put off by his interest in Laura and not in me. It was no doubt a product of my childish imagination."

"When our fathers were boys," Philip related, "and their father died, Adam Truff became almost like a second father to them—at least until Grandmother married again. Even then, I suspect, Dad and Uncle John, as well as Uncle Paul and Daniel Louis, were deeply attached to Adam. After all, he was a hero in his own right, and a man looked up to for the dignity of who and what he was. But why are we speaking of Adam Truff?"

"I wonder." Simon wore a distant expression. When Philip cleared his throat, the other quickly reached for his pocketwatch to check the time. "*The Eternal Light* should nearly be over. I wish to speak briefly with Augusta II and excuse myself. I must retire shortly thereafter, as it is an early train. I can sleep while riding, but I have several important matters to attend to once I arrive in Boston."

"I'll not go to the theater with you, Simon," Philip returned. "We'll get together back home. I suggest you come to the house soon and dine with us. Katherine always encourages me to invite you."

"I'll do that."

The cousins parted after a hearty handshake. Simon went toward the Majesty Theater, and Philip took off in the opposite direction.

"Ah, dear Cousin Simon!" exclaimed Augusta II as he entered her dressing room. "How delightful to see you!"

"I wanted to thank you again and say good-bye before I returned to Boston," Simon said as his cousin kissed him.

"Leaving New York so soon?" Augusta II questioned, making a production out of being dramatic. Her eyes ran over his handsome physique. There was no question that she found him seductively handsome. "We haven't had the opportunity to go out on the town, dear Simon, nor a chance for an intimate chat."

Simon began to feel uneasy under her aggressive appraisal. "Alas, there just wasn't time for us to get together, was there?"

"I do have an engagement for tonight," Augusta II said, "which I will gladly break if you would care to join me in seeing the sights."

"I can't possibly, Augusta. I've an early train to catch. But I assure you I'll be back in New York before long and we'll have a go at it then."

"A go at it?" Augusta II repeated with a suggestive smile. "I think I'll look forward to that." She embraced him again with a kiss and exploring hands.

Simon gently but firmly eased himself away from his cousin's provocative embrace, subtly making certain that he made his position clear without offending her. "I'll say farewell for Laura and Pru, too. They regret that they couldn't come in person."

"I trust you all will be back before the close of *The Eternal Light* and not wait for my next opening." Augusta II commented.

"I've no doubt that *The Eternal Light* will enjoy a remarkably long run, Augusta. And we're all certain to be back in town before it closes." Simon seemed anxious to leave. There was another embrace when Augusta II caught him at the door.

As Simon left Augusta II's dressing room, he encountered Leslie Brooks, fashionably attired and looking freshly washed, heading toward the star's quarters. Recognizing Simon as a Phenwick, the actor smiled broadly as if he were auditioning.

Simon glanced back as Leslie entered Augusta II's room without knocking. He had heard the gossip about Augusta II and the second leading man. Shaking his head as he continued to look back, he began to move forward. "Oops! I'm terribly sorry!" he apologized as he turned ahead on the impact of the collision.

"Excuse me, I wasn't watching where I was going," Phyllis Burdick said as she looked into his face in the dim backstage light.

"We meet again," Simon said.

"I was preoccupied," Phyllis explained. "I just received a note from Mr. Joshua Phenwick, stating that he could not have super with me tonight since another important matter arose. I dressed especially for the occasion. You can see why I was preoccupied in thought."

"In thought—or annoyance?" Simon questioned. "I know how terribly frustrated I feel when there is a last-minute cancellation to anything. I become infuriated."

"Circumstances are circumstances, and often unavoidable," Phyllis commented. "I understand. I'm certain I can convince Isaac Bell to take me somewhere inexpensive for a bit of something."

Simon examined his watch. A frown before a smile, as he looked into Phyllis's expression of anticipation.

"Mr. Phenwick had made reservations at a marvelous French restaurant, Pierre's, not far from here. I was so looking forward to going. But I know that poor

Isaac will never be able to afford such a place. Oh, well, there will be another time."

"Althought I feel I'm being victimized by your charm and beauty, Miss Phenwick," Simon observed, "I will risk a try and ask if I might take my cousin's place with you at Pierre's."

"Oh, Mr. Phenwick, I didn't mean—that is to say—I wasn't hinting that I would want you to take Mr. Joshua Phenwick's place."

"Don't you think I would make a suitable substitute for my esteemed cousin?" Simon asked, somewhat jokingly.

"I do believe you'd make a perfect substitute," Phyllis said before she caught herself. "Let me rephrase that. I'm certain I would be delighted and honored to dine with you at Pierre's, but I refuse to consider you a substitute for anyone."

"That is kind of you to say, Miss Burdick," Simon returned. "But I am fully aware of the circumstances under which this arrangement is being made. Regardless of that, I, too, would be honored to dine with you."

"I received a bouquet of roses before the performance tonight," Phyllis explained as they went toward the stage door. "I suspect they were from Mr. Phenwick— Joshua Phenwick. They were merely signed *'From a secret admirer.'* I had planned to take them to my room, but they would be a cumbersome bother. They'll keep just as well in my dressing room."

"Perhaps you are mistaken about the roses' coming from Joshua," Simon said as they went through the alley toward the street.

"I would like to think they might be from another," Phyllis returned. "Don't misunderstand, I find Mr. Joshua Phenwick charming and personable in his way. It's just that he appears to want to get serious too quickly, and I fear that his plans for the future are not at all compatible to mine. If you understand what I mean."

Simon laughed; and went to hail a cab.

Chapter Nine

"Has Miss Phyllis Burdick left for the night?" Augusta II asked the stage doorman as she prepared to make an exit from the theater with her arm in Leslie Brooks's.

"She left at least fifteen minutes ago," the doorman replied.

"Alone? Let me change that. Was she with my brother?" Augusta II corrected.

"She was not with your brother, Miss Phenwick," the man returned, "but she wasn't alone, either."

"Doubtless with one of the underling supporting players," Augusta II said grandly, turning back with a broad smile to Leslie.

"No, Miss Phenwick, she was with a gentleman."

"A gentleman?"

"I believe he was a Mr. Phenwick, too. In fact, I'm certain he was," the doorman stated.

"If not Joshua, who? Not Simon, I trust," Augusta II blurted.

"I believe it was Mr. Simon Phenwick, ma'am," the doorman replied.

"Impossible! Simon had to go directly to his hotel because he has an early train to catch in the morning."

"Perhaps Mr. Phenwick was only going to drop her at her home," the doorman suggested.

"Perhaps. Come along, Leslie," Augusta II said grandly. "I'll not bother myself with such mundane matters."

"Yes, Miss Phenwick."

The stage doorman had private thoughts about Augusta II and Leslie, but he tried to mind his own business and remain aloof from speculation about intimate situations. Still he had overheard Simon speak of dining with Phyllis at Pierre's. In his many years in his position, he had seen many, many things. Little or nothing shocked or surprised him.

Fortunately Phyllis recalled the address of Pierre's restaurant and was able to direct the cab driver. When they arrived, Simon held the door for her and helped her down. As they touched in passing, a startling reaction went through each of them.

"I'm afraid my old woolen coat is hardly fashionable for a place like this," Phyllis commented before they entered. "However, I confess I can't afford to buy an expensive fur coat. This old thing is good enough for another winter."

"You look exquisite tonight, Miss Burdick, and I am proud to escort you here or wherever else you desire to go," Simon said without sounding patronizing. "A beautiful woman is a compliment to the man she is with."

After they had been seated, in luck because Joshua had not bothered to cancel his reservation, they ordered wine and sipped it by candlelight.

"Did the performance go well tonight?" Simon asked as a means of continuing the conversation.

"Well enough," Phyllis replied. "I have so little to do anymore, after all the cuts, that it has become fairly

124

much of a routine thing to me. Oh, I love performing—that is my life—but I'm performing so little in *The Eternal Light* that it can be terribly frustrating at times."

"One day, perhaps, you will be a star like my illustrious cousin," Simon suggested.

"Oh, I do hope so. Not like, but better than," Phyllis added.

"Better than Augusta?"

"Miss Phenwick is an extremely accomplished performer," Phyllis replied. "I've been watching her—for a very specific reason. She takes command of the stage, but she has a tendency to overdo. She lacks subtle innuendo."

"You are most observant, Miss Burdick. My reaction to Augusta's performance was almost identical to yours." Simon smiled broadly. "You really are serious about this business of acting, aren't you?"

"Very serious, Mr. Phenwick."

"And how do you think your career on the stage will affect your private life?" Simon asked.

"I should hope it would enhance it."

"Even marriage?"

Phyllis looked deeply into Simon's face before she spoke. "I was led to believe that you are the perennial bachelor and man about town who has avoided the subject of matrimony with a passion."

"I have," Simon replied with a playful laugh. "Not that I'm opposed to the institution of marrage, not in the least. I simply haven't reached the point in my own consciousness where I am ready to give up my playboy freedom to settle down."

"Then you must consider that as my answer to your question," Phyllis said, "replacing the word playboy for actress."

"I see." Simon decided to drop the matter.

When they had completed supper, Phyllis suggested a short walk to aid with digestion. The winds of winter were approaching and a definite chill was in the night air. Still with a scarf pulled high about her neck, Phyllis was relatively comfortable.

"How adventurous are you, Miss Burdick?" Simon asked after they had covered close to fifteen blocks.

"That is a leading question, Mr. Phenwick."

"I meant it in a righteous and proper way."

"In that case, I consider myself quite adventurous. What did you have in mind?" Phyllis asked, a touch of amusement in her voice.

"I've always wanted to ride in a carriage up Fifth Avenue and into Central Park," Simon replied.

"I doubt that you would see much this time of the night."

"I disagree," Simon said. "Once one's eyes become accustomed to darkness, one's vision becomes quite sharp and keen."

"I thought you were concerned about catching a morning train."

"Only in that I catch it," Simon responded. "The fact is, as late as it has become, I suspect I would do well to remain up the rest of the night and plan to sleep on the train—to the annoyance of Laura and Pru, I dare say."

Phyllis laughed. "You're a bit compulsive, aren't you? If not impetuous."

"Despite the fact that I originate in Boston," Simon commented, "I am not your straightlaced, conventional Bostonian. Far from it. There are members of the Phenwick clan who think I'm a bit of a renegade. Frankly, I believe it is the renegades of the world, those who dare to be different, that are the ones who are most successful. I'm not, however, an advocate of unconventionality for the sake of not conforming. I believe there are those who must conform and toe the mark all the way. There's security in conventionality for most persons; for me there is really only security in unconventionality."

"What a peculiar observation."

"Not at all. I become stifled and thwarted if I must do the same thing all of the time," Simon related. "I need variety. For that reason, I feel that I will become buried in my father's law firm."

They saw a carriage for hire and Simon hailed it. Moments later, bundled in blankets and feeling substantially warm except for where the wind touched their faces, they settled back for a leisurely ride.

"You were saying, Mr. Phenwick?" Phyllis asked as she felt herself being magnetically drawn closer to the man.

"Was it important?"

"For some strange reason, I find everything you say seems most important."

"Then you are impressionable," Simon said with a jolly laugh. "What are we going on about, anyway? I confess a certain giddiness has come over me which is most unusual."

"I suspect it's the brisk air that has an intoxicating effect," Phyllis commented. "Look how crisp the stars appear in the clear black sky . . . and no moon in sight."

"Must be the dark of the moon." Simon was quiet for a few moments as he sustained his gaze upward. "Are you happy?"

"I beg your pardon?"

"I merely asked if you were happy."

"Do you mean all the time?"

"No, right now."

"I'm certain I am. Are you?"

"Most definitely," Simon reached to take her hand. "Do you mind?"

"Not in the least. My fingers were getting cold," Phyllis replied sweetly, enjoying the warm touch of his hand. "Are you happy *all* of the time?"

"I try to be," Simon replied. "The more I think of happiness, the happier I am. That's why I avoid thinking of sadness at all costs. For instance, when my mother passed away, it would have been very easy to fall into a mordant melancholy mood and think of sadness. Actually, I was happy for my mother. She had suffered a long time and her mind had been greatly troubled with what some might have thought of as insanity. I was happy that she had been released from the agony through which she had gone for so long. I could only be sad thinking that I wouldn't see her again. Yet I learned to think of the happy times we had had together."

"That's beautiful."

"That's when another thought occurred to me," Simon continued.

"What is that?" Phyllis eagerly asked.

"That all we really have is the present moment," Simon said. "Yesterday is gone, it will never come again. And who knows what quirk of fate may keep tomorrow from ever appearing? We only have right now, that's all we can count on."

"How funny, I made a statement similar to that not long ago," Phyllis commented.

"We must be in tune with each other." Simon squeezed her hand.

"Do you think so, Mr. Phenwick?"

The old carriage driver glanced back when their conversation ceased. Usually he played deaf and dumb to whatever transpired in the carriage, being of the opinion that his passengers had paid their fare and they had the right to every privacy. Still when there had been a stream of conversation and it suddenly broke off, his natural curiosity was aroused and he caught a glimpse. He smiled as he saw the young couple simply gazing into each other's shadowed faces. Looking beyond Phyllis and Simon, he saw the glare of approaching automobile lights.

"The danged contraptions should be outlawed," the driver mumbled.

"Did you say something, driver?" Simon asked, taking his concerted attention from Phyllis.

"One of them danged automobiles is behind us. Well, he'll just have to wait until there's a wide place in the road."

Simon glanced back, then to the side to see that they had entered Central Park.

The horn honked behind them.

"Let him go past as soon as you can," Simon called to the driver.

"There's a place I can pull over up ahead."

The roadster pulled alongside the carriage, moving slowly for a moment before it sped up and went on down the road.

A sweet fragrance wafted around the young couple as Simon again took Phyllis's hand. They leaned back against the seat and stared from each other to the sky above. The carriage started to slowly forge ahead.

"Is there a price on your thoughts?" Simon asked.

"I don't think I was even thinking, simply enjoying this moment, observing, sensing, feeling, appreciating the beauty of now," Phyllis replied. "And where are your thoughts, Mr. Simon Phenwick?"

"Right here on *now,* and thoroughly delighting in every moment of it," Simon said. "Boston seems so very far away, as if it were clear on the other side of the world."

"You sound as if you've developed a passion for New York City," Phyllis observed. "Is that the case?"

"A passion for the city?" Simon questioned. "I wonder if it is the city or for this moment we are enjoying in it. No. I find myself quite fascinated with Manhattan. It has a kind of magical enchantment. Oh, I must admit I have developed a passion for the place, the excitement, the hurry, even the confusion."

"It's the same reaction I have to New York." She laughed. "When I first arrived here, I was naturally confused by the vastness of the city; and all of the ethnic cultures that comprised it sometimes made me feel as if I were in a foreign land. The city becomes part of one. I would miss it very much if I were to leave."

"I haven't spent a great deal of time here," Simon said, "but each time I leave, I feel as if I am turning my back on an old friend." He laughed. "Aren't we silly speaking of a city as if it were a real, living thing?"

"Isn't it?" Phyllis asked.

An explosion rang out. The noise frightened the old horse pulling the carriage, and she started to move at a rapid trot. In the shock of the moment, Simon glanced to either side of the vehicle. The thick darkness was a protective cover for anything or anyone. However, he did see a fleeting reflection of light on metal.

"What was that?" Phyllis asked, reaching for whatever she could find with which to brace herself with the accelerated speed.

While Simon was still attempting to get his bearings, his attention turned to the old driver, who had slumped forward. Then, as the carriage raced around a curve, the inert body fell to the side of the driver's seat and toppled to the ground. "What on earth?"

He had difficulty standing, much less climbing over the seat to position himself to where he could take the reins. One of the leather straps had fallen to the ground. Simon did his best to guide the horse. The one hope was that the old animal would not have the strength and endurance to maintain a steady rapid pace.

When the horse finally came to a halt, Simon climbed from the seat and went back to check on Phyllis. "Are you all right?"

"I'll survive. It was a bit of a bumpy trip. What happened to the driver?"

"I don't know," Simon replied. "I'm not an expert at handling one of these carriages, but I'll give it a try. The old man may have been hurt."

A lantern hung on either side of the carriage, front and back. Simon took one and held it to examine the foaming, sweating horse. "We'll go slowly, old girl. We've got to go back and find your master."

The carriage turned around, Simon guided the horse to retrace its steps until they came to the body of the fallen driver. Alighting and taking a lantern with him, Simon went to examine the old man.

As Phyllis started to get out of the vehicle to join him, Simon called, "Stay back, Miss Burdick!"

"Is he badly hurt?"

"I think he's dead," Simon returned.

"Good Lord!" exclaimed Phyllis. "How may I help you?"

"Get up on the driver's seat. I'll try to get the old fellow into the back," Simon instructed. "We can't leave him here—dead or alive."

Shortly after riding from the park, Simon spotted two police officers and signalled to get their attention. A brief examination of the driver disclosed that he was dead and that he had been shot through the temple. Phyllis and Simon accompanied the officers to the nearest precinct where they gave statements of their accounts of what had happened.

"I believe we've had enough misadventure for one night," Simon commented as they left the precinct house.

"Naturally I've encountered death on other occasions," Phyllis said as she held tightly to his arm. "What bothers me most is the fact that we might have been badly hurt or—even killed."

"It just goes to show the importance of living for the moment, here and now," Simon remarked with humorous comment. "One never knows what the next moment may bring."

"I don't believe the driver could have been accidentally shot this time of the night—or should I say morning," Phyllis observed.

"I do recall seeing that flash of light on metal," Simon inserted.

"But why would anyone want to kill a sweet old man like him?"

"I don't believe the driver actually was the intended victim," Simon stated. "I rather believe that the incident occurred for our specific benefit or as a means of dispatching us into a world beyond this one."

"How can you think that?" Phyllis asked. They had started to walk in the direction of the boarding house wherein she lived.

"It follows if the driver weren't the intended victim—"

". . . that we were," Phyllis filled in. "Why? Do you have enemies in New York, Mr. Phenwick?"

"None whatsoever. I don't know of any enemies even in Boston."

"I have none that I know of," Phyllis added. "I suspect we might have been mistaken for someone else."

"That's always a possibility." Simon stopped, compelling her by his grip to remain with him. "Let us put speculation about the incident from our minds, and return to where we were before it happened."

"I fear that is easier said than done," Phyllis commented. "Too many perplexing thoughts are spinning around in my brain."

Suddenly Simon took her into his arms, holding her as close to him as he dared. "Miss Burdick, we're both in a state of intense emotion. We were frightened, there was fear; but there's also something more. Does it offend you that I've taken you in my arms like this?"

"No, Mr. Phenwick, not in the least," Phyllis replied. "I had hoped that you would."

"And do you wish that I will kiss you?"

"I don't know whether it's so much a wish, or if I simply assumed that you would under the circumstance," she returned.

Simon lowered his face to hers, their lips touched and together they applied pressure toward each other. The stimulation aroused intense excitement, and the excitement, passion that could very easily race out of control. Realizing how violently involved with each

132

other they were becoming, almost on cue, they both gently eased back until their lips separated. They stared into each others' faces in the dim glow of the nearby gaslamp. When neither seemed to find words, Phyllis softly lay the side of her face against his chest.

"I've purposefully made a point of avoiding intimate encounters with men, Mr. Phenwick," Phyllis said after considering the situation and her reactions to it. "I believe in virtue and moral dignity. I know what you want, Mr. Phenwick, and I would be a liar to say that I was unresponsive to you, or that I didn't want you to continue making love to me. It would be an unknown and new experience to me. Do you think ill of me?"

"You've never before been in an intimate situation with a man?" Simon questioned.

"Never."

"But I thought—I beg your pardon, Miss Burdick. I was led to believe that all actresses were—how shall I put it?"

"Experienced, morally weak, submissive? Are those the words you're seeking, Mr. Phenwick?"

"Do you think badly of me for thinking thusly?"

"No," Phyllis replied. "My thoughts of you are far from bad. In fact, at this point it would be very simple for me to lower my moral standards and permit you to allow me the new experience of being made love to. It would be for the enjoyment of the moment; but mustn't one be aware that one's actions in any given moment will be the cause of that which will result in another moment—perhaps not the next; but in some other time to come? We do reap the results of that which we sow."

Simon stood a few seconds in silence before he reached for his watch to examine it. "The night is quickly escaping us, Miss Phenwick. You require your rest and I must pack my baggage to return to Boston."

"Have I disappointed you, Mr. Phenwick?" Phyllis asked as they began to walk again.

"I'm not disappointed in the least. I've enjoyed being

with you. It was eventful. And I find that I am deeply attracted to you, not only to the gorgeous physical person that you are, but to your mind, your thoughts, and I might add, to your spiritual qualities."

"Do you think I have spiritual qualities?" she asked.

"That which is feminine about you is the quintessence of spirituality," Simon said. "Men are motivated by physical desires and drives to express themselves with women, when; in actuality, I believe that which truly motivates them is to receive the tenderness and fulfillment of spiritual compassion."

"What a strange thing to say," Phyllis observed. "Are you suggesting that women are strictly spiritual beings without physical desires of their own?"

"Not in the least," Simon replied. "The masculine is the physical aspect in both men and women, the feminine is the spiritual. As one gives physically, he receives spiritually—and that is a two-way street. That which you give me may only be a beautiful kiss, but I receive spiritually from it. If you analyze it, you'll find that that is why you had the reaction you did to my kiss."

"If that is the case, what is the purpose of going any farther than a kiss or kisses?" Phyllis asked.

"For the ultimate and complete experience of sharing one with the other."

After walking a distance and realizing they were farther away from their destination than they had been aware, Simon hailed a cab which took them to the boarding house in a short time.

Simon asked the driver to wait while he saw Phyllis to the front door. "You can never know to what extent I enjoyed this night, Miss Burdick. It's as if new doors have been opened to me. You've caused me to get a different perspective, and I see the possibilities of new dimensions opening to me."

"Are you always this philosophic, Mr. Phenwick?" she asked.

"Do you object?"

"Certainly not," Phyllis said. "I believe you've opened new dimensions for me, too. I've had a wonderful evening."

"It's almost time for the morning star. The evening had been long gone." He laughed. Then, as he halted at the top of the steps, he looked again into her eyes and let his lips reach to touch hers.

"Am I to ever see you again, Mr. Phenwick?" Phyllis questioned at least a full minute later when they disconnected their lips.

"I doubt if I'll be back in New York before early spring," Simon replied. "But, if I may, I would like to write to you. Will you answer my letters?"

"I will." She eagerly put her lips again to his, standing on tiptoe to do so. "Thank you—thank you for everything, Mr. Simon Phenwick. You are a beautiful man."

"And you are a beautiful lady, Miss Phyllis Burdick."

One last kiss and Simon insisted it was time that they part. Phyllis stood at the door, watching as the cab moved down the street and out of sight. She leaned her face against the cold brownstone at the doorway. As she did, she became aware of the spicy sweet aroma of roses. She raised her arms high at either side of her and shrugged as she threw her head back. It was as if she were taking a curtain call and she expected to hear the sound of applause.

A solitary figure stepped from the doorway across the street and slowly strode toward where Phyllis was standing. When she caught sight of it, she quickly fumbled for her keys and turned to unlock the door.

"Miss Burdick, it's me."

"Who is it?" Phyllis asked as she turned part way around.

"Leslie Brooks. I've been waiting for you."

"Waiting for me? Whatever for?"

"I wish to speak with you."

"Have you any idea what time of the night it is?"

"It's a little after four. I've been waiting nearly an hour for you," Leslie asked.

"I'm tired and I need my sleep."

"I'm deeply upset and need someone with whom to speak."

"Why did you choose me?"

"I can explain. May I come to your room and talk?"

Suspiciously, Phyllis looked down at him as he began to climb the steps toward her. "I think it would be best, Mr. Brooks, if we were to go to an all-night restaurant in the next block. This is a boarding house for young ladies, and no young man is permitted on the premises after eight in the evening. Actually, I am extremely tired."

"Please, Miss Burdick, I must speak with you," he persisted. "I don't in the least mind walking a block or two."

"Very well." She crossed down the steps to him. "You might as well begin with what you have to say while we walk. I'll only give you the time that it takes me to drink one cup of tea."

There was no doubt in Phyllis's mind that the handsome second leading man was distressed over something. She attempted to take a sympathetic and understanding attitude.

"May I speak perfectly frankly to you?" Leslie asked. "I mean be absolutely candid with you?"

"I don't think I embarrass easily, Mr. Brooks, if that is what is worrying you." They walked with a brisk stride in the cold morning air.

"Since I am an actor like yourself," he began, "I believe you must understand how desperately I wish to be successful at my profession. I will go to any lengths to see that I succeed."

"Any lengths, Mr. Brooks? That seems most drastic to me."

"Wouldn't you?"

136

"Not to extreme lengths, Mr. Brooks, if in so doing it appeared that I was sacrificing other values that were dear to me," Phyllis stated.

"I obviously do not possess the moral fortitude with which you are blessed, Miss Burdick."

"Be precise with what it is you wish to tell me."

"I suppose it's no secret," Leslie said after giving the matter further consideration, "that Miss Phenwick and I—well, that we are closely associated."

"Do you mean *intimately* associated?" Phyllis asked, certain he needed drawing out.

"Yes." Leslie held the door for Phyllis to enter the restaurant, and led her to a booth isolated from the other customers. "I knew Miss Phenwick was not impressed solely by my acting talent, yet she seemed absolutely fascinated by me. It took little to realize what aspect of me so fascinated her. I used my attributes to impress her and ultimately to get cast in *The Eternal Light*. An actress of Miss Phenwick's caliber wields tremendous influence in the casting—and I might add, the dismissal—of actors in the company."

"You seemed to underline the word dismissal with your inflection, Mr. Brooks. Are you trying to warn me of something?" Phyllis asked perceptively.

"Let me continue with what I have to say before I answer that," Leslie said. "I've become quite thick with Miss Phenwick. She even imagines that she is in love with me. But, I assure you, I am not in the least bit in love with her. Even if I were inclined to such emotion, Miss Phenwick would be far from my choice."

"Does Miss Phenwick know of this?"

"I don't believe so; as a matter of fact, I'm certain she doesn't." Leslie ducked his head.

"Have you led her on to believe that your emotions for her are sincere?" Phyllis perceptively asked.

Leslie nodded his head without looking up.

"Then you were deceptive with her from the beginning?"

"I readily admit that to be the case," Leslie said. "Now the situation between us is becoming progressively complicated. I'm beholden to her, and if I dare defy her wishes, I will not only fall from grace with her, but I will also lose my role in *The Eternal Light.* I think you can comprehend the situation I'm in. I'm literally trapped."

"Why have you come to me with this?" Phyllis asked as she sipped from the cup of tea.

"Why? Because I can relate to Miss Phenwick's attitude toward you," Leslie explained. "You know that she is tremendously envious of the fact you received praising comments from the reviewers. Furthermore, she fears that her brother is becoming romantically interested in you."

"What if he is? Hasn't Mr. Joshua Phenwick the right to be interested romantically or otherwise in anyone he chooses?" Phyllis snapped. She did not like the implication.

"Let me go a step backwards," Leslie explained. "When I first established a liaison with Miss Phenwick, I thought of her simply as an eccentric actress with singular ways—quirks, if you will. Now I realize that her eccentricities are far more complex than I had at first imagined them to be."

"Meaning?"

"I quite frankly question her sanity," Leslie replied. "There are times when she acts like a madwoman and treats me as a crazy person would. I admit she frightens me when she is like that."

"Like what?"

"When she becomes a slithering, hissing creature, spitting venom and gazing with evil in her eyes," Leslie informed her. "She has a hypnotic stare and there are times when I feel as if I'm succumbing to her dominant will."

"Explain yourself," Phyllis said as she felt a prickly sensation moving over her.

138

"It's just that I sense that at times I am under the spell, that she has tremendous influence over me and can cause me to do whatever she wishes me to do."

"Except fall in love with her?" Phyllis added as a curious whim.

"A person can't be hypnotized to do anything against his will."

"Does that mean that your will bends to accommodate her other desires?" Phyllis asked.

"That well could be," Leslie replied after a tense several seconds. "I sometimes believe she is a witch."

"You still haven't told me why you're telling me all this."

"Miss Burdick—if I may, Phyllis—I must warn you to be extremely careful around Miss Phenwick and exert all your force and will to keep from antagonizing her. She can be extremely vindictive if she is crossed or doesn't get her way in things."

"I am well aware of Miss Phenwick's extreme temperament," Phyllis replied. "If that is all you have to tell me, Mr. Brooks, I must ask that you walk me to my home. It is extremely late and I am exhausted, with a full day ahead of me tomorrow."

Leslie appeared as if he had something more to say. If so, he didn't express himself.

"Was there another reason you wished to tell me this, Mr. Brooks?" Phyllis inquired as they reached the boarding house.

"No—no, I think not. I was being impetuous, I suspect. It may have been a mistake for me to wish to speak to you in the first place. Good night, Miss Burdick."

"As abruptly as that?" she asked.

"Yes, good night."

"Good night, Mr. Brooks. And thank you very much for the tea."

Curiously, Phyllis watched as Leslie strode down the street, his eyes cast toward the street, his shoulders slumped. His attitude indicated that he was distressed about something far more serious than anything he had mentioned to her. She felt compassion, but she also needed sleep.

Chapter Ten

The autumn colors were vibrant in Boston that day in October when white-haired, full-maned, stately, slender John Phenwick left the courthouse and went directly toward his office. His long strides had rarely faltered over the years. A majestic being, he was well-respected among his colleagues in the law profession as well as the acknowledged patriarch of the Phenwick family. The second born of Peter Phenwick's second marriage, to Nancy Cox, John had managed to be successful in practically every aspect of his life. The four children born to Peter's first marriage were dead. Older brother Thadius had acquiesced to his assuming the title of patriarch because he preferred to live in the isolation of Greenfield, Maine, with his devoted wife Nellie. John was the logical choice, with third brother Paul in San Francisco, and youngest brother Daniel Louis succumbing to an early death. None of the family disputed the fact that John was the head of the clan, a position he maintained with quiet dignity and authority.

His feet shuffled through drifting piles of leaves with the wonderful autumn fragrance in the air which he so enjoyed. His head held proud, John nodded to familiar faces along the way and spoke when names were remembered. Boston had greatly changed over the years of his life. He liked change, the fresh, the new. Daughter Laura Donnally was the pride of his eye; son Simon was less the apple of his father's eye, but he nonetheless had never given him any difficulty. Now a widower, John tried not to live with haunting memories, but he could not help occasionally falling back into periods of reverie.

As John closed the large oak outer door to the waiting room, he glanced around at the empty seats and went about putting things in order. He had always liked to have things in their proper place, neat and tidy. The other attorneys in his firm had left for the day along with the clerical help. The rooms were quiet.

Upon entering the inner office, John perceived that some other person was present. He glanced over at the large wingback chair, where he saw a hand casually reclined on the armrest.

"Simon!" exclaimed the older man as he threw his arms open wide to welcome his son to a warm embrace.

Simon was immediately to his feet and wrapping his arms about his father. "Dad!"

"What a joy it is to see you, my boy," John stated as if he were welcoming a prodigal who had been away for years, instead of the proper young man who had been in New York for two weeks. "Does this mean that Laura is back, too?"

"It does. We arrived this afternoon."

"Come. Sit down. Tell me about your trip."

Simon spent the next half hour relating highlights of the New York excursion, Augusta II's play, the parties, the club.

"Hold on, Simon, hold on!" John ordered. "You're talking far too fast for my ears to keep up with you. That is, I hear your words, but I perceive you are hiding something beneath them."

"That's a clever observation, Dad." Simon laughed in response.

"What is it?"

"Tell me about yourself first."

"I've been asked to take a seat as a federal judge," John replied, beaming with pride.

"You will take it, of course," Simon encouraged.

"I'm giving it serious consideration."

"Imagine! A federal judge!" Simon rose and went to embrace his father again.

"If you make me feel like a king over such news," John commented dryly, "imagine how Laura will make me feel!"

"It's the appointment you've been wanting for a long time," Simon remarked as he returned to the chair on the opposite side of the desk, but he did not sit. "Now you can put your lawbooks away."

"I said I was to become a judge, not to go into retirement," John protested.

"In that case, Your Honor," Simon said, "I would like to present the case of your esteemed son and heir."

"Counsel may address the bench."

"It seems your learned son has grown weary of the environs of Boston," Simon stated. "It further seems he has a desire for more of a permanent change of scene."

"What are you saying, Simon?"

"Dad, I want to leave Boston—perhaps not forever," Simon continued. "I need a change of pace. Boston has become too stodgy for me."

"A change of scene? Am I hearing properly, boy?"

"While I was in New York, I interviewed with several law firms, several of which offered me immediate positions with them," Simon related. "I'm very seriously thinking about the legal aspects of the theater, of

143

handling contracts and all phases of what they call show business."

John frowned and folded his hands beneath his chin. "The theater?"

"The theater has held a fascination for me for years," Simon said enthusiastically. "I might even try my hand in producing. Several attorneys have gone into that. And—"

"Simon," John said softly but firmly.

"You don't approve?"

"Before I approve or disapprove," John insisted, "I must know more of the facts surrounding this lunatic notion of yours."

"The very fact that you call it a lunatic notion indicates that you disapprove."

"I do, on principle." The older man scratched his head before he returned the hand to be folded with the other beneath his chin. "Before you go any further, answer one question. Is there a woman involved in this?"

"A woman? That seems a strange question."

"Not in the least. Women have ways of making sound young men do erratic things. Is she an actress?"

"I didn't say there was a woman involved whatsoever," Simon fired back, annoyed over his father's supposition.

"I had always counted on you heading this law firm, Simon. That had been my dream since you were a small boy."

"You have capable men in the firm now. Capable men, whom I might add, resent the fact that I'm your son with far less practical experience than they have."

"Nonsense. All of the partners respect you."

"Yes, because I'm your son, not because of what I know or how I can handle a case."

"I hadn't realized that you had felt such antagonism from any of the men in the firm."

"It's nothing blatant, just subtle little things that

put me ill at ease," Simon replied. "Dad, I need a change of scene."

"She *is* an actress, isn't she?"

"What makes you think that?"

"Change of scene is a theatrical expression," John said attempting to shield an ironical expression.

"I prefer the lifestyle in New York," Simon persisted. "There is far more to do and to attract my interest."

"She must be a remarkably beautiful woman." John sighed.

"Why are you taking that attitude, Dad? It's most irksome."

"Because I can see that you've already made up your mind about this," John said, "and no matter what I think or say, you are determined to have your way in it. Well, I would be foolish to advise you not to follow the wishes of your heart. Things may not turn out in the long run as you would have them, but hopefully you will profit from whatever experiences you have."

"Then you're not going to object?"

"Oh, yes, I'm definitely going to take objection," John commented, "but I doubt if my objections will be sustained. We each see life from the point of perspective we chose. And, since no two people can be in the same identical place at the same time, there are bound to be different points of view." He stood up and went toward his son with an extended hand. "I wish you well with whatever you undertake in this life, my boy. What I want, or your sisters want, or anyone else wants for you may influence you in some way, but what you want to do with your own life is your responsibility. Yet, if for some reason you don't succeed in accomplishing your dreams, you know that there will always be open arms awaiting you here and a place of extreme importance. Wisdom is hard to come by, and when it arrives, it just sort of sneaks in. If anything can be said about me and the life I have lived, I trust it will be that 'he was a wise man, who offered

145

his opinions but who never tried to impose them on anyone.' "

"How will such a philosophy affect your role as federal judge?" Simon asked.

"Opinions and decisons are two different things. Opinions are predicated on senses and feelings of an subjective nature," John said, "while decisions are based on evidence of cold facts and must be reached as objectively as possible. I rest my case."

John pumped his son's hand until the two fell into each others' arms and clung to each other for several minutes.

"Go with my blessings, Simon, and with my love."

The R. Pruman Donnallys had purchased a good sized house near Edward House on Beacon Hill before Donald and Peggy decided to take up residence at Triumph House after Millijoy's death. Other of the Phenwicks lived nearby, and the Donnallys senior resided only three-quarters of a block away.

Laura had taken a nap after returning from New York, while Pru went to his office to catch up on what had happened during his absence. When she was awakened by her maid, Laura bathed and prepared to dine with the Gordon Thomas Phenwicks and Donald and Peggy at fabulous Triumph House, the mansion built by the late Millijoy, Mrs. Gordon Phenwick.

When the butler announced that she had a caller, Laura looked alarmed because she had budgeted her time precisely to the minute.

"Who could possibly know I was home?" Laura asked with annoyance as the servant stood without a change of expression.

"It's your father, Mrs. Donnally."

"Daddy? Oh, dear. I should have called him earlier." Laura tried to hurry with her preparations. "Ask him to come up here. He's seen me in a frantic state of preparation before, this won't come as any shock to him."

The butler left as the maid assisted Laura into her gown, springtime green encrusted with rhinestones in two vertical rows down the front of it.

"Hurry, Nan, fasten me in back before Daddy gets here."

"Daddy *is* here," John said at the doorway. "I was just waiting outside in the hallway. Never mind about your back, I've seen it bare on more than one occasion. You didn't let me know you'd arrived back in Boston, Laura."

"I was drained of energy by the time we got back," Laura related. "I was going to call you before we left for Triumph House."

"I presume that means Donald and Peggy are back, too."

"I believe they've been back for two days."

John coughed. "That's what comes of being a widower with no one to keep my social calendar for me. Your mother always saw to such things."

"What are your plans for tonight, Daddy?" Laura asked after Nan had finished hooking her gown. She went to kiss her father.

"The usual. A quiet supper, the newspaper, early to bed after a glass of sherry," John recited.

"It sounds dull, Daddy. I'll call Peggy and have them set a place for you."

"That's foolish, Laurie," John complained. "I don't want to barge in on you young people."

"You won't be barging, and I won't take no for an answer."

A short while later Laura returned to the room where her father was patiently waiting. "Well, now, that's all settled. It's roast mutton—your favorite. Peggy is delighted that you can come."

"Before we fly off into the social whirl of the evening," John said after clearing his throat and striking a serious pose, "there are a few questions I would like to ask you in private."

"Nan, do you mind?"

The maid scurried from the room.

"What is it, Daddy?"

"One of our favorite topics: your brother," John said as he went nearer to where she was standing appraising her appearance in the full-length mirror.

"What about Simon?"

"What was he up to in New York, do you know?"

"Simon didn't spend much time with Pru and me," Laura replied.

"You're going to be evasive, are you?"

"What do you want me to say?"

"Easy, Laura, you are under tension," John said softly. "I'll get to the point. Your brother told me he was interested in relocating in New York."

"Simon likes the city very much. He told us that he wanted to try to establish with a firm there," Laura answered mechanically as she checked her eyes. "Simon also mentioned the possibility of putting up money to back a Broadway show."

"Hmm." John stood with folded arms. "Is Augusta II behind this?"

"I shouldn't think so," Laura returned. "Simon didn't seem to get along too well with her this time around. He didn't mention specifics. No, I shouldn't think Augusta would have influenced—or if so, in an indirect way."

"Meaning?"

"If he does want to back a show," Laura speculated, "it may be to spite Augusta. I don't really know about it."

"Was there a young lady?" John asked.

"A young lady?" Laura blinked. "I saw Simon a time or two with an actress who is in Augusta's play."

"An actress? Just as I suspected."

148

"I only met her once. Both Peggy and Katherine spent more time with her than I did," Laura went on. "She's quite a beauty, as I recall."

"I see."

Since Laura had little more to say about Phyllis Burdick, and did not even recall her name, John decided to wait until he got to Triumph House before he enquired further about his son's new acquaintance.

John managed to get Katherine and Philip aside before supper at Triumph House. Philip had little to contribute to the conversation and, with a sign from his wife, he excused himself to join the others.

"When Aunt Isabelle was chosen to be a Phenwick woman," Katherine said mysteriously as her husband left the room, "she became aware of her selection through the scent of violets. Isn't that the case?"

"I believe Isabelle mentioned something about that at one time."

"Now Phenwick women are chosen with the scent of roses," Katherine said, "and both Phyllis Burdick and Simon have encountered such a phenomenon."

John stood with an incredulous expression, his mouth slowly sagging open. Then a laugh before he shook his head. "Roses?"

"Uncle John, I know you're too practical, too earthy to believe in such things of the spirit," Katherine said softly as she went to touch him. "Have faith. I know you've lamented because your son hasn't chosen a wife."

"But if his choice of a wife takes him away from me—"

"He's virtually been away from you for a long time, Uncle John," she smiled as she spoke with a reassuring expression. "You never owned him, you simply had the opportunity to raise him and love him as a precious gift. But he has his own destiny to live."

John shook his head. "I had such hopes for him here in Boston."

"If your desires don't coincide with his, the the chances of Simon fulfilling your hopes are extremely slim," Katherine advised. "Simon could well fail if he doesn't work toward the ambitions of his heart. He became an attorney because that is what you wanted him to be, and he felt he was pleasing you by so doing. But, Uncle John, I dare say he won't truly be happy until he is doing that which he wants to do to satisfy no one but Simon."

"Hmm. You may be right, Katherine." He sighed. "You may just be very right."

Chapter Eleven

March, 1911

The winter seemed longer than usual, as winters seem to do when the snows have been heavy and January and February have been bitterly cold. *The Eternal Light* nearly had to close down during the most severe part of the inclement weather; but there were those devoted souls who braved the elements to have the opportunity of seeing Miss Augusta Phenwick II playing the leading role in the play.

Keeping to his rooms, Madison Davis had completed the first draft of *Triumph and Passion* by the end of January, and the polished manuscript by the 27th of February. Hampton Colwell was the first to be given the opportunity to read the play, and he immediately became convinced that it was far better than any of Davis's earlier works.

With Hampton Colwell's enthusiasm Madison was

elated, and arranged, through Colwell, to get the manuscript to Mortimer Gree, the producer. Two days later Hampton went to call on Cree.

"I suppose you've come to hear my opinion of Davis's new play, have you?" rotund and moustached Mortimer Gree asked. "Well, I can't call it an absolute masterpiece—but it's damn well close to it. He has outdone himself."

"Oh, I'm very glad you feel that way about it, Mr. Gree," Hampton returned. "That was my feeling, but I wanted another's opinion."

"It's an ideal vehicle for Miss Phenwick," Gree said with a beaming expression. "She will make it into a bigger triumph than *The Eternal Light*."

Hampton's face fell.

"Don't you think that possible, Colwell?"

"The heroine of the new play is a girl of eighteen or nineteen," Hampton stated. "Not a woman of thirty-five or forty."

"Miss Phenwick has always played heroines years younger than her actual age. That's artistic license in the theater," Gree declared. "The role is perfect for Augusta."

"I must disagree with you, sir."

"Disagree? What? With me?"

"And I'm certain that Madison Davis will disagree, too."

"Why, that young whippersnapper, what does he know about the theater? Miss Phenwick is one of the biggest drawing names in the business. Why, I can get investors just like that." He snapped his fingers. "Miss Phenwick's name means instant backing."

"Miss Phenwick is no longer the actress that she once was," Hampton said softly. "I don't mean to be disrespectful. You haven't been to the theater in two or three months. There is hardly any appreciable crescendo in the applause from the time the supporting cast bows and Miss Phenwick arrives. She chews the
152

scenery. Her histrionics are often embarrassing, even though I specifically call her attention to what she is doing wrong. I suggest you go to the theater and see for yourself, Mr. Gree."

"I will do that, but I find what you say difficult to believe."

"It is true, Mr. Gree, frighteningly true."

Mortimer Gree pushed his head down toward his chest so that his physiognomy appeared to be one large double chin. He drummed his fingers on the desk as thoughts formed in his mind. "Did Davis have someone in mind to play the leading role in *Triumph and Passion?*"

"He does," Hampton replied. "However, before I disclose who that is, I would like you to catch Miss Phenwick's performance at your earliest convenience."

"I will see her tomorrow night. In fact I'll make a point of catching every performance throughout the rest of this week," Gree declared. "One cannot completely judge by seeing one performance alone."

"That's an excellent idea, Mr. Gree, an excellent idea."

The following evening, as promised, Mortimer Gree was in the seat he constantly reserved for himself. It was wider than the others to accommodate his girth. Hampton Colwell occupied the seat next to his. The house was only about three-quarters filled, a fact that distressed Gree.

Augusta II had not been forewarned that Gree would be in the audience that night. She arrived at the theater at the last possible minute, hurriedly got into her makeup and costume and was somewhat winded for her entrance. Immediately her timing was off and she had difficulty with several speeches.

"Has she been drinking?" Gree whispered.

"I don't believe so, sir, no more than usual," Hampton replied. "If you ask me, it seems as if her memory is failing her."

153

There was hardly any applause at the first act curtain. Disgruntled comments were heard by the producer and director as the audience filed out for intermission.

"What has happened to her?" Gree asked.

"I don't know," was Hampton's response.

"When she's on stage with that saucy little black girl," Gree commented, "the Molly, you know, why, Augusta acts as if she were playing against her, not with her."

"I know only too well what you mean. The actress playing the slave girl is extremely talented."

"I realize that," Gree replied. "I caught myself watching her far more than I was watching Augusta. It may only be tonight's performance, and she is off with her timing. I will be better able to judge after watching her tomorrow night."

By the third act, less than half the house was full. Three people had fallen asleep and the chorus of their snoring was distracting to the rest of the audience and actors alike. Gree said nothing. He got up and left the theater during the curtain calls without going backstage to let his presence be known.

"Did he say anything?" Madison enquired of Hampton as the house lights came up.

"He wasn't favorably impressed," Hampton replied. "Now I've got to get backstage and have a word with our star."

Hampton Colwell's mission backstage was brief. He merely asked Augusta II if she could arrange to have an early dinner with him the next night before the performance. She agreed to the arrangement and suggested that he come to her house on Riverside Drive. He accepted.

"I was so terribly embarrassed over tonight's performance," Phyllis said to Madison Davis when he met her at the stage door. "I was embarrassed for Miss Phenwick. Several times she looked at me with such a blank expression, I was certain she had completely forgotten the rest of the play. Miraculously, she found her place and went on. The audience was terribly restless—and I can't blame them."

"Did she say anything to you?" Madison asked before he raised his hand for a cab.

"She hasn't spoken a word to me since Christmas," Phyllis replied. "I don't think she's even acknowledged any of the rest of the cast since then. She seems to be trapped in her own little world."

"Trapped? That's a curious usage."

"It seemed appropriate."

"Have you been rehearsing regularly with Hampton Colwell?" the writer asked.

"I've over-rehearsed with him. I know Miss Phenwick's part backwards and forwards, and if I don't get the opportunity to play it soon, I can't guarantee in which direction I'll recite it."

"It only seems that way now, dear Phyllis," Madison said grandly as he waved a cab to the curb. "You'll find all that rehearsal will be to your benefit when your time comes—which may be much sooner than you anticipate."

Madison sat on the seat beside Phyllis. Without looking at her, he knew she was staring at him with a puzzled expression.

Carlyle showed Hampton Colwell into the sitting room the following afternoon at four-thirty. Because of her performance, Augusta II wished to have dinner over and done with no later than five-thirty, which would give her sufficient time to digest before curtain-time.

At precisely four forty-five, Carlyle announced that dinner would be served in the dining room, where Miss Phenwick was waiting.

"Hampton Colwell?" Augusta II enquired of him with a startled expression.

"Why, yes."

"Oh." A distant look. "I thought I was dining with Madison Davis tonight. How queer of me to have become so confused. Now I recall it was you with whom I was to dine. I should have remembered when Carlyle said you were waiting for me in the sitting room."

"Are you feeling well, Miss Phenwick?" Hampton asked.

"I've been having a series of headaches recently," Augusta II admitted. "They come and they go. For the past three nights after the performance, I've had screeching headaches that were so severe I asked Leslie to leave me to my own devices at a ridiculously early hour. Poor Leslie, he's so confused by my condition. He's a dear and terribly accommodating, but my goodness, I do confuse him." She laughed loudly as if she had said something extremely humorous.

The soup was served. Augusta II took two spoons of it and pushed the bowl aside. She sipped from the wine-glass, then rose and went to the far window.

"I saw a ray of sunlight come in through here the other day," she said in a sing-song manner, "but it escaped before I could catch it."

While Augusta II was adjusting the draperies at the window, in hopes of catching another look at the elusive sunray, Hampton took three small tablets from his vest pocket and quickly dropped them into her wine-glass. He continued spooning his soup as he watched her histrionics at the window. By then, she had wrapped one of the draperies about her waist and had taken a pose.

"I don't know what's come over me," she said suddenly as she flung the drapery aside. "I catch myself doing these most peculiar things from time to time." She crossed back to the table. "It's like I don't realize I'm doing them until I'm in the middle of doing them. If that makes any sense. Doesn't matter if it does, because I am a star. S-T-A-R. A star! Ta-da! Oh, Hampton, haven't you any sense of humor, I'm performing for you." She took the wineglass and raised it as if to propose a toast. A fierce look came to her face. "Damn her! Damn her! Damn her, I say!"

Hampton feared she was going to slosh the drink before she got the glass to her lips. With another dramatic gesture as if she were holding back anyone who might wish to restrain her, Augusta II downed the entire contents.

"I like a lusty drinker, don't you?" Augusta II questioned.

"I've seen sailors who couldn't put it away that well," Hampton commented. "Who were you damning a moment ago?"

"Was I damning someone? Oh, yes. That silly fool, Molly."

"Molly?"

"Black Molly—only she isn't really black." Her expression became dazed and she made a sweeping movement of her head as she attempted to focus on Carlyle when he came to remove the soup things.

"Is everything all right, Miss Phenwick? You hardly touched your soup," the butler commented.

Augusta II scowled as she gazed at him without saying a word.

"Is there something troubling you, Miss Phenwick?" Carlyle asked. He passed a cautioning glance to Hampton.

"Molly is troubling me, that's who!" Augusta II fired.

As Carlyle placed the next course before her, Augusta II took one look at it, glanced back at the butler, lost consciousness and collapsed, her head in the plate.

"Good heavens! What's happened to her?" exclaimed Hampton, displaying why he was a better director than he was an actor.

"I don't know, sir. This is quite unlike her," the butler said as he raised her face from the plate. "She is

157

a bit of a mess, isn't she? And totally unconscious, too. Did you ever?"

"I never, did you?" Hampton returned. "Can I give you a hand with her?"

"I'll just take her into the kitchen and clean her up," Carlyle expressed. "To my knowledge she has only had this one glass of wine. It couldn't be intoxication."

"Does she take medication?"

"Only to help her sleep and to ease those interminable headaches, sir."

Hampton assisted the butler in getting the unconscious Augusta II into the kitchen, where she was placed in a large chair as the heavy-set cook curiously came to see what had happened.

"I'll serve the rest of your dinner, if you are ready, sir," Carlyle said properly after he instructed the cook to wash Miss Phenwick's face.

"I don't believe I have much of an appetite left after all of that," Hampton replied. "Has she gotten like this before?"

"Not to my knowledge, sir," Carlyle replied. "She and Mr. Brooks go at it at night, I mean to say, they tipple a little and tend to get a mite rowdy. It sounds to be all good fun—but I, of course, do not hear it."

"Yes, of course." Hampton smiled. "At your convenience, Carlyle, you may get my coat, hat and gloves. If Miss Phenwick doesn't rally within half an hour, you'd better call a physician."

"Yes, sir. I'll do that."

"All I can say," the cook said, "is I am grateful she didn't drop her face into my chocolate meringue pie. It would have been a waste of good chocolate."

Carlyle went for Hampton's things as the director took one last look at the unconscious actress.

"Pleasant dreams, Miss Augusta II," Hampton said before he left the actress with the bewildered cook.

Thirty minutes later, still unconscious, Augusta II was stretched out on her bed. The maids had removed
158

her clothing and dressed her in sleeping attire. There was no indication that she would regain consciousness. Her breathing was heavy as if she were in a deep sleep.

"I'm a little late," Leslie Brooks said as he entered the front hallway and caught sight of Carlyle as he hurried down the stairway.

The butler hesitated briefly at the foot of the stairs. "Miss Phenwick is indisposed, Mr. Brooks. I was just on my way to call a doctor for her."

"Indisposed? Ill?"

"Unconscious, sir. She's been that way for the past half hour," Carlyle related.

"She hasn't been drinking too much, has she?" Leslie asked.

"I don't believe so, sir. I suggest that it would be best if you were not to disturb her, Mr. Brooks."

"Thank you, Carlyle." Leslie appeared concerned. "I'll have to let them know at the theater. Miss Augusta doesn't have an understudy, so the performance will have to be cancelled. What a pickle this is!"

Without bothering to personally check on Augusta II, Leslie left the mansion with a sense of urgency.

Coincidental with the events at the home of Augusta Phenwick II, Madison Davis arrived at the small apartment which Phyllis Burdick had taken immediately following the first of the year.

"You're early, Madison," Phyllis stated as she opened the door to him. "I'm right in the middle of getting ready."

"Wear one of your nicest dresses, Phyllis," Madison said emphatically. "This is going to be a big night for you."

"What do you mean by that?" she asked.

"I can't tell you yet. I guarantee this will be a night that you will long remember."

Phyllis appeared confused. But she had come to know Madison well enough over the months to realize he had a way of playing little games, always an edge of mystery and an element of surprise. "Any hints?"

"None whatsoever." Madison was beaming boyishly.

Phyllis studied him for a short while before she went to finish her preparations.

Hampton Colwell was waiting at the Majesty Theater when Phyllis arrived with Madison.

"The dressing room next to Miss Phenwick's has been cleared for you, Miss Burdick," Hampton said, attempting to sound casual. "The costumes are waiting for you."

"I beg your pardon, Mr. Colwell." Phyllis was obviously confused as a rush of excitement flamed through her. "What is this all about?"

"Miss Phenwick is indisposed tonight. You will have to go on in her place," Hampton replied. He put his arm about her shoulders in a fatherly gesture. "I know you can do it. And it's important that you give the performance of your life."

Words failed Phyllis for the moment and she permitted herself to be maneuvered into the assigned dressing room. She was still in a state close to shock when Cynthia, Augusta II's attendant entered the dressing room. She was a woman in her late thirties, tall and strong.

"They tell me Miss Phenwick is sick," Cynthia commented. "They tell me you know her part and are going to play it. Although it's against my wishes, I will help you dress. I feel as if I am betraying Miss Phenwick."

"You mustn't think that, Cynthia," Phyllis returned. The servant's attitude seemed to snap the young actress back to the stark reality of the moment. "Miss Phenwick is unable to perform tonight."

"There should be no performance if Miss Phenwick is indisposed," Cynthia stated. "I'm certain you'll be a poor substitute for Miss Phenwick, and it'll be a miracle if you aren't booed off the stage."

"I regret that you're not more favorably disposed to encouraging me."

"I would be a traitor if I did."

Phyllis would liked to have done without Cynthia's service, but in the flurry of excitement and sense of apprehension that had come over her, she did her best to abide with the servant's attitude.

Hampton Colwell personally went to meet Mortimer Gree at the latter's office a short distance from the theater. Despite the fact that Gree had promised to view all performances that week, something had come up that he would prefer to do instead of sitting through the agony of watching *The Eternal Light* again.

"It's important that you see the play tonight, Mr. Gree, most important," Hampton insisted.

"If Miss Phenwick's performance is as bad as it was last night," the producer stated, "I fear I will be inspired to close the play."

"I don't believe Miss Phenwick's performance will be anything like it was last night."

"Have you been working with her today?"

"Not exactly."

Mortimer Gree had become curious since he had never seen Hampton Colwell in such an enigmatic attitude.

Just prior to curtain time, Hampton Colwell stepped before the curtain to announce that Miss Augusta Phenwick II would not be appearing that night. A murmur of disapproval and disappointment rose through the audience.

"Don't pay any attention to that," Madison Davis told Phyllis as he stood beside her in the wings. "That sort of reaction was to be expected. You're going to have to give it everything you've got, Phyllis. This is your one-in-a-million chance."

"It is?"

"Mortimer Gree will be in the audience."

Sharp feared jabbed at Phyllis. "I wish you hadn't told me that. I'm certain to forget every line, each movement and gesture."

"It will all come back to you once you're on stage and feel the audience beginning to respond to you," Madison said.

After making the announcement, Hampton Colwell stepped backstage, quickly embraced Phyllis and wished her luck.

"Madison," Phyllis asked after Hampton abruptly left to go join Mortimer Gree in the audience, "when did you know that Miss Phenwick would not be performing tonight?"

"Only moments before you did," Madison lied.

"Are you certain of that?"

"There's suspicion in your eyes, Phyllis," the writer commented. "I don't believe it's important when I knew about Miss Phenwick. What is important is that you give a fantastic performance. Now get out there. I'll be watching from the front of the house."

Phyllis's first entrance was met with quiet indifference where Augusta II usually got an ovation of recognition. Her first line was hesitant, but she soon gained the confidence she needed to take control of the situation and command the stage.

"What's the meaning of this?" Gree whispered to Hampton when he sat beside him in the rear of the theater. "How did this girl learn the part?"

"I'll explain after the first act," Hampton assured him, and motioned for him to turn his attention toward the stage.

Once the members of the audience got over their disappointment and became involved with the action of the play, Phyllis felt less hostility aimed at her, and by the end of the first act she had the viewers in the palm of her hand. The ovation at the end of the act was far greater than the automatic polite response Augusta II had received the night before.

"She's not bad," Mortimer Gree condescended to testify. "In fact, she certainly brings a new life, and, I might add, a brighter dimension to the role. I'm impressed. How did she learn the role? You know Augusta II would never permit an understudy."

"I've been working privately with Miss Burdick over the past few months," Hampton admitted. "Miss Phenwick has been acting peculiarly for some time now. I thought it important that she be covered."

"I'm pleased that you did," Gree commented and offered the director a cigar to smoke during intermission as the two men went out to mingle with the audience in the foyer.

Everyone was talking about Phyllis and her performance. While some reacted with annoyance at being deprived of seeing Augusta II, the general feeling was that Phyllis was a powerful and extremely talented actress. Everywhere the producer and the director went among the people, they heard surprisingly astonished remarks about the substitute; and those who had seen the play before favorably compared Phyllis's performance to that of Augusta II's, conceding that the younger actress was probably better suited to the role, and just possibly her interpretation was far more believable than Augusta II's had ever been.

"Miss Burdick is the one you want to play the lead in *Triumph and Passion?*" Mortimer Gree asked as he and Hampton made their way back to their seats.

"She is," Hampton replied with conviction. "Furthermore, Mr. Davis wrote the new play with Phyllis Burdick in mind for the leading role."

"Is Davis sweet on her?"

"I don't believe it's that as much as he thinks, as I do, that Miss Burdick has a tremendous amount of talent and great potentialities for the future."

"Hmm. Well, there are still two more acts."

Madison had been backstage to offer Phyllis words of

encouragement. His present was the pat on the back she needed.

At the apartment on Riverside Drive, Carlyle went to have a look in on Augusta II about the time the curtain dropped on the first act of *The Eternal Light*. He moved practically noiselessly, but his presence in the room caused the actress to stir. She suddenly opened her eyes and shot a sharp glance at the butler.

"Are you awake, Miss Phenwick?" he asked.

"I can tell that I've been asleep," she replied, "but I seem to be in a state of confusion. My senses are distorted, and I feel most peculiar."

"You suddenly lost consciousness while seated at dinner, Miss Phenwick. If you hadn't rallied, I would have called your physician."

"What time is it?"

"Shortly past nine, Miss Phenwick."

"The play! The theater!" She sat up as a rush of pain hit her head. Her equilibrium seemed to be off balance. "I've got to get to the theater!"

"I suspect they've cancelled this evening's performance by now, Miss Phenwick," the butler opined.

"I was dining with Hampton Colwell, wasn't I?" Augusta II asked suspiciously as if her memory were clouded.

"Yes, you were, Miss Phenwick."

"How long did he remain after I lost consciousness?"

"Not long at all," Carlyle replied.

"You've got to help me up, then immediately go to the kitchen to prepare extremely strong coffee for me while the maid helps me dress," Augusta II instructed. "I've never had an understudy. But I have strange premonitions—and suspicions."

Carlyle didn't quite comprehend what his mistress was getting at, but he went to do her bidding.

"I must say I was greatly impressed by your first act

performance," Leslie Brooks complimented as he stood beside Phyllis before the second act rise. "Your characterization was an inspiration to play opposite. Keep up the good work."

"Thank you, Mr. Brooks." Phyllis waited for the curtain to go up, timed an appropriate pause before she hurried onto the stage. At first it appeared as if she had become a bit over confident because of the acclaim she had received in the previous act; but she soon managed to regain control and soon had the feeling that she once again had the audience in her hands. The romantic scenes with both Leslie Brooks and the other leading man were far more believable than the way Augusta II had played them. There was tenderness and warmth and the sense that here was a virginal young lady who was confused by the romantic pursuit of two dashing men. As Leslie kissed her, she fell into his embrace and her response to his touch at the moment was such that ladies in the audience fluttered their fans, and gentlemen uneasily altered their positions.

Augusta II arrived at the theater shortly after the curtain rose on the third act of *The Eternal Light.* She slipped in through the front door which had not been locked after the intermission. The head usher eyed her suspiciously. He started to comment on her late entrance, but assuming that she was one of the paying customers who had been detained for some reason during intermission, he did not pursue the situation.

Finding an unobtrusive place to stand at the back of the theater, Augusta II became enraged when she saw Phyllis enter attired in the costume of the leading lady. She might have caused a scene had she not realized that the audience had probably been told that she was indisposed; and for her to suddenly make her presence known might not be to her advantage.

By the end of the play the audience was tumultuous in their response to Phyllis's performance. Never had Augusta II received the applause that Phyllis did for her role in *The Eternal Light*. Augusta II was livid.

Augusta II made herself inconspicuous as she went among the departing members of the audience. The over-all enthusiasm was a bitter blow to the actress. Even greater was her disappointment that not a soul recognized her in their midst. She observed Hampton and Mortimer Gree leave the auditorium with extremely pleased expressions.

When the auditorium was empty and the stagehands were busily putting finishing touches to the stage for the night, Augusta II sauntered down the aisle in the darkened house. She took a seat half way back in the house and stared at the stage.

"Miss Burdick," Augusta II heard Mortimer Gree exclaim, "your performance was perfectly marvelous. I was duly impressed."

He was duly impressed, Augusta II thought.

"Thank you for saying so, Mr. Gree," the older actress heard Phyllis return. Bitter rage stormed through Augusta II's body. Her mind began to scheme a vindictive plot.

A short while later, Mortimer Gree, Hampton Colwell and Madison Davis crossed the stage in the company of Phyllis Burdick, like three doting admirers. Augusta II seethed. A moment later, Leslie Brooks appeared to be hurrying after them.

When all became quiet, Augusta II rose and went to the stage, climbing the steps at the left side. Grandly she walked to the center of it. Her fur cape began to slip from her shoulders.

"Why, dear God, why?" Augusta II stared forward into the darkened house. Had she reached the place where she had to step aside in favor of a younger actress? Surely, she could still play the roles of women much younger than her actual years. Her initial thought was to immediately tender her resignation. Then, realizing the success Phyllis had been that night, that was the last thing she wanted to do.

Augusta was standing in the dim stage worklight when Cynthia left the dressing room. The cape slipped from the actress's shoulders and fell behind her in a heap.

"Miss Phenwick? Is that you, Miss Phenwick?" Cynthia asked.

"Don't you recognize me either, Cynthia? I was standing at the back of the house when the audience left," Augusta II explained. "No one recognized me. How fleeting success and fame are."

Cynthia impulsively went to the actress and embraced her. "I was told you were indisposed."

"Did you watch *her* performance?"

"I didn't have the heart to, Miss Phenwick."

"I did see her last act, and she was damned good! That's what worries me," Augusta II said sharply. "It's an omen, but I won't go down without fighting. I vow that!"

Cynthia could sense the intensity of emotion charging through Augusta II as she held her arms about her.

"You must never tell anyone that I was in the theater tonight," Augusta II said. "Let them think that I am oblivious to what has happened here."

Chapter Twelve

"I demand to know what that woman was doing playing my role!" Augusta II's voice had become shrill, her face crimson with rage and her hands trembling with mounting fury. "It was clearly specified that I was not to have an understudy of any sort."

"Now just a minute, Augusta," Mortimer Gree said as he leaned back in his desk chair, rolled the large cigar around in his fingers and thumped his enormous belly with impatient drumming. "No producer in his right mind would permit a production without having each of the parts covered by other actors—certainly the principal roles must have understudies. There's too much invested in this play not to be insured that the show will go on."

"I've never had an understudy!" Augusta II exclaimed. "I've never missed a performance."

"You missed last night's."

"I was drugged," Augusta II insisted.

"Are you certain of that?"

"Why else would I have passed out?"

Mortimer shrugged. "I don't know. Sit down, Augusta, I want to have a serious talk with you now that you've vented your emotions."

Augusta II stared at him strangely. She had appeared in starring roles in four shows that Mortimer Gree had produced. They had had their ups and down, their disagreements, their battles royal, but in the end satisfactory resolutions had been worked out. She could also tell when he seriously meant business, and he did at that moment. "I can stand."

"I said for you to sit down, Augusta."

"Do you realize to whom you're speaking?"

"Yes, to you, Augusta Phenwick II." He stared back, waiting for her to take a chair. "I caught your performance the night before last, as I have at other times during the past few weeks. I must say I was shocked by what I saw. Whatever magic or skill, or whatever it was that once made you the toast of Broadway, is rapidly deteriorating. You blew lines, took awkward pauses and at times appeared as if you didn't even know where you were or what you were doing."

"I knew perfectly well where I was and what I was doing!" Augusta insisted. "I've simply been under a bit of strain."

"You have been hitting the bottle, that's what it is."

"How dare you insinuate such a thing?"

"Isn't it true, Augusta? Be honest with me."

"Perhaps I've had a drop or two more than is my custom, but only because of the strain." Augusta II was beginning to seethe. "Then that—that—woman! She's only a bit player, no one of consequence—she got notices for her performance. And she gets applause. For what? It's a conspiracy."

"What are you talking about? A conspiracy?" Mortimer lit the cigar. "It's your imagination. Are you referring to Miss Phyllis Burdick?"

"I am."

"Well, let me tell you about Miss Burdick," Mortimer continued as he put more intensity behind his words. "Miss Burdick's performance was ten times—no, twenty times the performance yours was the night before."

"How dare you say that to me?"

"Because I am the producer of *The Eternal Light*," Mortimer fired back. "You may be a grand leading lady of the theater and a stellar attraction, but you'll not maintain that status if you continue as you've been doing. That's all. I don't want to discuss the matter any further. But I will tell you this, I will be watching your performances from here on out, and if I don't see a noticeable improvement, changes will be made."

"Are you threatening me, Mortimer Gree?" Augusta II stormed.

"I'm giving you an ultimatum, Augusta."

"I have a run-of-the-play contract."

"Then I'll close the play rather than have you besmirch my good name as a producer," Mortimer stated as he rose and went to the door. "I've made my position clear." He smiled benevolently. "I will make a concession. If you would like to take a few weeks off—perhaps you require rest from all the strain you've been under—I'm certain your performance would improve."

"I'll not take a day off!" Augusta II said defiantly. "I'll not have my role ruined by a completely unknown nobody."

"You're afraid, Augusta," Mortimer replied firmly, "afraid that Miss Burdick will so outshine you that the comparison would do irreparable damage to your career. Take that into consideration. Either straighten yourself out—or take the consequences. Now I've other matters at hand."

"Mortimer—Mortimer—" She looked pathetic. "Please try to understand what I'm going through."

"I understand only that I have a play that is running and I intend to keep it going for as long as it can possibly survive," Mortimer stated. "I don't care about your problems, or your private life—the play is the thing."

"Very well. I accept your ultimatum, Mortimer, and I shall see that my performance improves." Dramatically, Augusta II took a stance, and with a sharp turn of her head, she marched from the office.

"Whew!" Mortimer Gree exclaimed as the actress firmly closed the door behind her. Then he went to an adjoining office and opened the door. "I don't know how much of that you heard, but I think you realize we have a problem on our hands."

Madison Davis and Hampton Colwell were standing near the door where they had been attempting to hear the conversation that had just taken place.

"Augusta Phenwick II is a force with which we have to reckon," Mortimer said. "She does have a run-of-the-play contract, which must be honored as long as she is capable of carrying out her part of it."

"But is she capable, Mr. Gree?" Hampton asked.

"Let me point out another aspect of this situation that you boys may not have considered," Mortimer went on. "I have several backers, large investors who have put money in *The Eternal Light,* not because they like the play, or because Davis wrote it, or you, Colwell, directed it, but because Augusta Phenwick II is the star of it. They invested in her name alone. Suddenly we're talking about Madison's new play. My backers will want Augusta, I know they will. I'm being put on a spot."

"But if Miss Phenwick is failing in *The Eternal Light,*" Hampton questioned, "how do you think she can possibly carry *Triumph and Passion?*"

"Where will I get investors without her?" Mortimer asked.

"Maybe Miss Phenwick could open in *Triumph,*" Madison suggested, "and let Miss Burdick take over the lead in *Eternal Light.* Then, when the investors see

171

how successful Miss Burdick is, they will back her."

"It wouldn't work," Mortimer replied. "Augusta always manages to get the sort of contract that is iron-clad, all the conditions she wants. And I'm certain she would not want Miss Burdick in either play."

"I see your position, Mr. Gree," Hampton said.

"I think it is quite clear."

"May I ask a question, Mr. Gree?" Madison enquired.

"What is it?"

"What if new backers were found, or a single investor who would put up the entire amount of cash necessary to produce *Triumph and Passion?*"

"That would be another matter, but an impossible situation. That sort of thing is rarely if ever done in the theater," Gree said. "Oh, it would be nice—but—"

"I have an idea," Madison said. "It's a gamble. But I think we're gambling here, anyway. If one backer or one source of backers could be found, would you consider producing *Triumph and Passion* without your usual backers?"

"With Miss Burdick in the leading role?"

"Precisely."

"Do you know someone who might back her?"

"Very possibly—yes."

"Anything is worth a try," Mortimer commented. "Who do you have in mind?"

"I can't tell you that now," Madison said enigmatically. "I'll have to leave New York for a few days, and with luck I should have an answer for you within a week or two." With that he hurriedly left the office.

"Davis believes in his new play, Mr. Gree."

"I can see that he does. But I wonder just how successful he can possibly be at arranging what he's trying to do." Mortimer relit his cigar and let smoke curl up from his thick lips.

The performance that night was strained. Augusta II was doing everything she possibly could to prove that she had not lost her ability to perform. For the most part, she had command of the situation. However, when she had scenes with Phyllis, the tension became noticeable. The younger actress was able to sustain her role as the slave Molly, but Augusta II could not divorce herself from the idea that she was playing opposite competition, an adversary.

"That must have been difficult to endure," Madison said to Phyllis when he met her to go to supper after the performance.

"It wasn't the easiest thing I've had to do," Phyllis returned brightly, "but I'm certain it was far more difficult for Miss Phenwick than it was for me. If she hadn't insisted that so many of my lines were cut, I might have had more difficulty."

Madison laughed. "Let's let that matter drop. Have you heard any more from your friend in Boston?"

"My—? Oh, you mean Mr. Phenwick?" Phyllis's face brightened and an almost dreamlike quality came to her eyes. "You mean Mr. Simon Phenwick, don't you?"

"Yes."

"I received a letter from him last week," Phyllis explained. "His letters are quite marvelous. It's just like he was talking to me, they're so conversational. He's quite an amazing man. It's funny, when he was here we were just beginning to get to know each other. Now, via the post, we have become quite well acquainted."

"You like this Mr. Phenwick, don't you?" Madison said. "I can see it in your eyes and your smile."

"You're making me blush, Madison," Phyllis responded, ducking her head. Suddenly she glanced up into his face. "Would I be too obvious if I said I like Mr. Simon Phenwick very much?"

"And not too long ago you told me all you were interested in was your career."

"Things change, don't they?"

"How does Simon Phenwick feel about you?"

"I think he likes me quite well," Phyllis said shyly. "Oh, aren't I being silly? Here it is months before spring—and I think I've got the fever already." She laughed. "Don't mistake me, Madison, I'm still very much in earnest about my acting. And I want more than anything to play the leading role in *Triumph and Passion*. Maybe I'm only having pipedreams about Simon Phenwick, and maybe I'm trying to read too much into his letters."

Madison put his hand atop hers. "Phyllis, in a short while you've become my best friend. I'm not romantically inclined—I don't know why that is, but it just is. Still I feel closer to you than I've ever felt to anyone—ever."

"What are you trying to tell me, Madison?"

"Just that I want you to be both successful and happy," he replied, "and I will do everything in my power to see that that happens. I'm going to try something."

"I don't understand what you're getting at."

"Just trust me. I want you to give me the address of Simon Phenwick in Boston," Madison said.

"Whatever for?"

"Trust me, Phyllis. If I succeed, I'll tell you all about it. If my plan doesn't work, then I don't want you to know what it was. Just trust me."

Phyllis stared at him for several seconds. "Do you have something to write with?"

Madison Davis arrived in Boston the next afternoon. He carried only one satchel and took a room in a fairly inexpensive hotel. After he had freshened from the trip, he called at the law firm of John Phenwick and asked to see Simon.

"Mr. Simon Phenwick is in conference, sir. If you would care to leave your card, I will tell him you wish to see him. I don't know how long a wait it will be."

The receptionist took Madison's card to the inner office and returned shortly with a message that Simon would meet him in the Mayfair Hotel lobby at six p.m. That arranged, Madison left and took a leisurely stroll around the Commons.

"Madison Davis! What a surprise this is!" exclaimed Simon at the appointed hour in the hotel lobby. "I didn't think I would ever see you here in Boston."

"I made a rather sudden decision to come," the playwright explained.

"We'll go to my club for supper, if it's all right with you," Simon suggested. "I've a lot to catch up with you."

That agreed upon, the two men went to the exclusive men's club in Tremont Street. The fraternity was housed in a monstrous old building, stodgy, stuffy and sedate in appearance, well over a hundred years old. Additions had been made to the building through the years, mainly for physical facilities and a swimming pool. Upon entering the place, one had the feeling that it was occupied solely by elderly gentlemen well past the age of retirement. Despite the almost moribund atmosphere, the heavy, moody rooms, the whispered silence, many younger men were members in good standing and had inherited their membership from fathers, grandfathers or uncles. John Phenwick had long been associated with the Pythian Club, as had his father, Peter, before him.

The dining room was less austere in appearance, but it held a quiet conservativism that properly suited most of the members. Simon and his guest were shown to a secluded table at the far end of the enormous room where they could chat without being disturbed.

"It is rather like stepping into a tomb, isn't it?" Simon joked as he watched Madison gaze at the high beamed ceilings. "Several of the younger members have sought to change the ambience of the entire place, but those men with much longer duration have always

175

been quick to veto any suggestions of modernization. I suppose by the time the younger among us have the influence to sway change, we will have become set in our ways and will want the place to stay as it is, out of tradition or some nonsense like that."

Madison laughed politely. His background was far less affluent than the Phenwicks' and he had had little association with such places, other than through his fairly recent membership in the Pythian Club of New York. He could not help but find the place interesting. "I would dearly love to be closeted away in a place like this to write my next play."

"Boston's the place for you if that is your preference," Simon commented. "Fact is, you'd probably fall in love with old Edward House, the original of which was built before the Revolutionary war by the first Augusta. Personally, I prefer the grand Triumph House, which was designed and constructed under the direct supervision of the late Millijoy Phenwick, a woman who was more of our time than of her own. We Phenwicks of Boston have a thing for old mansions."

"And you, too, Simon?"

"Perish the thought! I prefer a nice simple apartment with three or four rooms, enough to cater to my needs without feeling that I'm lumbering about in an old museum," Simon replied. "My sister Laura tends a little toward tradition, but even she is considered a bit of a modernist by some of our relatives."

Dinner was ordered and leisurely enjoyed as the men conversed about mundane matters. There seemed to be an avoidance of that which was paramount in each of their minds.

"I have never been one to like to lie back or lounge around with a full belly," Simon said at the conclusion of the meal. "I don't recommend strenuous exercise, but I do like to keep active. If you don't mind, I'll show you around the club. That will keep us active. Then in half an hour or so, we can get a bit more physical, do some light exercise and take the sauna and steam. Or is that totally adverse to your constitution?"

"No, that will be fine," Madison agreed. Because he knew that Simon enjoyed such activity, he was ready to conform with whatever he suggested.

The tour of the club was informative, but not particularly interesting. Simon's routine of exercise was far more rigorous than Madison was able to keep up with, but the playwright put forth admirable effort.

After bathing and a relaxing swim, Simon directed the way to the sauna and then the steam room.

"I am reminded of that night we met in the steam room of the Pythian Club in New York," Simon said as the two of them became enshrouded in clouds of moist vapor. "This room is not as expansive as the one you're used to. But it serves its purpose. I like the pine scent they add to the steam."

Madison had begun to feel the effect of the exercise. Happily, his supper was well digested. "I find the pine scent pleasant."

"When last we met in New York," Simon commented at last, "you were planning to write a new play. I've heard that it has been finished and that it may well be your masterpiece."

Madison laughed with a kind of embarrassment. "The play is indeed finished. But as to it being a masterpiece, well, your source of information was undoubtedly exaggerating."

"*Triumph and Passion*," Simon recited. "I like the title."

"If my suspicions are correct, Miss Phyllis Burdick must have told you about the play."

"She did. We've had quite a correspondence going between us," Simon explained. "We met in New York and knew each other briefly, but we have become well acquainted via the post. I feel extremely close to her, despite the distance, for it's as if we each have revealed more of ourselves to the other than we've permitted anyone else to know about us."

"Phyllis and I have become very good griends—strictly friends, I must add," Madison stated. "I know she greatly looks forward to receiving your letters. She is in an awkward situation playing in *The Eternal Light* with your cousin."

"Phyllis has written about Augusta's strangeness and eccentricities, none of which come as great news to me. I've never been particularly fond of Augusta."

"If that's the case, why is it you go to New York to see her opening night performances?"

"It's simply a chance for a holiday with others of my relatives," Simon replied. "Besides, the more I visit New York, the more I desire to live there—at least for a while. I have been doing quite a bit of research about the theater and theatrical enterprises. The more I read, the more enthusiastic I get about it."

"In what aspect?" Madison asked.

"Oh, in the legal part of it at first," Simon replied. "In time, I might even consider going into producing. I just recently received an invitation to join a law firm in Manhattan whose specializes in theatrical ventures. I'm very seriously thinking of taking them up on their offer."

"Will that please your father?"

"Not in the least," Simon returned with amused laughter. "He's become a federal judge and would dearly love for me to take over his law firm here in Boston. My cousin Morgan has come into the organization, and I believe he would be far better equipped to take over in such a capacity than I."

"From my understanding, the Phenwicks are an extremely wealthy family," Madison commented, inching toward the proposal which he had come to make.

"Collectively, the Phenwicks are worth several millions of dollars," Simon assured him. "That's what comes of having a close-knit family. Personally—and this is without boasting—I could live the rest of my life without ever working another day and still leave an opulent legacy to any and all heirs that I have."

"If that's the case, why do you continue to work?"

"People who are without means often question that," Simon replied. "The truth is one must continually work to keep his mind and body active, or he is liable to become lazy. I work for the sheer pleasure of accepting challenges and seeing them through to completion. It isn't the money derived from such ventures that is important as much as it is the very act of accomplishment that spurs me on."

"You mean you work more for the pleasure of actually working than for the remuneration you receive from it?" Madison asked.

"Precisely. To me that is the problem with the laboring masses," Simon inserted, "they work for what little money they can eke out of it, rather than for the exhilarating joy of succeeding in the task at hand. I should think you as a writer would understand that. Surely, you must write for the pleasure of accomplishment, rather than for the projected monies you may gain from your efforts."

"I have to agree to that."

Simon paused, inhaled deeply of the steam and coughed as a result of doing it.

"Is something wrong?" asked Madison.

"Do you still smell the pine fragrance?"

"Yes. Don't you?"

"I think I do," Simon replied, "but something's different about it. It seems far more sweetly pungent than it was a few minutes ago."

"Sweetly pungent?"

"If I didn't know better—and I have to take your word for it—I would say it had almost become the scent of roses," Simon said.

"Maybe you've taken too much steam. I still smell pine."

"Perhaps. It isn't important. One's senses can get distorted in a place like this."

"Have you ever considered investing in a theatrical play?" Madison asked as if the thought had just occurred to him.

"I recall that Millijoy Phenwick invested fairly heavily in dramatic productions for the stage," Simon returned. "Millijoy liked to encourage Augusta in her endeavors. A time or two before her passing, I discussed with Millijoy the possibilities of backing productions and she suggested I might be interested in pursuing such ventures. I never have to date, but the thought of so doing has been in the back of my mind for some time."

"I'll tell you the situation," Madison said, taking the situation in command. "I've written *Triumph and Passion* as a starring vehicle for Phyllis Burdick. She's an excellent actress. Mortimer Gree, the producer of *The Eternal Light* feels he can't get financial support for the new play unless Augusta Phenwick plays the leading role. She's far too old for it, and, quite frankly, her acting has become artificial appearing."

"Augusta's acting has degenerated from what it had been when I first saw her perform," Simon commented. "I suppose one does become jaded in a profession like that. Chances are one becomes too subjective concerning one's self-esteem."

"That appears to be the case with several actors I've met," Madison returned.

"Are you suggesting that I might be interested in investing in your new play, Madison?"

"That was what I was getting to," the playwright replied. "I so very much want Phyllis to play the leading role."

"Aha! I see the situation only too clearly," Simon said. "Let's get out of this steam and discuss it further. I will tell you, however, from the outset that I am

180

extremely interested. It may be that you've brought a solution to a problem I've been puzzling."

Madison felt relieved, both to be out of the steam and because Simon had so readily picked up on what he had come to propose.

Simon stood at the door to the steam room and turned back to take another whiff of the fragrance. "It is pine scent, but for a while there, I would have sworn that it was roses."

The following evening, Simon had previous plans to go to Triumph House, which was now the dwelling place of Donald and Peggy Phenwick. Dinner was planned wherein Laura and Pruman Donnally, Philip and Katherine Phenwick and Gordon Thomas and Lanny Phenwick were to be guests. Peggy had suggested that Simon might like to bring a lady friend, but he called that afternoon and asked if he might bring Madison Davis along instead. Since it was family, Peggy had no hesitation in agreeing to the situation.

Customarily Donald and Peggy Phenwick wintered in their mansion in San Francisco, but that fall Donald had developed a lung ailment that kept him to bed for several weeks when they ordinarily would have gone west. Peggy took advantage of the situation and propelled herself into the midst of social endeavors and quickly fluttered to the center of socialite activities. Donald could rarely attend the gala functions with his wife, but she managed to fit in quite well without his constant presence.

The swarthy beauty, Lanny Phenwick, who was not known as a Phenwick woman, but was very much at the hub of family matters, had not wanted to take up residence at Triumph House at the death of her grandmother, the grandest lady of all, Millijoy. Her parents, Thomas and Evelyn Phenwick, had taken up residence in Switzerland since most of their concert appearances were in Europe; hence, they did not wish to be bothered with the maintenance of the round-shaped mansion overlooking the ocean just north of Boston. Donald expressed a desire to purchase the house and acquired it at a bargain.

Katherine and Philip Phenwick lived in a comparatively small house near her parents, the Alexander Phenwicks. Along with Laura and Pru Donnally, the four young couples spent much time together and had become the nucleus of all family gatherings. Simon, as well as other single Phenwick members, were often included in the family affairs.

Before Simon and Madison Davis arrived at Triumph House, Peggy had commented that she felt it was time that they all put forth a concerted effort to see that Simon, eligible bachelor that he was, would find a wife. Simon objected strenuously to interference in his private life.

"My brother is hanging on with tremendous tenacity to his bachelorhood," Laura responded to Peggy's statement. "However, from little things he has said, I get the feeling that someone has very strongly attracted his interest."

"I'm certain a young lady has," Katherine observed.

"Is that another of your psychic premonitions, Katherine?" Lanny asked. "Or do you know that for a fact?"

"Since most of my psychic premonitions invariably turn out to be fact," Katherine replied in a simple, straightforward manner, "I would be willing to say it is a certainty."

"Who is the girl?" Laura asked.

"I feel we will inadvertently know that before this evening is over," Katherine said mysteriously.

Although they had been warned that Simon was bringing a friend for the evening, the Phenwicks were a bit taken aback when flamboyant Madison Davis appeared with him. Three of the four couples had met the playwright in New York, making him a stranger only to Gordon Thomas and Lanny Phenwick.

During the course of the evening meal, mention was made of Augusta II. Thoughts and opinions were exchanged about her.

"She may be the best known of the Phenwick women," Peggy commented, "famous or infamous, as the case may be, she has never allowed herself to be an intimate part of the family."

"Augusta II has changed over the years," Laura added. "She used to have a sweet disposition. Now it seems that success has changed her. Frankly, I don't think we'll go traipsing off to New York the next time she opens in a play."

"Augusta II is going through a very difficult period," Katherine remarked, "one from which she may not evolve as the person we knew her to be in the past."

"Why do you say that, Katherine?" Simon asked.

"First, she is coming to that time in life where women make a change. Secondly, she has existed on the raw edge of emotions for so long, that there is a chance her sanity might be affected by prolonged living in such a condition without developing a balance."

"Augusta has become extremely domineering," Simon observed. "I had the misfortune of watching her browbeat her brother Joshua into submitting to her domination. It was pathetic."

"There is a karmic attachment between the two," Katherine related. "It could turn out to be disastrous for both of them if their present course is not averted."

After each of the family members had expressed thoughts about Augusta II, and they seemed to be in accord in their opinions concerning her, Simon managed to get the center of attention and related the events that had been happening in New York, about Madison Davis's new play and the conditions surrounding the proposed production of it.

"Don't you have a say in it, Mr. Davis?" Peggy asked.

"I've had my say, but Mr. Mortimer Gree knows that Miss Phenwick is a money-making actress who can assure public interest and adequate backing," Madison said.

"The fact is," Simon interrupted, "Madison has written *Triumph and Passion* expressly for Miss Phyllis Burdick. Augusta would be terrible in the part in her attempt to play an eighteen-year-old girl."

"And this Miss Burdick isn't a money-maker?" Laura questioned. "Is that the case?"

"She could be made into quite a money-making actress," Madison explained, "once she had a substantial hit behind her."

"What is your proposal, Simon?" Peggy inquired. "Let me say this before you answer. I had a delightful time with Miss Burdick in New York. She is lovely, charming and quite enchanting. She won my approval from the start; and I personally would do anything in my power to assist her to become successful."

"If Augusta has taken the attitude toward Miss Burdick that she has," Lanny wondered, "wouldn't backing the young lady imply that you were in opposition to Augusta—your own cousin?"

"Augusta has been in basic opposition to the family for as long as I can remember," Philip stated.

"If each couple would put up one-fifth of the backing," Simon said, "and I put up the final fifth, it would not be a tremendous amount of money out of anyone's account. Although I've locked horns with Dad concerning this—which is why he isn't here tonight, I suspect—I've decided to reestablish myself in New York. I've been offered a position with a theatrical law firm. In time I may get into producing myself. The theater fascinates me and I can see where a tremendous profit could be made."

Exact details were discussed and before the evening

was over it was unanimously agreed that they all would back Madison's new play.

"Instead of *Triumph and Passion*," Katherine cryptically said later when she had drawn Madison aside, "you might have done well to have called your play *The Scent of Roses*."

"I like the title," Madison replied, excited because. his mission had been accomplished. "Whatever made you think of it?"

"You might say it's part of a premonition I have," Katherine returned with a sly twinkle in her eye. "You'll see."

Chapter Thirteen

Madison Davis was away from New York for a total of two weeks, during which time financial arrangements were made with the Phenwicks. It would be another two weeks or more before Simon could make the move. Despite John's objections, the young Phenwick gentleman was determined to make the change. Laura was on his side, and convinced their father that he should support Simon's desire to do what he was convinced he wanted to do.

John Phenwick was not easy to persuade. Even when the time of Simon's departure came, the older man gave his blessings only with certain reservations. John decided that he would simply have to take the attitude of the father of the Prodigal Son if Simon made a dismal failure of the venture.

During the night before the day Simon was to leave for New York, Katherine had a prophetic dream. Philip tried to get her to discuss it, but she refused to say anything other than that she had had a nightmare.

"Can't you tell me what it was about?" Philip asked as he tenderly caressed his wife.

"It's not so much what it was about," Katherine replied, "it's what it meant that is horrifying."

"Then can you tell me what it means?"

"I can only say this," Katherine said mysteriously, "that I fear Augusta II is on the brink of insanity. I can say no more about it at this time. But I must be ready to go to New York when I'm needed."

Philip held his wife even more tightly and tried to understand. As much as he loved her, he realized beyond a doubt that she was different from most people, with a psychic sense that let her see into the future. Often what she beheld were things she wished she not been witness to.

Mortimer Gree was overwhelmed when Madison Davis had returned to New York with news that he had arranged for the complete backing of *Triumph and Passion*. The producer immediately began making plans for a production of the play, to open either in late spring or early autumn. As part of the pre-production work, he would make arrangements for Phyllis Burdick to receive a great deal of publicity, so that by the time the play opened, her name would be known among theatergoers and people who might be curious to know why this beauty had risen from obscurity to fame in such a short time.

"We've had a terrible time with Augusta," Mortimer told Madison. "Not only has she been temperamental, but she's been downright difficult and cantankerous."

"That's been coming on for quite a while," Madison observed.

"She has even dared to demand that Miss Burdick be dismissed from the cast," the producer continued, "but her grounds for wanting it done are illogical."

"Has she made matters difficult for Phyllis? That is, for Miss Burdick?"

"I suspect her strategy now is to make life so miserable for Miss Burdick, since I refused Augusta's demands to dismiss her, that she will want to leave of her own volition."

"Have you considered letting Miss Phenwick go?"

"I have. Unfortunately she has a run-of-the-play contract," Mortimer replied. "And she's got enough money behind her that she could take me through a lot of legal hassles that could be most uncomfortable."

"Perhaps when Simon—that is, Mr. Simon Phenwick arrives, he will be able to handle his cousin," Madison said.

"While I appreciate what you have done, Davis," Mortimer commented, "I'm not looking forward to the moment that Augusta discovers that her own relatives are backing Miss Burdick in *Triumph and Passion.*"

"That's a bridge we can cross when we reach it," Madison returned.

Later Madison called on Phyllis Burdick at her small apartment. He took a small bouquet of hothouse carnations.

"Madison! Oh, am I ever glad to see you!" Phyllis exclaimed. "I missed you, you know."

"If you can't miss a friend, who can you miss?"

"What lovely carnations."

"I've excellent news for you," Madison said as he entered and removed his coat and hat. "I have the backing for *Triumph and Passion,* and the only thing I had to agree to is that you will play the leading role. Naturally, I was only to anxious to agree to that."

"Miss Phenwick is putting me through the horrors of the damned," Phyllis said a short while later. "I simply don't know how one human being can act that way to another. She has threatened on several occasions to have me fired from the company. So far she hasn't been able to do it. Her attitude confuses me. I feel I'm playing against her and not with her."

"She saw the last act of the performance in which

you replaced her," Madison admitted. "I fear we should have taken greater precautions that she would not find out about that."

"That damage is done. I wonder if there's any chance of picking up the pieces and soothing her ruffled ego," Phyllis commented.

"We'll go out after the performance tonight," Madison suggested as he checked his pocketwatch, "and discuss this further. Don't worry, Phyllis, this will all work out." He started to leave. "Oh, by the way, I have another surprise for you—but I can't tell you what it is right now."

"You're full of surprises, Madison." She caught him in an embrace and kissed him.

"You'd better find out what the surprise is before you get too generous with your kisses," he teased. He turned to leave.

"Madison . . ."

"What is it?"

"I just want you to know how much I appreciate your friendship," Phyllis said. "I really mean that from the bottom of my heart. I didn't realize how much I would miss you—until you were away."

"Am I the only one you missed?"

"That seems a strange question."

"Is it? I'm your friend, your pal. We care for each other in a special way," Madison remarked. "Maybe that's why I have the feeling that you are, or on the verge of being, in love with someone else. If that is true, I am happy for you."

"I told you my career—"

"Phyllis—Phyllis Burdick, we've each come to know the other pretty well over this comparatively short time. Deny or pretend with others, not with me. I must go now." He smiled brightly before he hurried from the apartment.

Phyllis stared a full minute at the closed door without altering her position in the least. Then she stepped

189

to an oval mirror near the door and examined her reflection. What had Madison seen in her face to betray the emotion generated by her thoughts of Simon Phenwick? She went to a table from which she picked up the most recent letter she had received from Boston. It wasn't a love letter as such, yet she read so many double meanings into what appeared on the surface as innocent conversational statements.

She held the paper on which Simon's words were written to her breast as an image of the man filled her thoughts. Still what an impossible situation it was. He was one of the wealthy Phenwicks; she was from an impoverished home background she was trying to forget. He was a well established attorney; she was a starry-eyed actress just beginning to get a foothold in the profession of which she had so long dreamed. They were really worlds apart. Yet there must have been something to attract them to each other in the first place.

The thing that distressed her most about her feelings for Simon Phenwick was that he was the cousin of the one person in the world she had come to hate. Hate? In a sense she felt sorry for Augusta II, and she pitied that which was obviously happening to the famed actress, the mental degeration, illusion, fear that her status was being threatened. Fear? The word caused her to tremble in reaction. One cannot hate anything unless he first fears it. It was apparent that Augusta II feared that Phyllis's fresh, young and perhaps even greater talent was a threat to her own security. She naturally would hate Phyllis because of that fear. But did Phyllis fear Augusta II enough to hate her?

Phyllis realized that Madison had her best interests at heart, but she wondered if he might be jeopardizing her career by pushing her toward stardom too fast. Still she had to consider his point of view: Madison was an ambitious playwright; he felt that Augusta II was not doing justice to *The Eternal Light,* so he purposefully set about to write a play that the famed actress would be unsuitable to play. In a way, it seemed that Madison was using Phyllis and their mutual friendship to obtain his own personal ends. Was there anything wrong with that? Only, she thought, if he had purposefully cultivated her friendship in the first place with ulterior motives in mind. She could not believe that was true of Madison Davis—but it was a possibility.

Two weeks after Madison returned from his trip, the destination of which he had kept a mystery from Phyllis, the playwright invited her to a leisurely Sunday afternoon dinner at a restaurant in Greenwich Village that had a small private dining room.

"How intimate, Madison," Phyllis commented after they had been seated by the waiter. "Are you thinking of taking advantage of me?" She giggled.

Madison arched his eyebrow and tried not to appear annoyed at the insinuation. "And if I said that you had guessed my intentions?"

She blinked. "I don't know quite how I would react, other than I might think you had been deceiving me all this time."

"Then you must immediately put aside such foolish speculations," Madison returned.

"Most men would have ulterior motives in bringing a young lady to a place like this," she persisted.

"Oh, I assure you I do have ulterior reasons for inviting you here," he replied. "Ulterior reasons are not necessarily always bad." He suddenly laughed. "Don't look so serious, pussy cat. Have you ever known me to do anything that wasn't in your best interests?"

"No. But I've often wondered why you've acted toward me as you have," Phyllis said.

"I once told you that a writer's life is an extremely lonely existence," Madison stated with a touch of irony in his voice. "In all honesty you are the one person in my entire life whom I have considered a real and close friend. Acquaintances come and go, but true friends

191

are difficult to come by. You are the sister, the daughter, the special friend I've always wanted. If I am playing a game, it's with your greatest good at heart, Phyllis. I want you to understand that now and always."

Phyllis put her hand on his. She gazed deeply into his eyes. "I honestly believe that, Madison. I trust you."

Tears began to well in Madison's eyes. Embarrassed, he asked to be excused for a few moments, saying that he would order champagne as an excuse for leaving.

A strange sensation came over Phyllis. She had the feeling that something was about to happen, and she wondered if it might not be a change of attitude as far as Madison Davis was concerned.

"It is the time, you know."

Phyllis suddenly turned around to find the source of the mysterious voice, and at the same time she became aware of an overpowering scent of roses. "Who—who is it?"

"I should think you would know the voice by now."

"Am I hallucinating? Are you an illusion in my mind?"

"All things are possible, aren't they?"

"You once said that I had been chosen. For what? When?"

"I told you that it is the time."

"I do wish you would be more explicit," she said and felt herself blush as she heard the door to the small room open. Had she been overheard talking to what would seem to be herself?

Believing that it was Madison who had returned, Phyllis remained with her eyes looking downward. Still the scent of roses was so strong that she almost felt stifled by it.

When nothing was said by the intruder, and her eyes were still held on the table, for the first time it occurred to her that there were three place settings on the white tablecloth. Three?

"Miss Burdick . . ."

The voice was music. She glanced up shyly, but not without an expression of surprise. "Mr. Phenwick?"

Simon had never appeared so handsome as he did that moment. His eyes were dancing with laughter and a hint of another kind of emotion. His smile was as she remembered it just prior to the moment he had last kissed her. Attired in powder blue, gray and glistening white, he seemed to radiate an aura that was almost unearthly, yet, at the same time, sensual and curiously fascinating.

Slowly Phyllis rose and, as if responding to a compelling magnetic attraction, she crossed to him. Their eyes met at close range before Simon reached his hands to touch her and gently drew her into his embrace. Words could not speak the emotion or explain the attraction. Lips became ablaze with excitement that trembled until they met. The sheer magic of the moment was the thrill of transformation, delight, discovery, fulfillment.

"Oh, Phyllis Burdick, I have missed you," Simon said with deep sincerity. "You'll never know how I've dreamed of this moment and the joy of holding and caressing you, the absolute beauty of kissing you. How utterly foolish of me not to return to New York before this."

"Mr. Simon Phenwick, I've missed you far more than you can ever possibly know," she said just above a whisper, emotion causing raspy huskiness in her throat, a dryness that could only be quenched by several more kisses. She pushed her face toward his, her mouth reacting with a famished hunger. "Kiss me, Simon, before I burst with anticipation," she said, her lips lightly brushing against his as she formed the words.

Simon held her in an all-encompassing, romantic

193

embrace. His strength firmly around her caused her to respond with what appeared to be sheer animal passion. And when his lips parted from hers, they traced over her cheek and down to her throat, the softness of her neck and back up the other side. Again their lips were locked in an expression symbolic of passion, desire and fulfillment of every dream fantasy either of them had ever held.

"Simon—oh, Simon! I wasn't prepared for this."

"You're doing a marvelous job of improvising," he replied softly. "However, I suspect our friend will be returning soon. If nothing else, it would be impolite of us to display such an intimate exchange in front of him."

"Madison?"

"He hadn't told you that I would be here?"

"No. I don't believe he has ever mentioned your name—at least not recently," Phyllis replied. "Do you mean that he purposely arranged this?"

"He was my accomplice," Simon corrected. He gently led her back to the table and held the chair for her to sit. Then he bent forward and kissed her again on the neck, letting his lips tenderly slide up to her cheek. She turned her head, permitting their lips to touch again in a passionate kiss.

When Madison returned, he pretended surprise to see Simon.

"I'm on to you, Madison Davis," Phyllis stated in mock annoyance. "You and Mr. Phenwick were in cahoots concerning this evening."

"Were we, Simon?"

"Weren't we, Madison?"

All three laughed.

Although there were a few awkward moments when the conversation lagged and it might have seemed that there was one too many people present at times, the afternoon and early evening were spent in lighthearted chatter and friendly discourse. Nothing was purposely mentioned about *The Eternal Light*.

"Before I depart," Madison said long after the last course had been served and the three had lingered over coffee, liqueur and continued talk, "I think it only fair that Phyllis be told the source of the backing for *Triumph and Passion*."

"Haven't you told her?" Simon asked.

"You?" Phyllis questioned incredulously.

"Me, yes, and other members of my family," Simon admitted. "I thought you already knew."

"No, I didn't."

"Well, with that tidbit, I'll sneak away and leave you two to your own devices," Madison said. He kissed Phyllis on the cheek and shook Simon's hand.

"I hope you didn't think I was so responsive to you," Phyllis said a few minutes after Madison left, "because I knew you were to put up the backing money for *Triumph and Passion*."

"No, that thought never entered my mind," Simon assured her. "I reacted to you because of things that were written between us, and because of the wonderful feelings I've developed for you."

"Simon—" She reached for him and he was immediately by her side, once again kissing her with even more passion and emotion—if that were, possible— than he had earlier done. There was promise, beauty and magic in their embrace, their kisses, the process of their becoming one.

The following day Simon called on Mortimer Gree, who had arranged for both Hampton Colwell and Madison Davis to be present.

"The damnable depressing thing about this whole business with Augusta," Mortimer said after they had broached the subject, "is that *The Eternal Light* has now reached the place where it is beginning to show a

195

healthy profit. I'd hate like the devil to close it while it's doing so well."

"Why should you even consider it?" Simon questioned, including all three men in his glance.

"Word concerning Augusta's peculiar behavior has gotten out, and admittedly, it has resulted in a decline in attendance," Mortimer explained. "She has a contract that gives her the advantage."

"I would like to see a copy of that contract," Simon said.

"It seems the brunt of Miss Phenwick's rage is vented toward Miss Burdick," Hampton commented while Mortimer Gree went to the file to find a copy of Augusta II's contract.

"In that case, it might be advisable to take Miss Burdick from *The Eternal Light* company and begin preparing her for her role in *Triumph and Passion*."

"I can readily agree to that," Mortimer said as he produced the contract. "However, if Augusta doesn't change, I will simply have to close the show."

"Or replace Augusta," Simon suggested as he scanned the contract. "I'm not too familiar with these contracts. I know the standard form, but this has obviously been written with certain specifications specifically for Augusta."

"We did haggle a bit over it," Mortimer admitted. "I don't see how she can be replaced."

"There's only one person who could possibly replace her," Hampton said. "Miss Burdick."

"It could be a helluva touchy situation," Gree returned. "And I should think it would be even more of a touchy situation with you stepping into it, Simon. After all, she is your cousin."

"All the more reason why I may have luck with it," Simon said with a broad grin which masked the inner conflict he was experiencing. "I wish to take this contract with me to go over and confer with the attorneys in the firm with which I'm going to be associated. My father has a saying that contracts were written to be broken, it's simply a matter of finding where the loophole is."

"Will you actually take sides against your cousin, Mr. Phenwick?" Hampton Colwell asked.

"In the first place, Augusta and I are distant cousins," Simon confided. "We're little more than strangers. You see, I witnessed something when I was last in New York which has deeply disturbed me—a scene played by Augusta and her brother Joshua. Any feelings of respect I had for Augusta prior to that were diminished when I beheld what I saw."

"Do you recommend that we hold off on our promotional campaign concerning Miss Burdick?" Mortimer asked.

Simon considered the question before answering. "No, I don't believe that will be necesary. In fact, I would suggest that you proceed with it immediately. Can I drop you someplace, Madison?"

"No. I've still several matters to discuss with Mr. Gree and Mr. Colwell," the writer replied.

Upon leaving Mortimer Gree's office, Simon decided to walk to the firm of Levitt, Blair & Morgenstern, with whom he had made arrangements to become associated.

Two doors away from his destination on Broadway, Simon was startled to hear his name being called from a short distance away. He turned and scanned in all directions before he saw the familiar figure of his cousin Joshua Phenwick.

"Joshua! Good Lord, what are you doing in New York?" Simon questioned. "I thought you had long since gone back to Portland."

"I did go back home, but I've returned. Do you have a minute, Simon? I would like to speak with you."

"Certainly. I'm in no hurry to get to where I'm

going," Simon replied as he more closely scrutinized the man before him. "What's happened to you, Joshua? You've changed."

"I've lost weight," Joshua admitted.

"You appear as if you had been sick."

"No illness of a serious nature," Joshua answered, trying to force a hearty smile.

"You were so robust-looking when I last saw you," Simon said. "What's happened to you?"

"Over a cup of coffee, Simon. People are beginning to watch us."

"Sure. Fine." Simon motioned to a small coffee shop across the street.

Joshua found it difficult to speak before the coffee was served. Then he turned and stared at Simon for a full minute before he could find the words. "They say that love—that is, being in love affects one physically. Being in love and knowing that your love is returned, gives one a joyous appearance. However, when one is in love and that love is not reciprocated, then, as you see, it can have adverse effects on one's appearance."

Simon frowned. "You are in love with someone here in New York?"

"Much to Augusta II's chagrin," Joshua confessed, "I am frantically in love with Miss Phyllis Burdick."

Simon tried not to scowl, but Joshua wasn't watching his expression, anyway. "And your sister doesn't approve?"

"Far from it." Joshua looked forlorn. "Augusta II now thinks of Miss Burdick as her mortal enemy, and she has chastised me for having the feelings I do. When she learned that I had attended many of the first performances of *The Eternal Light,* unbeknownst to her, and led the audience in applauding Miss Burdick's performance, Augusta II became absolutely livid." He seemed to be attempting to control his emotions. "I'm staying at the Astor. I'd rather continue this conversation later." He pulled money from his pocket and put it on the counter. "Call me at the Astor."

Simon stared after his cousin as the full impact of what Joshua had said hit him. He found himself in a difficult and complex situation which did not seem to have a solution wherein one or more persons could not be deeply hurt.

Chapter Fourteen

Sigmund Levitt, the senior partner of Levitt, Blair & Morgenstern, scrutinized Augusta Phenwick II's contract with Mortimer Gree. He made peculiar noises during that examination and glanced several times over the top of his glasses at the concerned expression of Simon.

"You say this woman is your distant cousin?" Sigmund asked when he finally dropped the papers to his desk and removed the reading glasses. A man in his sixties, he was quite bald and shriveled-looking. A hawklike nose gave him a severe appearance that was almost frightening. "She's had a clever lawyer draw this up. I presume Mr. Gree was anxious to have her as his leading lady and, therefore, gave her every advantage that he could allow. He did himself a disservice."

"Do you see no way out of it, Mr. Levitt?" Simon asked.

"Only if it can be proved that she is incapable of

fulfilling her end of the agreement," Levitt replied. "I mean to say, if she becomes physically or mentally unable to give a reasonably accurate performance. Frankly, I would suggest closing the show, allowing a period of time to lapse and possibly reopening with another actress in the role. That could be costly to Mr. Gree, as you must surely realize."

"I can see that," Simon said. "The fact is, Mr. Levitt, if we are able to resolve this satisfactorily in Mr. Gree's favor, we are certain to get his business in future cases."

"That sort of statement does not impress me, Mr. Phenwick," the older man stated. "We cannot take the law into our own hands. Since this woman is your cousin, perhaps you can deal with her on a personal basis."

"Are you familiar with Augusta Phenwick II?"

"I have met her on several occasions. In spite of the public acclaim in her favor, she has never been one of my favorite actresses. Her performances have an artificial ring to me. It's as if she is acting at acting, playing the role of leading lady without actually being one," Levitt said.

"I don't understand your meaning."

"I should think it was simple enough," Levitt went on. "Rarely does one run across an actor or actress who plays with such ease and conviction that it would seem they were living the part rather than acting it. To me, Augusta Phenwick merely acts whatever part she is portraying, she doesn't live it. I prefer realism in all things. You may say that it is a matter of choice, to which I will agree; but that is my choice, ergo, I don't care for Miss Phenwick."

"Before I present an even gloomier picture to Mr. Gree," Simon commented as he gathered the contract and folded it into his inside coat pocket, "I will make one more desperate try to communicate with my cousin."

"There's always a chance you may get through to her." Levitt cleared his throat and fingered his glasses as he studied the young man before him. "I perceive that you have a personal interest in this other young lady, Miss Burdick, is it?"

"Yes, Phyllis Burdick," Simon answered, sensing a faint blush come to his face. "I have come to know Miss Burdick on personal terms."

"Yes, that is obvious," Levitt returned. "I must say I wouldn't wish to be in your position. You might get Ben Morgenstern to mediate this for you as a disinterested party."

"I don't think that will be necessary, Mr. Levitt," Simon said. "I am quite able to remain objective despite my relationship with either Augusta or Phyllis."

"You're treading on eggs, my boy, treading on eggs. And you might find yourself in a most precarious situation," Levitt offered. "I shall be most interested to hear the outcome of all of this."

"Thank you, Mr. Levitt."

That evening Simon made a point to attend the Majesty Theater and catch the performance of *The Eternal Light* from opening to final curtain. It was if he had seen a totally different play from the one he had seen on opening night. Augusta II's performance was ragged, sloppy and in many instances inarticulate. She engaged in histrionics which appeared to be spur of the moment improvisations, often abandoning the blocking given her by Hampton Colwell. During the scenes in which Phyllis was on stage with her, Augusta II took every opportunity to up-stage her and seemed to invent business—if not dialogue—to confuse the young actress, who, miraculously was able to adapt to whatever the leading lady did without becoming thrown by it. Augusta II's interpretation of the role gave it an entirely different meaning, unsympathetic and not particularly likeable.

There were several moments during the play when

Simon actually felt embarrassed for his cousin's actions. During intermission he saw Hampton Colwell, who claimed he could only watch bits of the performance because it so sickened him to see what Augusta II was doing.

"She obviously isn't playing the role as it was intended to be played," Simon commented. "That in itself would seem to me to be a breach of contract."

"Miss Phenwick has always pretty much been given free reign of interpretation," Hampton said. "I had to accept that stipulation if I took the task of directing her. In the beginning she was pliable and cooperative. Now—well, you've seen her perform tonight."

"Yes—unfortunately."

At the end of the play, the audience response was dully polite. The applause was lukewarm, and many of the viewers didn't bother to remain seated after the final curtain to acknowledge the performance.

Simon heard disgruntled comments of harsh criticism, and even demands that the price of admission should be returned for having to endure such a travesty.

Cynthia opened the dressing room door to Simon when, after mingling with the audience to overhear their verbal reactions to the play, he went backstage.

"Simon? Is that you?" Augusta II asked as she lowered a glass from her lips and gazed at her cousin's reflection through the mirror.

"Yes, Augusta."

"I thought you were in Boston." She took another sip from the glass. The room had the definite aroma of liquor. "I must say I'm surprised to see you."

"I must admit I was surprised to see your performance tonight, Augusta. It's a wonder there's any scenery left the way you were chewing at it," Simon said, maintaining the charismatic smile that added to his attractiveness.

"Chewing the scenery? Chewing the scenery?" Before Augusta turned to stare at him head-on, she took a cigarette and, with shaking hand, lit it. "Did you actually say 'chewing the scenery,' Simon?"

"I did. It's a wonder you don't have a dreadful case of dry-mouth."

"Are you purposely trying to be offensive, Cousin Simon?"

"I am attempting to be truthful, Augusta."

"I see." Augusta II rolled large eyes toward the ubiquitous Cynthia. "Will you leave us, Cynthia?"

The maid hesitated a moment before making an exit.

"Cynthia is a dear, but her ears are far too big, and her tongue too loose, if you know what I mean," Augusta II stated and puffed on the cigarette. "Now then, what is this all about?"

"I think it would be more to the point to ask that question of your performance, Augusta."

"My performance? I gave the performance of a lifetime tonight!" she proclaimed with a broad gesture.

"It was far different from the one I saw you give on opening night."

"My performances improve with repetition."

"Improve? What I saw tonight was hardly an improvement over what I saw before. As a matter of fact, it was embarrassing."

"How dare you come in here with such a remark?" Augusta II demanded to know. "Who do you think you are? What do you know about acting, much less the theater, Simon?"

"I know what pleases me, what excites me, what appeals to my sense of values," Simon returned. "Augusta, we're cousins, and if I can't be bluntly honest with you as a relative concerned for your best good, then I don't know who can."

"We share the same last name, Simon, and perhaps a similar strain of blood," Augusta II asserted, "but other than for that quirk of nature we have nothing in common. Why should you dare take it upon yourself to criticize me as you have done tonight?"

"Because my name is Phenwick and I have recently transplanted myself to New York City to associate myself with a firm of theatrical lawyers," Simon returned, as if he were presenting a case in a court of law. "Regardless of what reputation I may build here as an attorney handling theatrical clients and matters of the business, there is no way that I will ever be able to divorce myself from the fact that I am cousin to the notorious Augusta Phenwick II."

Augusta II glared. "Why have you made such a move?"

"I have my personal reasons for that."

"Is the theatrical world big enough for two Phenwicks?" Augusta II questioned. She suddenly broke out in mocking laughter which verged on hysteria. "You're mad, Simon, quite mad for attempting to invade my territory." She snuffed out one cigarette and reached for another, which she put in a long cigarette holder. With effort, her trembling hands managed to light it. "Well, I'll tell you something, Simon Phenwick, I know precisely why you've come back to New York."

"Do you?" Simon braced himself.

"It's because of her and her conspiracy to destroy me!" Augusta II declared with a wide-eyed expression that was frightening. "She is trying to usurp my position, depose the Queen! Well, damn her, she'll have a fight on her hands."

"Of whom are you speaking?"

"First, she made a play for my brother, then for you," Augusta II raved on. "I know she's struck up an alliance with Madison Davis as well as Hampton Colwell—and probably Mortimer Gree. It is her systematic way of attempting to topple me. I know the queer ambitions of young actresses, their unscrupulous means and tactics. I can see what she's been up to from the very beginning. And she has sucked you into believing that she is the innocent victim of a deparved grand lady of the theater. Oh, yes, Simon, I can see that only too well. It makes me laugh to think how gullible men are. Miss Burdick isn't the innocent victim she represents herself to be. Oh, no, Simon! You are, Joshua is, Mortimer Gree, Madison Davis and Hampton Colwell are, even obnoxious little nobody Isaac Bell is. You've all been duped by her. You're all innocent members of the conspiracy of Miss Phyllis Burdick. How nastily and connivingly methodical she has been in all of this!"

"I suspect you have an overly active imagination, Augusta," Simon stated. "You're acting like a drowning woman grasping for straws; but a few random straws won't keep you afloat, Augusta! And, even if what you suspect is true and Miss Burdick is as contriving as you depict her to be, you are the only one who appears to be affected by your suppositions."

"Meaning?" Augusta II took a grand pose. While she waited for Simon's reply, she emptied the contents of the glass and again took a pose.

"The truth is you've become so jealous of Phyllis Burdick that you have permitted your reactions to her to make a travesty of your performance—as I witnessed tonight." Simon stepped toward her. "But I'll tell you this, Augusta, I think you're wrong about Miss Burdick in suspecting her of conspiracy. The only conspiracy is in your demented mind. And if you don't change your attitude and get hold of yourself, you will force the closing of *The Eternal Light,* but not before you've established yourself a harmful reputation that will prevent you from ever appearing on the New York stage again."

"Don't you realize I am a Phenwick woman? A member of one of the wealthiest, most influential families in this country?" she proclaimed grandly as if she were speaking to a complete stranger.

"And don't you know, Augusta, that I am also a member of the Phenwick family?" Simon questioned. "The difference between us is that I have taken a lifetime to closely align myself with the Phenwicks, earned their loved and devotion, while you have done much to alienate even the most sympathetic members of the family. Oh, yes, you've achieved fame and notoriety, but you've contributed little or nothing, only taken from. If it comes to a showdown between us, Augusta, there's little doubt in my mind who will rally the sympathy and support of the Phenwicks. It's time you realized the truth and stopped deceiving yourself. Your performance tonight was absolutely embarrassing, and a complete disillusionment to the audience. I regret having to be so blunt about this."

"Bastard!" Augusta II heaved. "Get out!"

"I'm going, dear Cousin, Remember, you've been warned." Dramatically, Simon stepped from the dressing room and firmly closed the door behind him. Several persons had gathered outside. They all suddenly appeared to be nonchalantly going about their business.

Cynthia crossed to Simon, glowered, and quickly went to tend to her mistress. Simon followed her movements with his eyes and held them on the closed door.

"The dressing room walls are not especially thick," Phyllis said as she came up behind him. "I fear you and Miss Phenwick have had a more attentive audience than was in the theater tonight watching the play."

"Phyllis? Did you hear what we said?"

"I overheard part of it. The sound was distorted, but I got the general drift of what it was all about," she replied. "I made the mistake back around Christmas of bringing two or three of your letters to the theater to reread while I was offstage. I later learned that Cynthia, Miss Phenwick's personal maid, had nosed around and had read them. I'm certain she reported back fully about their contents."

"I need a drink," Simon stated, "and I suspect you could use something to eat. Let's get out of here."

Simon took her to a quiet little restaurant in the theater district, where they found a secluded corner.

"If you think I should leave *The Eternal Light*," Phyllis said simply after listening to the reasons why and the arguments against, "then I will do it. I don't know what I will do as a means of income, but I've managed to put a little money aside."

"I'll see that you are put on a salary preparatory to the new play," Simon replied. "In fact, I'll personally see to your support and well being."

"Does that mean you don't believe I have created a conspiracy?" Phyllis asked innocently.

"Have you?"

"Not purposely, no, not at all. You can believe that, Simon, because it's the truth."

"I do believe you, my dear. Furthermore, I believe in you."

"That is very important to me," she said and allowed him to curl his hand about hers across the table.

"My cousin Joshua has confided in me today that he is very much in love with you," Simon said a short while later.

"I have done nothing to encourage that," Phyllis returned. "You must believe that."

"You're terribly on the defensive tonight."

"I think I have reason to be," Phyllis commented. "I have little patience with Joshua Phenwick. He is both immature and unreasonable. I have compassion for him because of the loss of his wife, but I think him foolish for not learning the lesson from choosing a woman whose interests in life were so diametrically opposed to his own—just as mine are. I know for a fact that Miss Phenwick initially took exception to the fact of Joshua's obvious interest in me—that, compounded by those silly reviews of my opening night performance."

"Yes, I'm fully aware of all of that," Simon said. "Let's not speak any further about it. And, as a matter of fact, I would like to leave here before too long. Although it's late, there's a call I would like to make."

Some time later, Simon escorted Phyllis to her apartment in a cab. During the ride they made close physical contact, to which they responded with excitement and deep feelings.

"If you didn't have other plans," Phyllis whispered, feeling so very much a part of him at that moment, "I would ask you up."

"No, I mustn't. There are things I must do, and I feel it is urgent that I act as quickly as possible."

Simon saw her to the door, where they sedately embraced. Then Simon hurried back to the cab and directed the driver to the Astor Hotel.

The imprint of Simon's kiss lingered on Phyllis's lips. She still felt remarkably warm where his embrace had been. As she climbed the three flights of stairs to her walk-up apartment, she could not, nor did she want to, dismiss the image of Simon Phenwick from her mind.

As she reached the third floor, Phyllis was suddenly alarmed by the appearance of a man stepping from the shadows. His face was hidden in the darkness of the dimly-lit hallway. Since he was standing between her and the door to her apartment, her initial thought was to retrace her steps back down the stairs.

"Wait, Miss Burdick, I want to speak with you," a familiar voice called.

"Who—who is it?"

Leslie Brooks moved so that his face appeared in a show of light. "I didn't mean to alarm you."

"Why, Mr. Brooks, I'm surprised that you are not in the company of Miss Phenwick tonight," Phyllis said, somewhat sarcastically.

"I have an understudy in that capacity tonight, Miss Burdick." He stepped nearer to her, his eyes held fast on hers. "It seems I am slipping somewhat from favor with the esteemed Miss Phenwick."

"That seems careless of you," she returned, attempting to sound coldly sophisticated.

"Frankly, I've lost interest in her," Leslie said. "Not that I was especially attracted to her in the first place. I formed an alliance with her because it meant a means to an end. The situation is that I find myself deeply attracted to you, Miss Burdick." His hands went to her shoulders, he clutched and tried to draw her close enough to him that he could kiss her tempting mouth.

"How dare you accost me in this way?" she demanded to know. "Step aside and permit me to go to my apartment." She pushed him with enough force to cause him to lose his balance. "How dare you attempt such a thing?"

"Please, Miss Burdick—Phyllis—I thought—I mean, I've seen you look at me, and I perceived I saw an invitation in your eyes."

"Your perception is badly in need of adjusting, Mr. Brooks. Excuse me." She moved past him. Fortunately she had her keys in hand.

"Please, Phyllis, I must speak to you," Leslie almost whined. "I apologize for being so physical with you a moment ago. It was impetuous of me and presumptuous."

Phyllis put her key in the lock and opened the door. "I accept your apology. Now please go." She quickly stepped through the door and closed it behind her, putting the chain in place.

Moments later, Leslie hit his fist against the door. "Please, Phyllis, I must speak with you. It's of utmost importance. Just open the door a crack. I'll behave myself."

Uncertain of the judiciousness of it, Phyllis opened the door the width the chain would permit it to be opened. "What is it?"

"I am deeply concerned about Miss Phenwick's behavior," Leslie confessed. "At times she becomes sadistically brutal with me, with no particular provocation."

"That would seem to be your problem, Mr. Brooks, for taking up with her in the first place," Phyllis returned.

"True." Leslie seemed nervous. "The reason I came here tonight is to tell you that I have reason to fear for your safety because of Miss Phenwick."

"My safety?"

"Miss Phenwick is a woman who finds herself in a desperate situation, and for some peculiar reason she wants to blame all of her troubles on you."

"The woman is insane."

"That is the conclusion which I have reached," Leslie said sincerely. "She has given me every reason to believe that she is losing her sanity. I cannot go into details because they are of both a personal and sordid nature."

"You are serious, aren't you, Mr. Brooks?"

"Definitely. For a time I thought some of her antics were amusing, that she had a bizarre way of expressing herself," Leslie related, "but when I discovered the relationship she has with her brother, I was frankly appalled."

"With Mr. Joshua Phenwick?"

"Miss Phenwick takes the attitude that she is his mother," Leslie explained, "and he responds in a most infantile way. Then she cuddles him and reprimands him. She has a hypnotic way with Mr. Phenwick as if she has persuaded him that they're not really sister and brother, but mother and son. In either case, I've detected blatantly incestuous overtones in their behavior."

"I don't want to hear any more, Mr. Brooks."

"Please let me come in. I would very much like to make love to you."

"How dare you say such a thing?"

"Because I am in love with you. Don't you realize that?"

"No, you're mistaken," Phyllis returned, hardly able to believe her ears. "Besides, I'm in love with someone else."

"With whom? Simon Phenwick?" Leslie snapped an

ugliness coming over his handsome features. "I've seen you together. I've heard about your romantic letters from him."

"Go away, Mr. Brooks!"

"I also know that Mr. Madison Davis has written a new play in which he wants you to play the lead, Phyllis, and not Miss Phenwick."

"Leave me alone!"

"You're an unknown actress, Phyllis. How can Mr. Gree possibly get backing for an unknown such as you?" Leslie persisted.

"Simon has arranged for the backing—I mean—" Phyllis tried to retrieve her statement, but it was too late.

"Simon?" Leslie put his face close to the opening in the door. "I think you'd better let me in, Phyllis. I can imagine how Miss Phenwick will respond when she learns that her own cousin is backing you rather than her in Madison's new play."

Phyllis slammed the door in his face and securely locked it.

"Phyllis? It would be to your advantage to open this door."

One of the neighbors appeared, to complain of the racket with threats of ejection.

Phyllis remained with her back against the door until she heard Leslie's retreating footsteps. She sighed. If only she could contact Simon. She needed him. Suddenly the impact of the threats hit her, and she felt as if she wanted to collapse.

When Leslie hailed a cab, he directed it to the Astor Hotel.

Chapter Fifteen

The broad-shouldered man of medium height was standing near the entrance to the Astor Hotel. His catlike eyes scanned faces as they passed him. At that hour of the morning, there were few people on the street. He was just about to go inside for a cup of coffee when a cab pulled up. Readjusting his muffler about his neck and hitting his gloved hands together to stimulate warmth, he appeared nonchalant as he watched the passenger alight.

"Mr. Phenwick? Mr. Simon Phenwick?" he asked as he stepped forward to interfere with Simon's hurried entrance into the building.

"What if I am?"

"The name's O'Malley, Douglas O'Malley. Inspector, New York Police Department, homicide bureau."

"I beg your pardon."

O'Malley repeated his introduction. "I don't mean to inconvenience you, Mr. Phenwick. Perhaps you would rather step inside where it's warmer."

"Can you explain what this is about?" Simon asked as they went into the lobby.

O'Malley motioned to a secluded corner. "I've been working on the Lawrence Frazier case," he said as they walked.

"I'm sorry, the name isn't familiar to me."

"Frazier was an older man who drove a carriage through Central Park. You and a lady were in his vehicle at the time he was shot."

"Oh, that man. I didn't recall his name," Simon said with a congenial smile. Then he frowned. "You act as if you had been waiting for me."

"I had been. We received a tip that you would probably be here sometime tonight," O'Malley replied.

"I find that curious. Who would have presumed that I might have been here?" Simon asked.

O'Malley shrugged. "I don't know. I just followed instructions and came over here to wait for you. I'll be brief. Since it has been proved beyond a shadow of a doubt that Frazier had been killed by an assassin's bullet, we need to get a more comprehensive report about what actually happened that night."

"That was months ago."

"You'll have time to refresh your memory. Come into the 17th Precinct anytime tomorrow and someone will take the information from you," O'Malley said.

"Why should there be suspicion of foul play?" Simon questioned.

"There is a theory going around—but it's only a theory—that the driver, Frazier, had not been meant to be the intended victim. Instead, the shot may have been fired at you or your lady friend."

"Are you serious?"

"There would have been no reason to silence Lawrence Frazier," O'Malley replied. "There might have been a reason to want to get you—or your lady friend—out of the way."

"I see. I'll be in tomorrow first thing to report all I can remember," Simon assured him.

Confused and puzzled, Simon tried to dismiss the conversation with Douglas O'Malley from his mind. But there was too much involved in what he had said to pass the matter over lightly. The thing that most perplexed him was that someone had informed the police that he would be at the Astor sometime that night. Who?

Simon called from the desk. Joshua assured him that he hadn't been asleep, and he had only just arrived back at the hotel room a short while before. Simon was invited up.

Joshua greeted him with a forced smile and a half-hearted handshake. "Come in, Simon. I rather imagined that I would see you sooner or later."

"Have you been out on the town tonight?" Simon questioned.

"I've been wandering about, going nowhere in particular. Can I offer you sherry? That's all I have."

"Sherry will be fine," Simon replied as he gazed around at the furnishings of the room and reached the conclusion that it was not one of the more expensive accommodations. Then he watched Joshua nervously pour the wine. When he poured the second glass of wine, it slipped from his hand. Simon went to get a towel to help clean up the mess.

"What's troubling you, Joshua?" Simon asked as he observed the other's trembling hands and furtive, animal-like eye movement.

"I don't know," Joshua replied.

"How long have you been back in New York?"

"I went to Portland for a week the first of last December," Joshua replied, "and immediately came back."

"Haven't you business in Portland?"

"My father understood. Actually, he wanted me to go

215

to Boston to see Dr. Ornby. I probably should have done that." Joshua drank and followed it with a deep sigh. "What good did it do me to return to New York? I don't know. I'm very confused, Simon—and I can't explain why that is, either."

"Do you see your sister often?" Simon asked, recalling the evening he had dined with the brother and sister and the resulting fiasco that it had turned out to be.

"Yes. I see Augusta often. We have an extreme closeness." Joshua's eyes appeared watery, and the glass scraped over his teeth when he raised it to drink.

"I think you would do well to go to Boston as soon as possible and have Dr. Ornby examine you," Simon remarked. "I've never seen you in such a state."

"I know. I know that's what I should do. One part of me tells me that I must, while another part of me denies it. Augusta is violently opposed to my doing so. She insists that I'm as sane as she is."

Simon started to reply to that, but the statement caught in his throat and he reconsidered his words. "Augusta appears to have a strong hold over you?"

Joshua stared at him as if he didn't quite comprehend what he had said. "Augusta is my sister. She knows what's best for me."

"She might have known what was best for you when you were a child, Josh, but that doesn't necessarily hold true now. You're obviously not of the same temperament as your sister. She is a public figure, while you're basically a conservative business person. And what of your children? Have you abandoned them to stay in New York?"

"My parents are caring for them at Falmouth House," Joshua replied. "I feel very much apart from them. I sometimes have a feeling that they hold me responsible for Alice's death—and maybe I am. When does a man stop lamenting his own misfortune and begin to concern himself with the needs of others? I keep asking myself that. Augusta insists that my first obligation is

216

to myself. Yet, when I assure her that I need a wife, she reacts as if I am being childish. It's not childish for a man to want a wife."

"Perhaps she feels as she does because she has never married," Simon suggested.

"I've thought of that," Joshua sat with his head in his hands, elbows on his knees. "If I had stayed in Portland, undoubtedly I would have found a suitable prospect for a second wife. I didn't. I made the unfortunate mistake of falling in love with an actress. I thought Augusta would approve. She had liked Alice very much. Of course, Alice had never appeared in a play with my sister."

"You are in love?" Simon asked, trying to draw the answer from his cousin, and all the time knowing what the answer must be.

"Yes."

"And is your love returned?"

"No. My actions have made me totally repellent to her," he explained. "I've been a clumsy fool in the entire matter. Of course, it pleases Augusta that Miss Burdick rejects me."

"Miss Burdick?"

"Miss Phyllis Burdick," Joshua replied. "I believe you've met her. I'm certain you did at the opening night party for *The Eternal Light*. She's the one who plays the slave girl in blackface. Augusta has become terribly jealous of her. Again, I take part of the blame for that because I was overly enthusiastic in my pursuit of Miss Burdick. I led the applause for her at the curtain calls, and Augusta found out about it."

"Has it occurred to you that your sister may be punishing you for that?"

"How's that?"

"It entered my mind that Augusta bitterly resented the acclaim and acknowledgment that Miss Burdick received," Simon speculated, "and vindictively set about to not only punish you for your part in it, but to take out her outraged resentment on Miss Burdick as well."

"Why should she have such resentment toward Miss Burdick?" Joshua asked, something within him telling him that Simon was on the right track.

"Because she is young and talented," Simon replied as he watched for Joshua's reaction. "Youth has slipped Augusta by, and she obviously refuses to admit it. And in her attempt to maintain and play a youthful role she has developed unbecoming eccentricities."

"I never think of Augusta as an older woman," Joshua said in her defense. "I find her extremely youthful."

"And that, I dare say, is because you know she is chronologically older than you are, Josh; hence, as long as she appears to be young, so will you. An older man with a young wife is quite acceptable in our society, but an older woman with a younger man is crudely frowned on."

"I'm aware of Augusta's partiality for young men," Joshua replied. "However, it seems to me you're confusing two issues. What does Augusta's interest in young men have to do with Miss Burdick?"

"It's part of the same thing," Simon replied. "I suspect your sister feels competition from younger women in their attractiveness to young men, just as she feels threatened by their youth as up-and-coming actresses. Still, isn't it ludicrous of Augusta attempting to play the part of a twenty-year-old heroine at her age? And even more foolish surrounding herself with such young men onstage, as well as in her private life."

"Please, say no more about Augusta. I love her dearly," Joshua suddenly said. "Augusta has my best interest at heart."

"Has she?" Simon's words were like a knife.

"I believe she has. The problem is, I'm torn between my duty and devotion to Augusta and my excessive and unrequited love for Miss Burdick."

"But does Phyllis—that is, Miss Burdick—express any feelings for you?"

"I said it was unrequited. No, I doubt that she can abide me anymore. I did the wrong things. I pushed myself at her, prematurely and in an overly aggressive way. I was a fool."

"In that case, Josh, are you just pursuing a dead end relationship, by continuing in your feelings for her as you are?" Simon questioned.

Logically, the answer is yes. Emotionally, I want to shout no. I simply can't detach myself from my desire for her."

"You can't, I suspect, because Augusta won't permit you to do so."

"What a queer thing to say!"

"It was only a thought," Simon returned, "and I have nothing to substantiate it with. However, it seems to me that your sister may be using you as a pawn against Miss Burdick." Several other theories suddenly entered his mind, but he did not voice them. He needed to escape the immediate vicinity of Joshua and sort his thoughts. His preception was becoming extremely clear—and with it a curious sense of fear concerning that which might be a diabolic plot that could well be in the process of unfolding at that moment.

"I don't understand what you're driving at, Simon."

"Nor do I, at this point," Simon replied. "I'm extremely fatigued from the move and attempting to establish myself in New York. I suspect I'm not making much sense at all. With that, I simply must excuse myself and get back to my hotel. I expect to have an apartment within the next few days. You must come and visit me there, once I've moved in. Perhaps by then I will have sorted my thoughts and be better able to explain my theories."

Joshua stared strangely at Simon as if he didn't quite comprehend what he had said. "If you must go, then you must. We'll talk again, Simon."

As Simon left the room and went toward the lift, several conflicting notions came to mind. The most perplexing of which was how Police Inspector Douglas O'Malley had known that he was expected at the Astor Hotel. Had someone merely speculated that he would eventually call on Joshua?

Simon yawned in the elevator and decided he would do well to go to his hotel as quickly as possible and close his mind to all the theorizing thoughts that were clogging it with confusion.

In Boston, snuggly in the warm bed with her husband Philip, Katherine Phenwick suddenly awakened with a start. As she jerked herself upward, Philip reacted and regained consciousness.

"Is something disturbing you, my dearest?" Philip asked sleepily.

"Yes, Philip. Oh, gracious! It was that dream again," Katherine replied. "I must go to New York City as quickly as possible."

"Whatever for?" her husband asked.

"To avert tragedy," Katherine said.

"I can't possibly go with you until the weekend," Philip commented, knowing full well that it would do no good to object to Katherine's premonitions and her determination to do what she felt she must.

"I can't wait until then, my darling," Katherine replied. "I must go the first thing in the morning."

"Can you explain why?"

"No. But I will know why before I get there."

Philip took her in his arms and tenderly caressed her. "Can you tell me nothing about it? What prompted this sudden decision?"

"I dreamed of Adam Truff," Katherine said.

"How can you have dreamed about a man you've never known, who lived and died before you were born?" Philip asked and stifled a yawn.

220

"We've been through that before, Philip." Katherine snuggled against her husband. "Before I returned to life form as I am now, I chose Adam to succeed me in selecting the Phenwick women. I can't explain how that was done, because I don't know. I only know that that is the truth of the situation. We were closely associated when I was the first Augusta Phenwick and he was Clayton Latshaw."

"Please, my dearest Katherine, let's not get into all of that again. I love you as you are, not for what you might have been. And I'm very sleepy." He kissed her. "Very sleepy."

Katherine felt the intensity of his hold about her slacken and listened as his breathing became heavier. She kissed him on the forehead. She loved this man with all her heart and soul; yet she knew that he could never possibly understand what she understood—and perhaps that was just as well. Since she could not go back to sleep, she began making plans for her trip the next day.

Chapter Sixteen

Phyllis slept late the following morning. A light snow had fallen during the night. The apartment was warm and the windows steamed over. It was a good day to remain in bed as long as possible. In a dreamy mood, she thought of Simon Phenwick and the wonderful feelings she had for him. Had anyone told her a few months before that she would find that she was in love, and her thoughts were directed toward one man, she would have denied that such a thing was possible. Now, with fantasies she had never entertained before, she could not escape the picture of the man who was constantly in her thoughts.

A knock at the door and her heart skipped a beat in anticipation. As she hurriedly slipped into a robe, Phyllis wanted to believe that it was Simon come to call. She made a quick check of her appearance as the knocking came again.

Isaac Bell was standing outside the door, exuding a

boyish personality and a compelling smile. Phyllis tried not to look disappointed when she saw him. Why had she thought it might have been Simon?

"Isaac?" she questioned.

"You don't appear to be particularly delighted to see me," Isaac commented. "It's been snowing. Do you mind if I come in?"

"Please do," Phyllis replied cordially. "You must forgive my appearance, I slept late."

"I'll forgive your appearance if you forgive my intrusion," he said as he stepped in and removed his coat, cap and scarf.

"I must say I'm surprised to see you here, Isaac." Phyllis pulled her robe up high about her neck. "If you'll excuse me a minute, I'll change into a dress. I've put the teakettle on. Would you care for some tea?"

"I would like some coffee, if you have it."

"There's the things to make it in the kitchen. Why don't you do the honors while I dress?"

"Fine."

By the time Phyllis returned from the bedroom, dressed in a warm outfit and looking far more presentable for entertaining, the coffee was merrily perking, scenting the kitchen with a savory aroma. Isaac had put two cups and saucers out on the table.

"It'll be ready in a minute," he said. "I hope you don't mind if I made myself at home."

"Not at all." She eyed him curiously. Over the past two months she had not had many encounters with him, other than seeing him at the theater.

"I've got good news," Isaac exclaimed. "I'm going to be understudying Leslie Brooks's role in the play."

"Understudying? That *is* unexpected good news," Phyllis said enthusiastically. "I'm pleased for you." She went to the cupboard and took out pastries, put them on a plate and placed them on the table. "Does that mean that Leslie may be leaving the play?"

"I don't know about that. Miss Phenwick simply

thought it would be wise to have the role covered," Isaac returned as he poured the rich, brown coffee.

"Miss Phenwick?" Phyllis asked curiously and she recalled seeing Isaac leaving the leading lady's dressing room two nights before. "It sounds as if you've become on friendly terms with Miss Phenwick."

"She has taken an interest in my career."

Phyllis wondered if Leslie Brooks had fallen from favor with Augusta II, but she did not voice the question. She excused herself for a few moments to get a nailfile from the bedroom. When she returned, busily working at a broken nail, she observed Isaac with an appraising scrutiny.

"Is something wrong?" Isaac asked.

"I was simply observing that you have changed, Isaac."

"I've changed?" He laughed. "I don't think I have."

"There's something different about you." She sat and sugared her coffee. "I guess I always thought of you as just a boy. I don't mean to be unkind, but I see a hardness in your face. Maybe it's just a look of maturity."

"I'm very much a man, Phyllis." He was standing as he drank from the coffee cup. "I guess everyone sees in another person what they want to see. Miss Phenwick thinks I'm very much a man." He smiled suggestively.

"Have you been playing up to Miss Phenwick as a means of getting to understudy Leslie?"

"You might say that."

"In hopes of replacing him?" she asked.

"I was naive when I first got the job in *The Eternal Light*," Isaac explained. "But I've learned my way around. Acting talent alone isn't what gets a person ahead in the theater. It's who you know and how you play your cards."

Phyllis felt her mouth was gaping, so she raised the cup to it, but continued watching Isaac over the rim. "You make a very tasty cup of coffee, Isaac." An
224

uneasiness had begun to come over her which she was unable to dismiss. "What was your real purpose for coming here?"

"Just friendship, Phyllis. We used to be such good friends."

"Why do I have the feeling that you're up to something?"

Isaac laughed heartily. "Well, I did overhear a conversation between Miss Phenwick, Mr. Gree and Mr. Colwell." He suddenly sounded gossipy. "Miss Phenwick has been warned that if she ever gives another bad performance that she will be replaced—binding contract or not. Miss Augusta refused to be contrite, and, as a result, vented angry emotions toward you. She doesn't much like you, you know. But I suppose that doesn't come as news, does it?"

"No, I can't say it does." Phyllis drank again and made an awkward gesture as she tried to contain a yawn. "Basically, I'm an innocent bystander in the entire situation. I've done nothing purposely to harm Miss Phenwick in any way."

"Miss Augusta believes that you're in some way involved in part of a plot against her."

"How could I possibly be? That's just Miss Phenwick's singular imagination." Again she stifled a yawn.

Isaac emptied his cup and refilled it before he stepped to where Phyllis was seated. "You know, Phyllis, I have been fascinated by you from the first time we met. I find you very exciting and stimulating." He put his hands to her shoulders. "I would like very much to kiss you."

"No, I won't hear of it. What's come over you?"

"Manhood. I'm no longer a shy little boy—not as you've thought me to be," Isaac said, projecting strength and virility. "Miss Augusta has taught me many things."

"Please, don't touch me, Isaac."

"Do you find my touch repulsive? Miss Augusta doesn't."

Phyllis got to her feet and attempted to put the chair between him and herself. "I must ask you to leave, Isaac. I—" She reached for her head as a dizzying sensation came over her.

Isaac's eyes had a piercing intensity, his smile suggestively leering, his posture provocative, as he undulated toward her.

Phyllis's eyes were playing tricks on her. Her vision became distorted and cloudy. "Isaac, why have you come here?" She looked up at him, then shot a perceptive glance toward the coffee cup she had been drinking from. "The coffee—?"

Isaac stepped toward her, and she lost consciousness.

Late that afternoon, Simon Phenwick went to the police precinct to give his report. He asked specifically for Detective Inspector Douglas O'Malley, who was not due to come on duty for another fifteen minutes. Simon decided to wait.

"Yes, Mr. Phenwick," O'Malley said as he shook Simon's hand, "I recognized you. Won't you come back into an office where we won't be disturbed?"

"What is this all about?" Simon questioned a few minutes later as he sat at a large table opposite Douglas O'Malley.

"From the angle that Lawrence Frazier was shot," O'Malley related, "reconstructing the situation as best we can, it seemed that he may have accidentally got in the way of the bullet, which was probably meant for you or Miss Burdick."

"So you said," Simon replied, "but I see no reason for you to have such a suspicion. I was only visiting New York at the time. And I can't believe that anyone would have such ill feelings about Miss Burdick that they would attempt to kill her."

"Can you recall the events of that evening?" O'Malley asked.

"I met Miss Burdick at the theater after the show. We went out to dinner, after which we walked several blocks before taking the carriage."

"Did either of you recognize anyone at the restaurant?"

"I didn't. If Miss Burdick did, she didn't mention it."

"And when you walked," O'Malley pursued, "did you have cause for suspicion that you might have been followed?"

"No suspicion whatsoever. The thought never entered my mind," Simon said. "It was quite late and there were few people on the street. We hailed the carriage on Fifth Avenue, probably somewhere in the thirties."

"Did you have any conversation with Lawrence Frazier, the driver of the carriage?"

"Only to give him instructions to drive us to Central Park."

"Mr. Phenwick, search your memory," O'Malley said. "Did anything at all unusual happen during that ride?"

"Only when we were about to enter the park road," Simon recalled, "an automobile came up behind the carriage and wanted to get around. The carriage driver got to a wide place in the road, pulled over and let the car pass."

"What sort of a car was it?"

"A relatively small one—I'd say it might have been a roadster. As I remember the car slowed up before it passed us."

"How long after you entered the park did you hear the shot fired?"

"I don't know. Maybe ten or fifteen minutes." Simon suddenly snapped his fingers. "When the shot was heard, I recall turning back and noticing a reflection of light bounce off something metallic. At least that was the impression it gave me."

"The gun? Or perhaps the metallic reflection was

227

part of the automobile. You say you didn't think you were followed."

"Not on foot."

"But you might have been followed by that roadster."

"I had no reason to suspect we might have been followed at all," Simon replied. "I suggest that I compare notes with Miss Burdick and see if I can't get the facts straight."

O'Malley leaned back and drummed his fingers on the tabletop. "Mr. Phenwick, I have taken a curiously unusual interest in this case. As a result, I've done quite a bit of research regarding it."

Simon sat forward. "What sort of research?"

"Primarily seeking information about both you and Miss Burdick," O'Malley replied.

"Isn't that unusual?"

"When you returned to Boston," O'Malley went on, "I needed information. Frankly, I learned only that you were an attorney with your father's law firm in Boston and that you had been interviewing with several firms in New York, with an eye toward relocating here. Nothing suspicious there. On the other hand, in securing information about Miss Burdick, I learned that she has been appearing in the play in which your cousin is the leading lady. I have seen the play. I must say I wasn't terribly impressed by your cousin's performance. I did discover in the process that Miss Augusta Phenwick II and Miss Burdick aren't the happiest of co-workers—or should I say co-performers?"

"There seems to be a bit of professional jealousy on Augusta's part," Simon acknowledged.

"Possibly more than meets the eye," O'Malley commented. "Your cousin, Miss Phenwick, owns a roadster, doesn't she?"

"She may. It never occurred to me to ask."

"Well, she does, which she allows a young actor—one Leslie Brooks—to drive," O'Malley continued. "Recently another actor has been seen driving the automobile. Another young male actor, I hasten to include."

Simon shook his head. "I simply don't know anything about that. And again, I must suggest that I consult Miss Burdick who may be able to shed light on the situation."

"Yes. Why don't you do that and get back to me?"

"I'm curious why you haven't interrogated her yourself?"

"I'm getting around to it. But I wanted to confer with you first, Mr. Phenwick."

When Simon left the police precinct, he was perplexed by what had transpired. Moroever, O'Malley's attitude disturbed him. He found it extremely singular that the detective should be spending so much time on the case wherein an old man with no known relatives had been killed. It was his implications, however, about Phyllis's involvement without her awareness that troubled him.

Simon went directly to Phyllis's apartment. After knocking several times and receiving no answer, he went to the building superintendent, stated his concern for her and got the man to open the door for him.

The superintendent entered with Simon.

"No one here."

"I want to look through the house," Simon said.

"I'll have to stay with you."

"Fine."

In the kitchen Simon discovered the two coffee cups still on the table. A residue of liquid was in each. Taking a bit from each cup on his finger, he tasted it.

"What is it, Mr. Phenwick?"

"There's a peculiar taste to this one."

"Poison?"

"I don't believe so," Simon replied, "but a chemical of some kind."

Finding an old newspaper, Simon wrapped the coffee cup in it and took it with him. He thanked the superintendent for his co-operation and asked him to keep an eye out for Miss Burdick. If she did return to the apartment, she was immediately to contact Inspector Douglas O'Malley at the 17th Precinct.

Hurriedly departing, but making certain not to lose any of the liquid remaining in the cup, Simon went directly back to see O'Malley.

Chapter Seventeen

After O'Malley had had the contents of the coffee cup analyzed as a rather strong sedative known to induce unconsciousness, the police officer and Simon went directly to Augusta Phenwick II's mansion on Riverside Drive, where they were met by Carlyle.

"Miss Phenwick is occupied with the dressmaker," the butler announced. "She will be some time."

"We'll wait," Simon said forcefully. "You may tell her we're here.

"I sent two men to check at the theater to see if Miss Burdick is there," O'Malley said as they waited in the downstairs parlor. He paced about, periodically going to the front window to look out.

"If Miss Burdick has been drugged and abducted," Simon speculated, "I would think the theater would be the last place she would be taken."

"True," O'Malley agreed, "still it must be investigated. Hello. It seems a visitor is arriving. If I'm not mistaken, that is Mr. Leslie Brooks coming up the front walk."

When they did not hear the bell ring, Simon stepped to the front hallway and observed Leslie letting himself in.

"Mr. Brooks?"

Leslie was startled to see Simon. "Yes."

"Would you mind stepping in here for a few moments?"

"I was on my way to see Miss Phenwick."

"Obviously," Simon returned. "But Inspector O'Malley and I would like to have a few words with you first. My cousin is occupied with the dressmaker at the present, anyway."

"What's this all about?" Leslie asked apprehensively as he went into the parlor.

"You drive Miss Phenwick's roadster, don't you?" O'Malley said, getting immediately to the point.

"I have, in the past. It seems I've fallen from grace with Miss Phenwick, and driving privileges have been suspended," Leslie replied.

"May I ask how you managed to fall from grace, as you put it?" Simon enquired.

"I foolishly expressed my interest in another young lady to Miss Phenwick," the actor replied. "She didn't take kindly to that, since the lady is a person of whom Miss Phenwick is not particularly fond."

"Miss Burdick?" O'Malley questioned.

"Why, yes. How did you know?"

"A guess."

"Miss Burdick, I hasten to add, is not in the least bit interested in me—which I learned too late."

"Too late for what?"

"To maintain my driving privileges," Leslie said with an ironic smile. "You'll forgive me, Mr. Phenwick, but I must confess I followed both you and Miss Burdick from the restaurant last night. After you left, I encountered her; but she let me know in no uncertain

232

terms that my attention was not wanted. I didn't realize that she was in love with you. Please accept my apologies."

Simon merely nodded, but he was not happy with what Leslie had said.

The door to the parlor had been left ajar and footsteps could be heard coming down the stairs.

"The dressmaker?"

Simon put his index finger to his lips and crept to the door from where he saw Isaac Bell tiptoeing down the stairs. Simon motioned with his head, and both Leslie and O'Malley joined him in the observation.

"Isaac Bell," Leslie whispered. "Isaac, I suspect, is my replacement in Miss Augusta's affections and benevolence."

"He was with Miss Burdick the night of the party here," Simon said.

"I believe Miss Augusta has taken up with him," Leslie went on, "as a means of making me jealous. I've heard that he is going to understudy my role in *The Eternal Light*. If gossip is correct, Miss Augusta may ultimately see that he replaces me in the part."

As Isaac took the hallway towards the back of the house, O'Malley stepped from the room. Returning, he pulled Simon aside.

"It is now 4:10. I want to follow Isaac Bell. I will meet you at the office of Mortimer Gree at 5:15," O'Malley instructed.

"What do you want me to do about Brooks?"

"Find out anything more you can from him." O'Malley nodded, and quickly went in the direction Isaac had gone.

"You still have a key to my cousin's house?" Simon questioned.

"I was returning it," Leslie replied. "If you don't mind, I'd appreciate if you would give it to her for me. I just dropped by. I've things to do."

"Very well." Simon took the key and watched as the

young man hurriedly left the house. His first impulse was to follow Leslie, but he felt it necessary to speak with Augusta II.

Fifteen minutes later, Carlyle announced that Miss Phenwick would see Simon and he led the way to her second floor chamber.

"Augusta?" Simon asked as he entered the room. She gazed at him with a vague expression.

"I thought Carlyle said my brother wished to see me."

"You misunderstood."

"Well, what do you want, Simon?"

"You're not particularly cordial this afternoon."

Augusta II wore a blank expression and she appeared to be not quite focused on the situation: spacy. "I seem to be preoccupied." She put her hand to her forehead. "Did you say you wanted something in particular, Philip?"

Simon turned his head slightly as he eyed her. "What did you call me?"

Augusta II made a wiggly gesture with her fingers. "I'm sorry. I don't know what I can be thinking, Simon." Suddenly a hand clutched at her hair and the other slid over her face, pushing her features into a distorted expression. "What were you saying?"

"Are you well, Augusta?" Simon asked, registering concern.

"I don't know. It seems more and more of late that my mind is clouded and I'm not certain what is happening."

"Mr. Leslie Brooks asked me to give you this key," Simon said as he placed the key on the table next to where she was seated.

"Leslie? Oh, yes, Leslie. He's a fool. He could have had the world—*my* world—but he was a fool. Now Isaac—" She shot him a cautious glance. A sudden change. "Why have you come here? What do you want of me?"

"Do you take sedatives, Augusta?"

"I've been known to do so when I can't sleep at night. Why do you ask?"

"You act as if you've been drugged."

"How dare you criticize my acting? Do you know to whom you're speaking?"

Simon studied her a moment before he spoke. "To whom am I speaking?"

"To me! Augusta Eugenia Phenwick, the first!"

"The first?"

She broke into uncontrolled, imbecilic laughter. "I was Augusta, the first, now I'm Augusta, the second. I'm the greatest living actress in the theater! That's who I am! And who are you? Nobody, that's who!"

"I'm your cousin Simon."

Augusta II squinted. "Oh? I thought you were—I don't remember who I thought you were. It isn't important."

"You were having a session with your dressmaker?"

"My *what?*" Again the laughter. "I was being entertained by Isaac Bell." Suddenly she leaned forward with her head in her hands. Then she gazed strangely through the openings between her fingers. "I didn't say that. I couldn't have said that. Now I remember. I've got to make haste or I'll not get back to the theater in time." She stared at Simon. "Are you still here?"

"Augusta, I think you must see a doctor," Simon said, worry in his face.

"No! Never! I'm quite all right—quite." She smiled brightly, crossed her legs and took an elegant pose. "What were you saying, Simon? I'm sorry if I got distracted."

"Perhaps I should question you later when you've pulled yourself together."

"I am together, Simon . . . quite together."

Carlyle knocked on the door and entered. "I'm sorry to disturb you, Miss Phenwick. I just received a telephone message for you of utmost importance."

"Well, what is it, Carlyle?" Augusta II turned to Simon. "You will forgive the interruption, won't you?"

"Word has come from your brother's hotel, Miss Phenwick. It seems that Mr. Joshua Phenwick has put a gun to his head and killed himself."

"What!?"

"Good heavens," Simon exclaimed. "Are you certain of that?"

"That was the message, sir."

"Oh, no! No!" Augusta II wailed. "My baby brother—dead! No—no—no!!!" She arose and collapsed in a heap on the floor.

Simon was instantly at her side, followed by Carlyle. "She's unconscious. You'd better call her doctor."

"Yes, Mr. Phenwick."

"I might have averted this if I had properly interpreted the signs when I last saw Joshua. I knew he was despondent. I didn't realize how serious his state of mind was."

"Yes, Mr. Phenwick, I understand. I'll call the doctor."

"I'll remain with my cousin until you return. You had better send in one of the maids to look after her."

"I will, sir."

Simon lifted Augusta II onto the sofa and looked about for smelling salts as a maid came running in to tend to her mistress.

"Augusta can't possibly perform tonight," Simon announced a short while later, when he arrived at Mortimer Gree's office and explained the situation. Both Hampton Colwell and Madison Davis were present.

"Then Miss Burdick will have to—"

"Have you heard from Miss Burdick?" Simon asked.

"No. Should we have?" Gree asked.

Simon explained what he had discovered at Phyllis's apartment, and other findings. "The fact is, since
236

Augusta can't possibly go on tonight, and Phyllis has disappeared, you will simply have to cancel the performance."

"Yes, I'm afraid we will—unless, of course, Miss Burdick can be found before curtain time," Mortimer Gree said.

Shortly thereafter, the telephone rang. O'Malley was calling and asking for Simon.

"This is Simon Phenwick."

"I've followed Isaac Bell to an old house up in the Harlem area," O'Malley announced, "near Second Avenue on 127th Street. He parked and started to get out when he noticed me. Driving off, he lost me in traffic. I've come back to the precinct to get assistance. Can you meet me here as soon as possible?"

"Yes, by all means." Simon hung up, informed the others of the situation and quickly left the office.

"I demand to see Miss Phenwick!" Katherine Phenwick said as she confronted Carlyle at the front door of the house on Riverside Drive. "I am Mrs. Philip Phenwick and it is urgent that I see my cousin."

"Miss Phenwick is indisposed," Carlyle said officiously. "She has just received word of the death of her brother this afternoon."

"Whatever her condition, I must see her," Katherine insisted.

"I'll tell her, Mrs. Phenwick."

"I'll come with you," Katherine stated.

"Augusta II was propped up in bed, staring somewhat wild-eyed as Carlyle entered with Katherine.

"Augusta, dear," Katherine said as she rushed to the bed, "I'm so sorry to hear about Joshua."

"The ravages of war," Augusta II replied. "We don't know that he's dead, only listed among the missing in action."

"The war?" Katherine exchanged a glance with Carlyle.

"The Revolutionary war. What other war is there?" Augusta II asked.

"I fear the news about her brother has snapped her mind," Carlyle whispered. "She's been speaking peculiarly like that for the past half hour—ever since she regained consciousness. Excuse me."

"I was speaking of your brother Joshua," Katherine said.

"Joshua Phenwick is my husband. I married him because I liked the Phenwick name," Augusta II rambled.

"You're an actress: Augusta Phenwick, the *second,*" Katherine stated.

"No. I'm Augusta Phenwick, the first. Joshua is my husband. Or am I speaking of Charles Signoret, whom I've married and made arrangements for him legally to be called Joshua Phenwick—Dr. Joshua Phenwick."

"You've always wanted to believe you were the reincarnation of the first Augusta," Katherine remarked. "But I know for a fact that you're not."

"How dare you! How dare you!" Augusta II screamed and threw the covers back from the bed.

At the scream, Leslie Brooks emerged from the adjoining room. "She's quite out of her head, Mrs. Phenwick."

"I can see she'd demented," Katherine observed.

With that, Augusta II lunged at Katherine, hands reaching to clutch at her hat. Leslie swiftly moved behind Augusta II and restrained her.

"Inspector Douglas O'Malley was here a short while ago, from the 17th Precinct," Leslie explained as he struggled with Augusta II. "Maybe you'd better try to contact him."

"She'll contact no one!" Augusta II raged.

"Can you detain her here?" Katherine asked.

"I'll try my best," Leslie replied.

"You'll never see that brothersome Phyllis Burdick again, damn you!" Augusta II screeched as she struggled with Leslie. "I, Augusta, the first, have taken matters into my own hands."

Katherine did not wait to hear more.

Leaving the house, Katherine managed to hail a cab and directed the driver to the 17th Precinct. Upon arriving there, she learned that both Douglas O'Malley and Simon Phenwick had left not five minutes before. She explained the situation and managed to get four police officers to accompany her back to Augusta II's mansion.

When they reached the house, the police officers discovered that Leslie Brooks had been overpowered, tied up and was unconscious from a severe beating. Augusta II was gone.

Instructions were given to take Leslie to the hospital while Katherine quizzed Carlyle, only to discover that he was unaware that she was not still in her room.

"You might as well take me back to the police precinct," Katherine said, "where I'll wait until there's news from Simon. Why hadn't I gotten here sooner?"

Katherine went with two of the policemen.

Chapter Eighteen

The taste in her mouth was bitter. Dry. She tried to swallow, but there was no saliva. Her wrists were bound together, as were her ankles. Lying on the floor in an uncomfortable position in the cold room, she did her best to remember what had happened after she had regained consciousness. Tension filled her solar plexus with twisting pain. Phyllis wanted to cry; but she couldn't.

"Where am I?" she said aloud as her eyes strained to penetrate the complete darkness. Beyond, to her right, she detected the outline of a window with night darkness behind it. The streets were hushed as if a new snow had fallen. The cold was almost unbearable.

"Oh, God, what place is this?" she questioned. "How did I get here?" She tried to recall. "Isaac! Isaac Bell! But why did he bring me here?"

"You have a lot of questions, Phyllis," the voice said in the darkness. It had a menacing quality and an eerie timber to it.

"Isaac?"

"That sedative took longer to wear off than I anticipated it would," he remarked and struck a match to light a cigarette. The match glow gave his face a sinister quality.

"Why are we in darkness?" Phyllis asked.

"I was followed here earlier. Light will attract attention."

"Surely one little candle wouldn't attract anyone," Phyllis returned. "I'm very thirsty."

"I suppose I can give you some water," the actor said as he rose and left the room.

While he was gone, Phyllis decided that she would attempt to play up to him, even in a romantic way if necessary.

Isaac returned with a lit candle in one hand a cup of water in the other. "I guess one candle won't hurt. I'm tired of sitting without light." He held the cup for her to drink.

"Why am I being treated this way?" Phyllis asked. "Please release me, or at least untie my hands. They're bound so tight I have no circulation in them."

"You must stay here until Augusta arrives."

"Augusta? Are you so familiar with Miss Phenwick that you dare to call her by her first name?"

"You might be surprised about me, Phyllis—very surprised," Isaac returned. "When we first met, I was shy, inexperienced, naive. Like you, in many ways. I was so backward that when I found I was falling in love with you, I didn't know how to express myself. I was clumsy, awkward. I thought you laughed at me for being such a clod."

"I never laughed at you, Isaac," Phyllis said as pleasantly as she could. "I always thought of you as a good friend."

"A friend? I wanted to be more than a friend to you," he stated. "Then I saw how the Phenwick men came at you at the party and how you flashed them on with

241

your charm. You never did that to me. I was always available when no one else was—but I was only a friend."

"Like a brother."

"But I'm not your brother. I'm a man with the desires of a man," Isaac snapped bitterly. "Well, I watched what others did. I know how Leslie Brooks got the second leading male role in *The Eternal Light*. My ambition has always been to be a successful actor. Then, when I saw how annoyed Augusta was with you, I went to her. At first, she didn't take me seriously until she realized I could help her against you. I let her seduce me—at least that's what she thought she was doing. And I learned how to please her—far better than Leslie Brooks ever did. Well, I've progressively replaced Leslie in her affections."

"I never would have dreamed that of you, Isaac."

"Wouldn't you?" Isaac sneered. "I trailed you when you went out with Augusta's brother—and with her cousin. She told me if I really wanted to please her, I would kill you. That night she let me use her automobile. I followed you and Mr. Simon Phenwick from the restaurant. Then when you got in the carriage, I stayed close behind until you got to the park. My aim was off. I killed the old man instead of you."

"*You* killed—?" Phyllis gasped. "Do you intend to kill me now?"

"It will happen soon enough," Isaac threatened. "And then I will be right where I want to be in Augusta's esteem."

"How could you even contemplate taking another person's life?"

"Because it will help me accomplish my ultimate goal," Isaac said.

"Why does Miss Phenwick dislike me so much?"

"She's envious of your talent, for one thing," Isaac replied. "Another is your youth. When she saw you playing her part, I suspect she realized how wrong she was for it. Leslie made the mistake of complimenting your performance to Augusta. She became livid and flew into a rage."

"I can't believe I'm hearing this."

A door was heard closing in the distance.

"Shh!" Isaac quickly extinguished the candle. "Don't say a word. It may be Augusta. Then again, it may be someone else."

Footsteps came closer to the room. There were two sets of them.

"It must be Augusta. She knows right where to come."

"Why is there no light?" Augusta II all but shrieked.

"I'll get a lamp, Miss Phenwick," the other woman said.

"Who is with her?"

"That would be Cynthia," Isaac replied. He struck a match and relit the candle.

"So there she is!" Augusta II exclaimed as she saw Phyllis on the floor. "Act your way out of this, you little tramp!"

"What's wrong with you, Miss Phenwick?" Phyllis asked as terror filled her. "I've always tried to be cautious and not purposely do anything that would upset you. I think you're a great actress!"

"I'm not an actress," Augusta II charged. "I'm Augusta, the first, an empire builder!"

Cynthia entered the room with a lamp.

"You're considered to be one of the finest actresses in New York," Phyllis persisted.

"Yes, I am, aren't I? Oh, my God, I'm tremendous! Sensational!"

"Shall we get on with this?" Cynthia asked. She was a woman of imposing stature with intense dark eyes and a perpetual scowl on her face.

"What are you going to do?" Phyllis asked.

"Eliminate the competition!" Augusta II shrieked.

"Kill me?"

"How perceptive you are, Phyllis Burdick, how very perceptive."

"Why?"

"I accuse you! I accuse you of purposefully perpetrating a scheme wherein you worked some kind of magic on my poor brother Joshua in an attempt to become a Phenwick woman. Don't you think I saw the red roses? Don't you think I knew what you were doing?"

"No such a thing," Phyllis denied. "Furthermore, I've never tried to compete with you or seek to take your place as an actress. I'm innocent—perfectly innocent."

Augusta II became wild-eyed as she shot daggers of hatred at the pretty young woman. "It doesn't matter now. Joshua is dead. I accuse you of destroying him with your flirtatious ways and then taking up with his cousin. You're a harlot, that's what you are!"

"I'm not! I swear I'm not!" exclaimed Phyllis as terror trembled through her entire body. "You're deranged!"

"I'm deranged?" Augusta II charged toward her. "I should have your tongue cut out for saying that!"

"Please, Miss Phenwick, won't you listen to reason?" Phyllis pleaded.

"Joshua is dead! Joshua is dead! My baby brother is dead! You killed him! *You* killed him!"

"No! No! No!" Tears came.

"Step back, Miss Phenwick, let me handle this," Cynthia said forcefully. She took a crystal pendant and let it swing loosely, pendulum-like.

"What are you going to do?" Isaac asked.

"I'll show you, Isaac," Cynthia replied in a deep contralto. She held the crystal before his face. "I'll hold this before Miss Burdick's eyes like this, swing it back and forth, and as she watches it, she will fall into a hypnotic trance . . . fall into a hypnotic trance . . . relax . . . let go . . . and fall into a deep sleep . . . a deep, deep sleep."

Isaac's eyes began to get heavy. "Into a deep, deep . . . trance . . ."

"No, Isaac," Phyllis cried, throwing caution to the wind, "don't do it! They're trying to put you under, too."

Cynthia turned coldly to Phyllis. "He's already under. Now, Miss Burdick, it's best if you cooperate with this. Your death will be less painful if you are under hypnosis."

"You're as mad as Miss Phenwick!" Phyllis cried.

"I'm not mad! Not deranged! I'm a great actress!" Augusta II declared. "We'll give her another sedative. As long as Isaac is under, that is all that is necessary."

In the next few minutes, Cynthia and Augusta II struggled to force a portion of sedative down Phyllis. They managed to get her to take enough, mixed with that which she had already in her system, to be effective. Grogginess came over the young woman and she soon lost consciousness.

Cynthia went to Isaac. "Isaac, do you hear me?"

"Yes, Cynthia."

"You will carry Miss Burdick down to the roadster, place her on the passenger's side, then you will drive her across town to the Hudson River at the foot of 72nd Street," Cynthia commanded. "Do you understand?"

"Yes, Cynthia."

"You will drive as rapidly as you can and not stop when you reach the river. Do you understand?"

"Yes, Cynthia."

"Good, then go to it."

"Revenge at last! Revenge, sweet revenge!" Augusta II screamed.

"You must control yourself, Miss Phenwick."

By the time Isaac had lifted Phyllis and taken her from the room, Augusta II was raving incoherently. Cynthia went to the window to watch as Isaac put the unconscious Phyllis into the roadster. Moments later, the automobile was started and sped out of sight down the street.

"Please control yourself, Miss Phenwick," Cynthia said forcefully. "We've got to get back to the house. This way it will look as if Isaac took your car, abducted Miss Burdick and recklessly drove her into the river. But we must get back to make certain that suspicion is not thrown on us."

"Yes, Cynthia, you're so very thoughtful," Augusta II said. "I'll miss Isaac. He was interesting in his way."

The open police car in which Douglas O'Malley and Simon Phenwick were riding pulled into 127th Street as the roadster sped down the street. O'Malley stopped long enough to instruct part of the policemen in the other cars to apprehend whomever was in the house and detain them at the police precinct, while the rest of the officers followed them in pursuit of the roadster.

"He turned left at the next corner," Simon said. "You'd better hurry."

The ride was freezing cold in the open car, but both Simon and O'Malley were so keyed up in anticipation that they were practically oblivious of the temperature.

Isaac had the accelerator depressed to the floor. He came very close to just missing several cars as he recklessly navigated the roadster without stopping.

Phyllis stirred on the seat beside him, but she was so groggy that she had no comprehension of what was happening.

By the time the roadster reached Broadway and 72nd Street, O'Malley managed to catch up with it.

"There's Phyllis," exclaimed Simon. "She looks as if she's unconscious."

"Probably scared out of her wits," O'Malley speculated, "from the hair-raising ride. The man doesn't seem to notice us."

246

"He's headed for the river!" Simon yelled. "Is he in some kind of trance?"

"That would be my guess," O'Malley replied. "Brace yourself, Mr. Phenwick. I'm going to try to run them off the road before they reach the river. Then be prepared to get out of the vehicle as fast as you can. We may have to pull them from the car. If they go into the river they'll surely drown."

"I'm ready, if you are," Simon declared.

O'Malley forced the police car to ram into the side of the roadster. The concussion jarred Isaac and he turned his head slightly to the side. It also rocked Phyllis into semi-consciousness. She looked back to see the car behind. Her immediate reaction was to fall back to sleep.

Suddenly, Phyllis became aware of an overpowering scent of roses.

"Wake up, Phyllis! You must wake up and kick his foot from the accelerator. It isn't time for you to come over to this side."

"Wake up?" Phyllis mumbled. As she did, she became more aware of the impending danger. She braced herself as best she could and put her foot against Isaac's leg.

At that moment, O'Malley charged the police car again into the side of the roadster, the impact of which caused Phyllis's leg to straighten and dislodge Isaac's foot from the accelerator. The roadster slowed as she kept her foot tightly pressed against his leg.

When O'Malley forced his vehicle into the other a third time, the roadster spun around in loose, wet snow, and slammed into a treetrunk.

Both O'Malley and Simon jumped from the police vehicle. The crash had caused the door on the passenger's side to fly open. Phyllis's upper torso was hanging outside the car. She had been kept from falling out by the way her foot had become entangled in Isaac's leg.

247

Simon scooped Phyllis up in his arms and held her tightly. She was conscious enough to wrap her arms about his shoulders and rest her cheek against his chest.

The other police cars arrived.

"The man's dead," O'Malley announced after examining Isaac. "How is she?"

"She's barely conscious. I have the feeling she must have been drugged," Simon replied as he placed a kiss on Phyllis's temple. "We've got to get her out of the cold. Augusta's house is only a few blocks up on Riverside Drive. We had better take her there."

Carlyle was surprised to see Simon at the door carrying Phyllis. O'Malley flashed his badge and ordered the servant to make some coffee and fetch the brandy. Reluctantly, Carlyle obeyed.

Simon took Phyllis to the parlor and put her on the sofa while O'Malley went to get blankets.

Gently kissing her cheeks as he brushed back her hair, Simon spoke softly, "Phyllis, my darling, can you hear me?"

Phyllis partially opened her eyes. "Simon?" She smiled sweetly. "Do you smell the roses? He awoke me with the roses. I've been—I've been given—a sedative—I don't feel anything." She closed her eyes, then slowly opened them again. "I don't feel anything—except deep and undying love for you, dearest Simon."

Simon kissed her full on the lips and hugged her tightly until O'Malley came with the blankets to cover her.

Chapter Nineteen

The brandy forced down Phyllis caused her to cough, the convulsions of which brought her partially back to consciousness. Two cups of black coffee that Simon and O'Malley managed to get into her began counteracting the effects of the sedative she had been given.

"I feel as if I were floating suspended in a chasm somewhere on the edge of time," Phyllis uttered as she started to get her bearings. The closeness of Simon gave her the assurance that she needed to bring her back to a clear sense of reality.

"Do you recall anything that happened in the last hour or so?" O'Malley questioned.

"I remember coming to consciousness in a dark room," Phyllis recited, "to eventually learn that I was tied and Isaac Bell was guarding me. Then Miss Phenwick and her maid Cynthia arrived. Isaac was put under hypnosis, but I refused to allow it to be done to me. As a result, I was given more sedation. I don't think I took too much, but obviously it was enough to render me unconscious. I remember nothing else—except that I was riding in an automobile and I was made aware of the odor of roses and I thought I heard a man's voice attempting to awaken me. I recollect trying to extend my leg. It took tremendous effort. The next thing I knew I was in Simon's arms and he was kissing me."

"Isaac Bell was killed in the crash," Simon informed her.

Phyllis gasped. "Oh, I'm sorry. I had a soft spot in my heart for him. But he had changed. When I first knew him he was like an innocent little boy; but today he was a hardened animal. He had learned to play the vicious game many actors are forced to learn in their struggle toward success. I doubt if Miss Phenwick cared that much for him, but she found that she could use him against me. Isaac followed us that night in Central Park. He was driving Miss Phenwick's roadster—and he shot the carriage driver: his aim was off, Miss Phenwick intended that he kill me." She shuddered.

Simon embraced her as tightly as he could. "Jealousy is a cruel master that distorts one's senses. Augusta has literally let it destroy her."

"Do you feel strong enough to go down to the police precinct, Miss Burdick?" Douglas O'Malley asked.

"If it's necessary," Phyllis replied. "Just give me a few more minutes."

While O'Malley left the young couple alone in the parlor, he went to take a statement from Leslie Brooks. He testified to the belief that Augusta II had lost her sanity and cited several examples that indicated he was correct. He admitted a close relationship with the actress as a means of furthering his own career, but denied having any part in a conspiracy against Phyllis. Ultimately, he revealed that he was the one who had tipped the police that Simon was on his way to the Astor Hotel the night before, and he had told Joshua Phenwick that Phyllis was in love with Simon.

Leslie was taken to the police station in a second automobile, and would give a formal statement in private.

When Katherine Phenwick had gone to the police precinct, she waited eagerly for news of the events that were happening. Upon learning that Phyllis was safe, she convinced two of the police offers to chauffeur her on an errand. She returned to the precinct a short while later in the company of Joshua Phenwick, who was very much alive.

"This may be extremely difficult for you, Joshua," Katherine warned, "because your sister is in a very bad way."

"If she's done all you've told me that she has," Joshua replied weakly, suffering an acute attack of depression, "it is best that she is properly dealt with. I have a responsibility to her."

"And a responsibility to yourself, Joshua. Don't ever forget that." She had been able to persuade him that his sister was losing her mind. As a shock device to force Augusta II to show her hand, Katherine had convinced Joshua to have someone from the hotel call and say that he had killed himself. "Augusta was teetering on the brink. She needed that tiny shock of emotion to force her to go one way or the other."

"I feel guilty for doing that," Joshua said.

"Had you not done what you did, Miss Burdick's life well might not have been spared," Katherine explained.

When Augusta II saw Joshua, she became even more hysterical than she had been, and all signs of rationality escaped her. Two strong police officers had to restrain her. Strong sedation had little effect on her, and she had to be carried away to the mental ward of Bellevue Hospital where all attempts would be made to help her.

Fortunately for Phyllis, she did not have to have another confrontation with Augusta II, but she did come face to face with Cynthia. "Yes, I saw her hypno-

251

tize Isaac Bell. And she tried to do the same with me. Then I heard her instruct Isaac to drive the roadster into the Hudson River with both he and me in it."

"Miss Phenwick is my mistress," the devoted Cynthia said. "I would have done anything for her to help her sustain her position as the grand leading lady that she is. I resented Miss Burdick as much as Miss Phenwick did. Yet, I knew it was inevitable that some young actress would come along to cause Miss Phenwick's downfall. Long ago I recognized the slow creeping indications of insanity overtaking Miss Phenwick, many of which, I believe, only I was privy to. I tried to keep it a secret. Isaac Bell meant nothing to Miss Phenwick, but he presented a means by which she might destroy Miss Burdick. But if it hadn't been Miss Burdick, there would have been someone else. It was inevitable."

"How did it happen," Simon asked after all of the statements of fact had been made and he and Phyllis were free to leave, "that you decided there was a murder case of extensive proportions in the death of Lawrence Frazier, O'Malley?"

"It was just a hunch," O'Malley replied. "The circumstances were such that I realized more had to be behind it than met the eye. I like that sort of challenge." He shook Simon's hand. "We'll have to go for a little ride again sometime, Mr. Phenwick."

"Thank you anyway," Simon returned with a laugh. "You're a wild driver, Inspector O'Malley."

The morning headlines carried Augusta II's name and the accompanying story told the details of the great actress's condition. It also explained Phyllis Burdick's story and of how she had barely escaped death as a result of Augusta II's diabolic scheming.

"We'll use it," Mortimer Gree exclaimed after reading three accounts of the story. "We've got thousands of dollars of free publicity. Of course we'll use it!"

A meeting was arranged for three o'clock that afternoon in Gree's office between Hampton Colwell, Madison Davis, Phyllis and Simon and himself. The portly producer was wreathed in smiles when the others arrived.

"Miss Burdick," Gree began, "first, let me offer my sympathy for the harrowing experience you had yesterday. In a way, I suspect we are all of us responsible in one way or another for getting you into such a predicament. Still we had no way of knowing just how serious Augusta's condition was." He cleared his throat. "The afternoon papers will carry information stating that *The Eternal Light* will be presented at its usual time tonight, but not with its usual star."

"Miss Phenwick couldn't possibly—" Phyllis stopped as Simon squeezed her hand.

"Mr. Colwell, Mr. Davis and Mr. Phenwick have been in conference with me," Gree continued, "and we have decided the only hope of survival for our play will be if you, Miss Burdick, will agree to permanently take over in the leading role. I know you can do it because I've witnessed it—tricked into witnessing it, but I did see it with my own eyes. Mr. Phenwick has gone over the details in a contract I have here. All you have to do is sign it and I'll give word to have your name substituted for Miss Phenwick's on the marquee and in the program."

Phyllis gaped, stunned by the announcement. "Sign it?" She looked at Simon and he nodded approval.

"Not only will you be insuring the survival of *The Eternal Light*," Gree added, "but we will use your success in it as promotional publicity, which will make you a definite name drawing-card when *Triumph and Passion* ultimately opens. Well, Miss Burdick?"

"May I consult in private for a few minutes with my attorney?" Phyllis asked.

"By all means. Take your time," Gree stated. "I don't have to give word to the papers to release the story for another eight and a half minutes." He checked his watch.

Simon and Phyllis stepped into the adjoining room.

"Oh, Simon, hold me! Sqeeeze me tightly to keep me from bursting with excitement," Phyllis begged.

Simon complied to her wishes, augmenting them with several kisses.

"I can't afford an exorbitant legal fee," Phyllis finally said, "but I do need your advice."

"I can take part of the fee out in kisses," Simon teased and quickly kissed her. "You see, you've already taken care of the retainer fee."

They both laughed.

"Shall I sign?"

"I think you would do well to sign," Simon replied.

"But what will that do to us if I'm suddenly catapulted to stardom?" Phyllis asked.

"To us?"

"You do know I'm very much in love with you, Simon."

"I could tell, just as I'm certain you're aware of my love for you," Simon said. "Do you put our love above your chance to become the great actress you've always dreamed of being?"

"Right now, your love for me and mine for you is far above anything else to me," Phyllis replied. "I never thought I would ever say anything like that, much less feel at the core of my being as I do at this moment."

Simon kissed her again.

"We've got to watch for Mr. Gree's eight and a half minutes." Phyllis whispered as her lips parted from his.

"Will you marry me, Miss Burdick?" Simon asked as he held tightly to her as if attempting to squeeze a positive answer from her."

"My dearest Simon, I thought you would never ask," she returned. Their lips met again.

"Both Peggy and Katherine have been certain for a long time that you were destined to be a Phenwick woman," Simon said. "And we've only got two and a quarter minutes left." He stroked her chin with his index finger. "I want to strive to see that you become a far greater actress than Augusta ever was. In many ways, we'll do it together. And, in time, who knows, I may become your producer. By all means, sign the contract and set Mortimer Gree at ease."

After the contracts had received Phyllis's signatures and Gree began calling the newspapers, Simon and Phyllis returned to the other room, where they again fell into each others' embrace.

"You know, my darling, were we to get a judge to marry us this afternoon," Simon suggested, "you could be billed as Phyllis Phenwick on the marquee."

"No, Simon. I want Phyllis Phenwick to be a very private person, the adoring wife of Simon Phenwick. Phyllis Burdick will be the public figure. I think it's better that way."

"I was being impetuous." He kissed her again. "It isn't important that we see Joshua and Katherine off on the evening train to Boston."

"Poor Joshua Phenwick. I do feel sorry for him."

"I have faith in Joshua," Simon commented. "He is doing well to return to Boston to see Dr. Ornby, before going back to Portland and trying to get his life straightened out. I wonder if he might have been a victim of Augusta's domination to a greater extent than we realize—or than he realizes."

Phyllis put her lips over Simon's words to silence him.

A short while later, there was a polite knock at the door to the inner office. Simon went to open it. Madison Davis was standing outside.

"May I come in a moment? I know I'm intruding, but I just wanted to congratulate Phyllis before I left," Madison said.

"You must congratulate both of us," Phyllis replied. "Simon has asked me to marry him and I've accepted."

Madison gazed at her for a moment without speaking. His eyes sparkled as tears of happiness welled in them. "I'm overjoyed for both of you. I'm a sentimentalist. I suppose that is a necessary ingredient for a writer to have. I hope you both will always consider me as family. I feel very close to both of you."

"And we feel close to you, too, Madison," Phyllis assured him."

"This must be the most exciting day of your life, Phyllis," Madison observed as he wiped his eyes.

"The ever present *now* is the most exciting time of my life," Phyllis replied. "Give me this day, Simon's love and the chance to work at reaching every goal I set forth for myself, and the excitement will be unending."

"I don't know of two people who are more ideally suited to each other," Madison remarked. "I love you both."

"And we love you. Don't we, Simon?"

"Have you ever considered being a best man at a wedding?" Simon said as he shook Madison's hand.

"I've never been asked before," Madison returned. "But I'm certain, if the question arises, that I'll answer in the affirmative."

As they laughed, Simon again caught Phyllis in his arms. "Excuse us, Madison, some things just can't wait."

Madison started for the door as the young couple kissed. When he looked back, he became aware of a very sweet fragrance. Breathing deeply, he identified it. "Don't disturb yourselves. We'll talk later. Mrs. Katherine Phenwick may have been right when she suggested that *Triumph and Passion* should be called *The Scent of Roses*. Well, I can always use it as the title of my next play." He left the room.

When they let their lips part from each others', Phyllis and Simon breathed deeply, and knew beyond a doubt what had prompted Madison to mention "the scent of roses."